Paul Mannering was born, as we so often are, to biological parents (literally, his father was a Marine Biologist).

The youngest of 4 surviving children and an unknown number of others who never made it past zygote, or were simply sold for research purposes to make ends meet. (The 70's were a hard time for his family). Born in Kaikoura, New Zealand, where steep mountains plunge into dark seas with canyons so deep that colossal squid and whales duel it out in the crushing depths.

Moving to Christchurch at 14, after a year of boarding school, he fought his way through high-school and then started the first of many full time jobs. He became a father at 19, went through various life experiences, went to a community college as an adult student, studied nursing, traveled overseas, returned, worked and did all the fun things that you do when you are in your 20's and 30's.

Realising that he really missed writing, Paul started taking it seriously again in his late 30's. Since then he has had a dozen novels published, a pile of short stories released into the wild, and he has written and produced a lot of podcast audio drama. He even won awards.

Paul has recently relocated to Australia from New Zealand where he now lives under an assumed identity as a functional adult in Canberra, Australian Capital Territory.

THE DRAKEFORTH SERIES
PUBLISHED BY IFWG

Engines of Empathy (Book 1)
Pisce of Fate (Book 2)
Time of Breath (Book 3)
Heroes of Heresy (Book 4)

THE DRAKEFORTH SERIES BOOK 4

HEROES OF
HERESY

BY PAUL MANNERING

Heroes of Heresy

All Rights Reserved

ISBN-13: 978-1-922556-30-1

Copyright ©2021 Paul Mannering

V1.0

Printed in Palatino Linotype and Voodoo Eye Title

IFWG Publishing International
Gold Coast

www.ifwgaustralia.com

For Silvia and Patch

and for Number One.

CHAPTER 1

The city has an underbelly like a cat's: soft, warm, and inviting to anyone with a desire for a risky thrill. For those who explore without caution, multiple stab wounds and a disfigured face are the likely result.

Nearly an hour after midnight, Vole Drakeforth lay in a dimly lit alleyway outside an underground club, trying to ignore the two men hitting him with foam rubber swords.

"It's no good, Cole," one of the attackers announced, pausing for breath. He wore the brown robes, long hair and beard of an Arthurian monk. His larger companion, who wore the same vestments, stepped back from Drakeforth and leaned against the wall, panting.

"It'll take hours to kill him this way," the larger man said.

"Let me think," the first assailant said. "We could stab him instead," he suggested.

"Right." the second man straightened up and rammed the point of his foam rubber sword into Drakeforth's chest.

"Not with these toys, you idiot," the first attacker said. His companion frowned at the bent blade of his weapon. Tossing it aside, he went to explore the recycling bins for something deadlier.

Drakeforth worked a hand free of the cords that bound them behind his back. Reaching up, he pulled the gag from his mouth.

"You pointless prototypes," he sneered. "You pair of brainless broccoli!"

"'Ere, steady on. That's uncalled for," the first attacker said.

"You can tell your masters they will never stop me! I will find the truth!" Drakeforth snapped.

"Try this, Edwid," the second man said, returning with an armload of cast-off items.

Edwid sorted through the options: paper bags, string, empty food containers, magazines and newspapers. "And what am I supposed to do with this lot, Cole?"

"Paper cuts?" Cole suggested.

"Perhaps you could simply bore me to death," Drakeforth said, from their feet.

"Sorry, mate," Edwid said. "We aim to provide a high level of customer satisfaction."

"Yeah, sorry," Cole said, shuffling his feet.

"Well, how about you simply untie me, and we let this whole matter pass without further comment?"

"Right, yeah." Cole crouched down, and with fierce concentration began to work on the knots tying Drakeforth's feet together.

"'Ang on," Edwid said. "While we do aim to provide a professional service, our primary responsibility is to our client. Which in this instance is not precisely you, Mister Drakeforth."

"Who is paying you?" Drakeforth's eyes narrowed.

"That is confidential," Edwid said.

"The identity of whomever has hired you to kill me is confidential?" Drakeforth gave a snort. "Consider it the last request of a condemned man."

"Well, in that case..." Cole said.

"No, no, no. Professionalism must be maintained," Edwid insisted.

"Oh, fine. Is it someone I owe money to? Someone who didn't like my witty repartee at a recent public meeting? Oh, wait, let me guess, it's one of my insufferable relatives trying to avoid a repeat of last year's Hibernian dinner fiasco."

Cole finished loosening the knots binding Drakeforth's legs. "There you go, all done—err, undone," he said.

Cole and Edwid seized Drakeforth by the arms and lifted him onto his feet.

"Please accept our apologies for the delay. Your assassination is important to us," Edwid said, brushing dirt from Drakeforth's trench coat. "If you wouldn't mind 'olding for a minute, we will resolve some technical issues and complete this job promptly."

"Yeah, sorry," Cole said again.

"Right," Drakeforth straightened his suit jacket and glanced upwards. "Is that Arthur?" he said.

Edwid and Cole looked skyward. Drakeforth bolted like a rabbit. The rope tangled around his ankles, and he went over like a felled tree. The crack of Drakeforth's skull hitting the concrete echoed off the walls of the surrounding buildings.

Edwid and Cole looked at each other and then hurried over to the man lying unmoving on the ground.

"Is he okay?" Cole asked with concern.

"Let's 'ope not, Cole," Edwid said, rolling Drakeforth over onto his back. After a cursory examination, Edwid shook his head.

"Let's get out of here. Job's done and all that. No one said 'ow it had to be done, just get it done they said."

"Well yeah," Cole looked sheepish, "It kinda feels like cheating."

"We get paid when Vole Drakeforth is dead," Edwid said. He rummaged under his robes and retrieved a camera. "'Old his 'ead up," he instructed.

Cole got down on his knees and lifted Drakeforth's face up for a better angle.

"Cole, get your mug out of it."

"Sorry, Edwid, I thought a litho of the two of us together would be a nice souvenir."

Edwid snapped a picture of Drakeforth's slack face. "Okay, let's go before someone sees us."

The two assassins hurried to the end of the alleyway and joined the raucous crowd of revellers in the street celebrating the Arthurian festival of The Incomplexity of Cheese.

A shadow fell over Drakeforth's still form and cleared its throat.

"Excuse me, I wonder if I might ask you a favour." After a

second passed without response, the shadow continued: "You see, I need some help. It's all gotten frightfully out of hand and I require an agent to act on my behalf. My fault entirely, of course, I should never have let anyone write down half the things I said." The shadow paused. "You're not writing this down, are you?" Satisfied at the lack of response, the shadow looked up and down the alleyway and then stepped closer.

"I'll just lie down here and if you have any particular concerns, let me know."

The dark spectre aligned itself with Drakeforth's feet and then sat down, the ghostly figure disappearing through his body.

"Yes, quite comfortable, thank you. I think this will do nicely." The shadow lay down and a moment later Drakeforth sat up with a gasp.

CHAPTER 2

Habeas Yeast did not suffer the tempest of doubt that sometimes beset his fellow Arthurians. His personal revelation had come during junior school in the form of a dream. Arthur himself had visited young Habeas and said, "Hello? Hello? Is this thing on? What year is it? I think I have the date wrong. Sorry to have bothered you."

The dream stayed with Habeas long after waking, and he had spent many hours pondering its meaning. Entering a religious order as soon as he turned eighteen was a natural career path to follow. Now his beard brushed his chest, though most accurately it brushed his chest when he lowered his head a little. He had always worn his hair long, and now it draped over his shoulders like a yak skin, the brown eyes and perpetually calm expression underneath the fringe adding to the bovine impression.

As a follower of Arthur's teachings, Brother Habeas did not measure the passage of time in years. The change in his hair and beard were the only reliable indicators of the perception of time. He had smiled when his mum sent a card, wishing him a happy twentieth birthday. His reply had been an essay explaining the futility of observing time in a simply linear way. He included some Arthurian tracts in the form of brochures which illustrated his main points in an easily digestible form.

This tradition had come about when Arthurianism was moving away from the old-fashioned convert-or-die fundamentalism to the religion of peace and tolerance of the modern era. There were certain nations where the people remembered the days when

Arthurian missionaries would descend like zealous blacksmiths, beat the locals' ploughshares into swords, and then proceed to execute the populace with them.

As a result, many cultures prohibited the possession and distribution of Arthurian religious materials. This forced the faithful to develop edible paper so they could dispose of the incriminating evidence in an emergency.

Development of an easily digestible printing press, however, faced ongoing challenges.

Doubt, for Habeas, had finally arrived in the form of a cup of tea. Yesterday—and the monks of the Order of Saint Erinaceous used the term dismissively—Habeas had been out witnessing the glory of Arthur to weary travellers at the city's international zippelin port.

Arthurians were devoted people watchers; thus it had occurred to them exceedingly early on that international zippelin terminal passenger lounges are the one place in the world where people are most likely to be open to suggestion.

Habeas also liked to watch the zippelins coming and going. These vast silver cylinders, over a hundred feet long with aerodynamically tapered ends, moved like clouds as the reflected light of the afternoon sun bounced off the paper-thin alloy shell encasing the lighter-than-air cloud of gas and passenger cabin. He watched as a loaded zippelin rose from its boarding gate mooring, floating upwards like a soap bubble borne on the warm breath of a child's delight. With perfect delicacy, the balloon manoeuvred into position for the flight to distant Mocorro. Once the craft was pointed in the right direction, the jet engines rotated into flight position. A moment later, the empathic generators engaged the power and the sleek, silver bullet accelerated towards its destination at a velocity quickly approaching the speed of sound.

Habeas sighed; in his mind, the zippelin was the perfect combination of faith and technology. Watching these behemoths vanish over the horizon in a blur filled his heart with a righteous joy.

He slipped the remaining (vanilla-flavoured) tracts on Arthurianism into his satchel and wandered over to the nearby *Espression* café. Joining the queue of people waiting to order tea in a cup or pot, he witnessed something extraordinary.

A young woman with a heavy-looking bag over her shoulder, stood in front of Habeas and held a cup and saucer. The contents of the cup steamed gently, and Habeas wondered why she was standing in the queue rather than taking a seat in the half-full café and enjoying her tea.

Habeas stared, fascinated, at the back of the woman's head. Her shining hair was the colour of spun honey, so magical you could forget bees made it with their bums.

"Hi, my name is Owow, how can I help you?" the bateasta asked when she was within service range of the counter.

"Is this some kind of joke?" the woman asked.

"I… Hi, my name is Owow—"

"You can help me by answering my question," the woman said. Owow hesitated. Habeas watched with interest as Owow flicked through his mental catalogue of customer responses and then announced, "Have you tried our daily special?"

The woman took a deep breath; her shoulders rose and then fell as she released her inner tension.

"Thank you," she said to Owow, and walked away.

Habeas ordered a pot of Horse-eye with a bugnut cookie, and then went to sit at the woman's table.

She sat with a slim computer on the table in front of her, typing steadily with a cadence that suggested she was not mincing her words.

"No, thank you," she said without looking up.

Habeas poured his tea and did not respond, watching the way her fingers stroked the keys instead.

The woman stopped typing. She swept her golden fringe out of her eyes and regarded Habeas over the top of her screen. Habeas sipped his tea and sighed with content.

"I said *no, thank you.*"

"What exactly are you refusing?" Habeas asked.

She sighed and closed the laptop lid. "You are Arthurian. You are going to invite me to experience the change of self-perception that occurs when the observer and the observed interact. You will quote some quasi-quantum berkelsnert about the nature of reality and, because you expect me to be completely ignorant of the impenetrable nature of the fundamental state of the Multiverse, you will assume I am a suitable target for your nonsense."

Habeas marvelled at her. "You said all of that without once pausing for breath."

"Circular breathing; it's a difficult skill to master, but I like a challenge. Now, please go away."

"I was wondering why you were complaining about the tea."

"The tea?" she regarded Habeas for a moment. "Let me tell you about the tea. Firstly, they claim this is *Oolongjen*. Anyone who has tasted actual Oolongjen knows that the subtler qualities of the brew are achieved by allowing the leaves to be first consumed by the Bomby worm. It is only when the excreted matter is mixed with other dried and crushed—mind you, never cut—leaves of the Oolongjen, that the tea has the true Oolongjen flavour."

"Circular breathing?" Habeas asked.

"I could go on all day," she continued, ignoring his interruption. "About the complete lack of idiosyncrasies in this tea. It's as close to Oolongjen as I am to giving you my phone number."

"I'm Habeas, Habeas Yeast," he said.

"Felicity Goosebread," she replied, "But everyone calls me Pimola. Felicity was the name of my mother's pet silverfish and I cannot abide the idea of being named after an insect. Or a fish."

"So, you're some kind of tea critic?" Habeas asked, sipping his own drink.

"I am the best kind of tea critic. The kind who loves tea with an all-encompassing passion. I write a column for *The Weekly Word*."

"P.R. Fenstick's 'World of Tea'," Habeas said immediately. "But isn't Fenstick a man?"

"Fenstick retired and went treasure hunting in the Aardvark Archipelago four years ago. I've been writing his column ever since."

"Fascinating," Habeas said. Pimola immediately glared at him.

"Why? What exactly is fascinating?" she asked in a tone that dared him to respond.

"You," Habeas said. "Everything about you is fascinating. From the Fibonacci swirls of your hair to the way the photons reflect off your retina in such a chilling stare."

"Oh, please," Pimola said, rolling her eyes. "Do you know how much a tea critic writing a column for *The Weekly Word* earns?"

Habeas opened his mouth to offer an opinion, but Pimola continued without him.

"Nothing. Not a Kadozian bean. Why do you ask? I'll tell you why. I started out as an intern during my final semester of university. They've so far refused to change my contract to actually pay me for my fifteen hundred words a week."

"So why don't you quit?"

"Quit? Of course I can't quit. Can you imagine if someone who didn't know the difference between Oolongjen and a pot of *Capricious Grype* took over writing the reviews?"

"I actually can't imagine it," Habeas admitted.

"Exactly. The results would be disastrous. There would be people out there blithely putting milk in their tea with scant awareness of the consequences."

Habeas peered doubtfully at the green liquid swirling amongst the brown tea in his cup. "What sort of consequences?"

"Terrible consequences," Pimola said in a dark tone.

"You should also include a review of the café service in your column. That bateasta didn't seem very good."

Pimola raised an eyebrow at him, "I have more important things to worry about than the quality of hot drinks produced by a zippelin port lounge café."

"I thought you were here writing a column on the tea they served you."

"Whatever gave you that idea? I'm here for work."

"Which is not writing a column for *The Weekly Word*?"

"No, I'm here for…" She was interrupted by the sudden fanfare of a marching band. They blew long, tube-like horns and banged on wooden drums. Somewhere in their midst a male voice rose

9

in an undulating wail—as if he had opened his mouth to sing, and then promptly slammed his hand in a car door instead.

"Oh, good," Pimola said, closing her laptop. "The Escrutians have arrived."

She stood up, slipped the computer into her bag and walked out of the café. Habeas cast a final sideways glance at his teacup and then followed her.

Having settled whatever internal conflict appeared to have divided them in choice of key, melody, and chord, the members of the Escrutian marching band were now playing the same song, at the same tempo. Their singer was still wailing in apparent agony.

The band formed part of a procession, winding their way from the arrivals gate. At the head, a man in a high, plumed hat and uniform laden with medals searched in vain for someone to present himself to. Behind him, an entourage and the band were strung out in a conga line that wheezed, clanked, and honked.

"General Kow-Plan! General Kow-Plan!" Pimola called, waving over the noise and heads of the curious onlookers.

The general turned and marched towards her. The rest of his party falling into position behind him.

General Kow-Plan bowed and Pimola bowed in return. The general, on his way back up, noted that she was still on her way down, so he bowed again. Several moments passed while they bobbed up and down in front of each other like a pair of hens pecking at grain.

An aide managed to get a gold-trimmed cushion under the general's nose during an upstroke. He took the opportunity to seize a scroll from the cushion. Unrolling it, he declared,

"The Eternal Empress of Escrutia accepts the petition of the grovelling barbarian dogs. We hereby present to you the summation of the glory of the Eternal Empire."

General Kow-Plan stepped aside, and a rectangular wooden crate standing over six feet high was rolled forward on a cargo trolley.

"We are humbled and grateful for the kindness of the Eternal Empress. The gift of this technology will bring our two great nations closer together and enhance our collective understanding of the mysteries of the natural world," Pimola responded.

The aide leaned in and murmured in the general's ear. He nodded, gave a slight grunt, and with a firm, salute-like motion, he extended a hand.

"Your receipt. Sign where indicated."

Pimola did so, and the aide made finger whirling gestures at the ceiling. General Kow-Plan, his entourage, and the still-playing-band completed a carefully synchronised about-face and marched away towards the departure gate. Pimola, Habeas and the growing crowd of curious spectators were left alone with the large wooden box.

"What is that?" Habeas asked the question that was clearly on everyone's mind.

"This," Pimola said with a triumphant smile, "is the machine that is going to prove that you and your fellow paper-munchers are a bunch of raving wig-weavers."

With that she beckoned the zippelin port staff behind the trolley to follow her and headed towards the exit.

CHAPTER 3

The offices of Mint and Munt Personal Solutions Inc. were currently in the basement of an otherwise abandoned building.

Two desks huddled in a clear space, surrounded by the cut-off pipes that had once carried empathic energy around the building. It was, as Edwid explained to a frowning Cole, a beginning. One day they would look back at the time they spent in this damp, cold, rat-infested tourist trap of a basement with fondness.

Cole, who had complained about the fungus growing up the walls and not least because it *looked at him funny*, arrived that morning in a more positive mood than usual.

"I've found a way to get us lots of business," he said as soon as he managed to shoulder-charge the door open.

"Really?" Edwid didn't look up from the newspaper he was scanning for potential clients.

"I've taken out an ad in the *Blue Pages*," Cole beamed.

"You *what?*" Edwid folded the newspaper and regarded Cole with an expression of stunned surprise.

"Look, 'ere's a copy, the new edition comes out next week. Should get us plenty of business."

Edwid took the sheet and smoothed it out on the table.

Mint and Munt Personal Solutions Inc.
Quality Assassination Services.
Let us be the death of you!
Excellent Rates.

"You do realise we are meant to be entirely anonymous, don't you, Cole? A shadowy organisation 'idden from the public view. Like ghosts, we strike and leave no trace."

Cole nodded enthusiastically, "Oh yeah, and this is going to get us lots of work."

"It's gonna get us arrested. The green are gonna be on this like slime mould on cheese."

"Nah." Cole grinned like a puppy. "The police can't arrest us, we're a legitimate business now."

"Cole. We are hit men. We are offering specialist services to *ex-vitate* people for money. Our clients are discerning, and discretion is at the core of everything we do."

"That's good, Ed, I should put that in the flyer."

"The *what?*"

"Flyers. I'm going to stick them up around town. For walk-ins. You know, people who are thinking they really should get an assassin, but haven't committed to it yet. We can get them, the spontaneous shoppers."

"We're talking about toppin' people, Cole. It's not really a spur-of-the-moment decision."

"You're always saying we need to grow our customer base. We can't do that without getting our name out there."

"Yes Cole, but I was thinking more along the lines of *word-of-mouth*. Satisfied clients contacting us for repeat business. We're aiming for the corporate market. Not the average zeeb on the street."

"Like the Drakeforth job?" Cole said, his mood deflating with all the joy of a balloon left hanging for three months after the party.

"Exactly. Your initiative is to be admired, mate, but seriously, you need to talk to me before you start taking out adverts in the business directory."

Cole slumped behind his desk and stared at the phone. If the Universe was on his side, it would ring right now with a job. In three…two…one… In five…four…

The phone rang.

Cole overbalanced in his chair, arms flailing as he crashed

to the floor. Edwid leaned across the desk and snatched up the receiver. The video screen remained blank; this was a voice- only call. "Mint and Munt, how may I help you?" Edwid asked.

"You reported to us that the Drakeforth problem had been taken care of," the voice on the other end of the phone snarled.

"Yes, sir. Taken care of last night, sir."

"Then please explain why he is currently lurking in the metropolitan bus terminal."

Edwid felt a lump of melting ice cream materialise under his skin and slide down his spine.

"I-I don't understand," he managed.

"Let me use small words. Vole. Drake. Forth. Is. Alive. He is still engaged on his ridiculous crusade. He is making certain people uncomfortable. You were hired specifically to remove that discomfort. You appear to have failed."

"Yessir," Edwid's gaze fell on the advertisement. "Our results are guaranteed, sir. Remember our motto, *Let us be the death of you*," Edwid said.

"If Drakeforth isn't taken care of, his death will be the least of your concerns!"

The caller hung up. Edwid returned the phone to its cradle and frowned at it.

"Good news?" Cole asked from under the desk.

"You said Drakeforth was dead."

"'E is. No pulse, not breathing. 'E's as dead as a doorknob."

"Then why is 'e at the bus station, probably making a nuisance of 'imself?"

The desk bounced as Cole's head struck the underside of it.

"'E what?"

"We've got one very unhappy client. We need to get this sorted immediately."

"'E can't be alive. His peepholes were fixed and deleted."

"Pupils, Cole. And watching hours of 'ospital shows on the box doesn't qualify you as someone who can make a call on the state of someone's life signs."

"Well why didn't *you* check?" Cole crawled out from under the desk.

"Because I'm management, Cole. I delegate responsibility to you, and I expect you to do the job right."

Cole nodded. "Right, Eddie. I'll go out and find him then."

"You'd best do that right quick, Cole. If we don't put this job to rest, we may never get out of here."

Cole's downcast eyes flicked towards the creeping slime mould, which he was certain, froze as soon as he looked at it.

"Come on, mate, I'll give you a 'and," Edwid said. "We're a team, right?"

"Right," Cole agreed.

They left the cold, damp office together and in the empty space they left behind, the slime mould stretched a little and relaxed, delighted in its own way that the object of its affection had looked in its direction at last.

CHAPTER 4

Habeas rode the bus most days. He would ride to the zippelin port or the central city to distribute pamphlets and share the certainty of Arthur's teachings with his fellow people.

He felt conflicted about taking the bus, as using anything empowered by the double-e flux was forbidden by many sects of Arthur.

The young monk often questioned the wisdom of his elders, and they encouraged such youthful defiance, reasoning that nothing made you think more carefully about your beliefs than having some young pup suggest you were out of touch with modern thinking and about as relevant as a sundial in a gold mine.

When Habeas asked if it was appropriate for him to ride the bus, his elders responded with wisdom like: "Only your mind is in motion," and "In any time, in any place, that alone is where you are."

The truth of their words became no clearer after meditation, which inspired Habeas to devote more time to practice.

He got off the bus at the central terminus. The layout of the cathedral-sized hall, filled with bus-based commuters, had been designed to move people quickly and efficiently from the buses to the street.

In the afternoon, the polarity reversed, and the commuters returned home in a far more positive mood.

The flow of human traffic made the threshold leading to the street a prime spot for people wanting to take a moment of your time to enlist your support in all manner of causes, fund-raising efforts, and community projects.

An enterprising few came equipped with trays on neck straps so they could offer refreshments and souvenirs to the people leaving the bus station. The really enterprising ones recognised an untapped market and stocked items pitched towards the other merchants, such as throat lozenges, juice-boxes, spare pens, and icepacks for bruises.

Habeas nodded to the other regulars and took his usual spot next to a vending machine. He stood looking out into the street, not watching the pedestrians flowing past. The beep of a credit stick being inserted into the machine told him that someone was within range. At the sound he turned, and in a surprised tone greeted the person as if they were an old friend he hadn't seen in years.

By the time the target realised that they did not know this strange young man with the wild hair and plucky beard, he had managed to press one of his pamphlets into their hand and bestow some of Arthur's wisdom upon them.

Habeas smiled warmly at the back-peddling man in the business suit, nodding as the fellow made his excuses and hurried away into the sidewalk traffic. The sense of implanting a new idea in a mind filled Habeas with the same joy he knew a farmer must feel when the first green shoots of a new crop burst from fertile soil.

"Excuse me," an irritated voice said. Habeas turned around, his friendly smile vanishing in a flash of pain as a fistful of white-clenched knuckles filled his vision.

"What the Helium did you do that for?" the dishevelled man standing over Habeas' prone form demanded.

"I'm sorry?" Habeas asked, certain there had been some kind of mistake.

"You said we were going to talk to him. Instead, you cleaned his clock!"

"I'm sorry?" Habeas asked again.

The man waved a warning finger at the young monk. "You stay quiet. This is between me and him."

Habeas couldn't see who the man was arguing with, but after a moment of intense listening, the fellow with the fist interrupted the unseen and unheard conversation. "Well let's get one thing straight, from now on we talk to people. Express your views if you must, but the hands are mine."

Habeas wriggled up the wall until he was standing again, and stared at the act of lunacy playing out in front of him.

"No!—Just!—Stop that!" The dishevelled man wrestled with his own fists, which seemed intent on punching him in the face. He gripped his right wrist with his left hand until, in a sudden dowward strike, he punched himself on the fly. "Oooh..." he exhaled, and sank to his knees.

"Excuse me, sir, are you all right?" Habeas carefully touched the man on the shoulder of his coat.

"I'm fine," the man on his knees wheezed, his body still folded in a foetal position.

"I've never been hit before. I am changed by the experience, as no doubt you are," Habeas declared.

"Arthurian monk, are you?" the man muttered.

"Yes, sir." Habeas gathered up his scattered tracts and presented one to the man, who was making his way into a standing position with the careful attention to detail of the very drunk.

"My name is Brother Yeast, Habeas Yeast," Habeas said, extending a hand, the tract palmed in it as if performing a card trick.

"Vole Drake—Arthur—forth. Vole Drakeforth," he said through clenched teeth.

"Vole, have you ever taken the time to consider the incredible wonder of the physical Universe?" Habeas asked.

"Listen," Drakeforth said in a conspiratorial hiss, "you're making him quite annoyed."

Habeas went silent and looked around. "Who?" he whispered.

"Arthur," Drakeforth said.

"I'm sorry?" Habeas asked.

"I'm not sure if apologising is going to cut it. He's quite adamant." Drakeforth's right fist jerked up, and he hurriedly intercepted it and pushed it down to his side again.

"We need to talk. Somewhere less public," Drakeforth said, while trying to wink.

Habeas stared at him, concerned that this strange man might be having some kind of seizure.

Drakeforth gave up being subtle, "Come with me or I'll punch you in the face again," he warned.

The idea of being punched in the face in a public area, in the presence of witnesses, as opposed to going Arthur-knows-where with a clearly disturbed fellow with a proven penchant for violence, was only slightly more appealing.

"Where are we going?" Habeas asked, as Drakeforth took him by the arm and marched him out to the sidewalk.

"You're going to meet your maker," Drakeforth said, while looking up and down the street for somewhere discreet.

"Mum and Dad?" Habeas asked, the confusion evident on his face.

"What? No, you papoose, Arthur. He's got something to tell you."

Habeas felt his knees go weak; if Drakeforth wasn't gripping his arm, he might have fallen. "I am ready, Lord," he announced. Drakeforth ignored him.

Stepping into an alleyway, Drakeforth regarded the rubbish bins with suspicion. The feeling they were regarding him with an equal wariness deepened his scowl.

"Right, I'm going to leave you two alone to talk," Drakeforth said. "Yes, I said I would. You can have a couple of minutes. No, I don't care if it's going to take longer than that. You should be grateful that I'm letting you do this at all!"

A bewildered Habeas stared at Drakeforth as he argued with himself.

"Just shut up a minute," Drakeforth said. He took a deep breath and exhaled slowly, his eyelids slipping to half mast before his shoulders jerked and his eyes snapped open again.

"What's your name, boy?" Drakeforth asked.

"Habeas Yeast, I told you that a min—"

"Hush. No time, he's only given me a couple of minutes.

Which is what I want to talk to you about."

"What?" Habeas asked.

"More when," Drakeforth replied. "You lot think that time is static and malleable and—well, you know more than I do about what you think."

"I would like to think so," Habeas replied.

"That's the problem: far too much thinking. Let me put it in words you can understand but are unlikely to believe. I am Arthur. The Arthur. I am the founder of your so-called religion."

"How—" Habeas started.

"Don't ask questions, just listen. I am Arthur, the founder of Arthurianism.

"Bu—" Habeas tried again.

"Listen, gods exist because people believe in them. I exist in a strange state which even your self-proclaimed wisest elders cannot comprehend. More importantly, and it if isn't too much trouble, I need you to save the Universe."

"How do I know you are Arthur?" Habeas blurted before he could be shushed.

Drakeforth leaned forward, and with an exaggerated solemnity uttered, "'Hello? Hello? Is this thing on? What year is it? I think I have the date wrong. Sorry to have bothered you.'"

Habeas swallowed. "Arthur…"

"Yes, and you, young Habeas, are to be my prophet. Accompany this Drakeforth vessel. Go out among the people and ensure they remain oblivious. Follow the path and find the truth. There are still opportunities to correct what may happen. If you fail, I don't know what will happen."

"What…may happen?"

"Exactly. Ignorance is the engine that drives the Universe. It fuels uncertainty, and chaos, and change. You and Drakeforth are seeking answers. And when you find the truth, you must make sure no one else ever knows."

"What was the question?" Habeas blurted.

"Did I forget to mention that? Well it's quite simple. You are seeking a greater truth, and Drakeforth is seeking exactly what he wants to know. Together—"

Arthur's eyes narrowed and then crossed. He shivered as if someone had walked over his grave, and then straightened. "Time's up. I want to spend even less time soaking in my subconscious than most people," Drakeforth announced.

"That was really him? That was Arthur?"

"I've done my part. You, Arthur, all this custard… It's narwhal-snot and I'm not doing it anymore."

Habeas remembered he had knees in time for them to fold underneath him. He sank down between the rubbish bins, which shuffled nervously and made room for him to collapse gently.

"Why are you fainting? Get up and go away," Drakeforth insisted.

"Arthur has chosen me to be his prophet," Habeas said, and looked skyward.

"Yes, aren't you special." Arthur extended a hand and seized Habeas by the scruff of his robe. Pulling the boy to his feet, Drakeforth dusted him off and set him straight.

"You got the message, right?"

Habeas nodded. "I did," he beamed at Drakeforth.

"Beans and bacon…" Drakeforth muttered. "All right, away you go then. Go and do as commanded."

"It's a test," Habeas agreed. "Arthur has spoken to me and I must prove my faith to him by inciting the faithful to be, well, more faithful."

"He told you that, did he?" Drakeforth asked.

"I believe so," Habeas breathed.

"Dry docks," Drakeforth muttered. "He didn't perhaps say anything specific about finding the truth?"

"He said I was to accompany you on a holy quest. I must seek a greater truth. You, are seeking a great truth, too."

"Are you sure?" Drakeforth's face suggested he had just swallowed a cup of chilled slugs. "Listen, kid. From the way he is going on, it would seem that Arthur's instructions were to do something more important?"

"Of course, his message appears to say exactly that," Habeas replied. "Which is exactly why I must seek the truth of what he truly means."

"Does it not seem likely that Arthur might have been using the limited time he had to speak to you to extol the exact truth in as few as words as possible?"

Habeas nodded slowly, "Arthur has instructed me to accompany you in a holy quest to seek the truth."

"Technically yes, but it is important you focus on the context and intent of that message," Drakeforth said hurriedly.

"Once I know the truth, I must ensure that no one else knows it?" Habeas whispered, his eyes going wide.

"What in the turkey gobblers does that even mean?" Drakeforth snapped.

Habeas nodded. "Arthur's words have always required great dedication of spirit. We should study his message and meditate on the essence of its reality." He seized Drakeforth's hand and shook it vigorously. "Thank you, most sacred vessel of Arthur. Tell him I have heard his word and will not fail on this holy quest."

"Hang on," Drakeforth said, jerking his hand back.

"No time!" Habeas rushed out to the street. "We have to find the truth and then—" Habeas stopped and clapped a hand over his mouth. Hurrying back into the alleyway, he whispered, "Not tell anyone." Looking around furtively, Habeas skulked out of the alleyway, looking more suspicious than a police line-up of compulsive confessors.

Drakeforth opened his mouth and then slowly closed it again. "Arthur," he murmured. "I appear to have made a grave mistake and have clearly misjudged you. I was prepared to entertain your insistence and assist you with this plan. I did so with reluctance, because frankly, the idea of you seemed like the sort of delirium that may be brought on by a concussion. Which I am quite sure I recently suffered at the hands of those two 'assassins'—and I use that word loosely, much as you might use the word watertight for a boat made of toilet tissue." Drakeforth's voice rose in volume and sarcastic tone. "While it previously appeared possible that you might be on the right track, I can now conclude, conclusively, that you are an idiot with all the sense of a wallfish!"

Drakeforth went silent for a moment. "No, I am not following him. He's *your* apostle and therefore not my problem. Now, where do you fancy going for lunch?"

CHAPTER 5

Habeas went from bus to bus, consulting the almanac of the Metropolitan Transit Timetables. Like many carefully prepared documents for public consumption, the bus timetables were drafted and crafted with the purest intent by people who really believed they were making a difference.

Transport engineers, city planners, people who have studied the subtle effects of shades of colour on the human psyche, even bus drivers had been consulted to create the mathematical marvel that was the metropolitan bus schedule.

In theory it was perfect: a vast ballet of lumbering omnibuses; each leaving and arriving on a schedule as carefully monitored and massaged as a ventricle during open heart surgery.

Like all perfect theoretical models, it only required the introduction of the human element to descend into chaos. And yet, buses came and went, people got on and got off. Somehow, it worked. As it became apparent that the actual timetable was becoming far more complex than originally designed, there was an attempt to analyse the system.

A small team were assembled and given the task of confirming exactly how the municipal bus system worked. Their findings were never published and the fate of those involved was never made public. All enquiries into their whereabouts led nowhere, and none of the team were ever seen again.

Habeas took a step of faith onto a bus and swiped his credit stick to pay the fare. Taking his seat, he glowed with fervour. He needed to find the Great Truth and that meant trusting Arthur to guide him to the answers. He leapt out of his seat a moment later as the bus pulled out and he saw Drakeforth walking towards the terminal exit.

The monk wanted to shout for the bus to stop, but Arthur's words rang true in his mind and he stilled himself. In the perception of time and space, Drakeforth would be where he was needed to be when he was needed to be there. It would all come down to the will of Arthur.

The bus journey ended for Habeas at the campus of Vander Waals University. He walked among the buildings, through a myriad of students, closing his eyes and allowing the random probability of Arthur to guide his steps.

Every time he collided with someone or something, he would head off on a new vector until, eventually, he opened his eyes.

The School of Physical Sciences, the sign in front of Habeas read. Beneath that a second sign advised, *Arthurianism Is Located In The School Of Arts And Literature: Religious Studies Section.*

Content in his purpose, Habeas went up the steps and into the building. He approached the reception desk with the same air of openness and warmth that had snared many an unwary commuter at the bus terminal.

The woman behind the desk barely looked up from her computer screen. "No," she said before Habeas could say a word.

"I—"

"No. *Noho. Ex-nubi. Kapheek. Aihwa. Shnitz. Nahin. Zuuu-pok,*" the woman said.

"I—"

"Arthurianism is in the faculty of arts and literature. Religious Studies section. You can follow the signs outside, and they will take you to where you want to be."

"But—"

The receptionist continued with the same practised recitation of a zippelin aircrew member delivering the passenger safety briefing. "We are a faculty of scientists. While you are entirely welcome to practise your beliefs, we ask that you do so in an environment where they are less likely to be met with derision and ridicule."

Habeas waited until the receptionist was immersed in her work again. "I am here to see Pimola Goosebread," he said in a rush.

The receptionist frowned. "One moment please." She donned a headset and keyed a number on the phone.

"Sorry to bother you, Ms Goosebread. There is a...man here to see you. An Arthurian."

"Habeas Yeast," Habeas offered.

"Says his name is Half Beast."

"Yes, Ms Goosebread. Right away, Ms Goosebread." The receptionist disconnected the call.

"She will be right out. Word of warning, utter a single word of your pseudo-quackery and I will have Security deliver you to the mail room, whereupon you will be placed in a crate with minimal air holes and then shipped to Escrutia by boat."

"Thank you," Habeas replied.

"The long way round."

By Habeas' perception of time, five minutes had passed when a stairwell door opened and Pimola walked into the reception area.

"Hi," Habeas said.

"Uh, hello?" Pimola regarded him.

"Habeas Yeast; we met at the zippelin port café. You write the weekly Fenstick column."

"Yes...?" Pimola asked politely.

"There's something important I need to talk to you about. Not tea. Something—" Habeas caught the receptionist watching him with narrowed eyes. "Something about the box you received from the Escrutians."

"Oh?" Pimola folded her arms.

"Is there somewhere else we can talk?"

"You can come down to my lab." Pimola led the way.

"I have Security on speed-dial," the receptionist called after her.

"Thank you, Silphia."

The door closed behind them, and Pimola showed Habeas down the stairs.

27

"You have to forgive Silphia. She gets more than her fair share of Arthurians trying to gain access to the various researchers working here."

"Arthurianism is knowledge. Wisdom that needs constant study and exploration. Who better to lead us to greater enlightenment than leading physicists?"

"Well, in the opinion of many of my colleagues, it isn't a physicist you need, but a psychiatrist."

"There is always some madness in genius. To reach enlightenment requires us to cross a threshold of Self. For many people that seems like insanity."

"And sometimes, people are just mentally ill and in need of support and professional care," Pimola replied.

"Arthurians have always provided support to those in need."

"This is us," Pimola said, changing the subject and opening the door. Her laboratory struck Habeas as being like a temple, if put together by someone who had only heard rumours about what a temple does and had taken it all very literally. Which in essence was the main concern that the Arthurians had with particle physics and, ironically, was the only concern that particle physicists had with Arthurians.

Computers hummed cheerfully as they busied themselves in complex computations. Hard drives chattered and tossed out data like a domestic simplification guru on a house call. Whiteboards marked with arcane symbols of mathematics and logic stood around the walls, and only the tea set in the tiny corner kitchenette seemed out of place.

"Tea?" Pimola asked.

"Oh, yes please." Habeas said, feeling the spirit of Arthur filling him anew. Here in this room, the presence of the one true God filled the air and the computer printouts and the whiteboards.

Pimola made tea and returned with two cups. "Sit and tell me what is so important."

"I met Him," Habeas said, managing to enunciate the capital *H* with an eyebrow wriggle.

"That's sweet. My mother always said there was someone out there for everyone. Except me, of course. I'm not sure why you felt it necessary to track me down to tell me about your new relationship."

"It's not a new—Oh!" Habeas blushed. "I didn't mean like that. I met a man who claims to be Arthur. Then I actually met Arthur!"

Pimola sipped her tea. "Good for you. Anything else?"

"You must understand. I met him. I met the true Arthur."

"Yes, I understand you think you met your god. Which must have been very exhausting. You should probably go home and get some rest. Maybe call a friend or family member and talk to them? I could call someone for you if you like."

"I am not crazy!" Habeas yelled.

Pimola set her cup down. "Habeas, if you shout at me again, you will have to leave, and I will never speak to you again."

"I'm sorry. I'm having a hard time understanding it all myself." Habeas tasted his perfect tea.

"Perhaps you could start at the beginning?"

"I was assaulted by a man who called himself Vole Drakeforth. He appeared quite ma—err, enlightened. At the bus terminal. He was engaged in an argument with Arthur himself."

"And that convinced you that he was the genuine article?"

"No, that came later. When Arthur made himself known to me. It was *The Revelation of the Alleyway*."

"The revelation of the alleyway?"

"Well yes, it's where it was revealed to me."

"You had a vision of profound importance in an alleyway?

"Yes."

"Are you sure there isn't someone I can call for you?"

Habeas regarded Pimola with his warm cow-eyes from under his yak-like fringe.

"I'm fine, thank you. I wanted to tell you, because as a journalist, I thought you might be interested and would have the means to help me find the Great Truth."

"Habeas, I write a tea-review column. I'm not a journalist."

The young Arthurian monk waved her words away. "I'm not a neurosurgeon, but I can still tell a fish from a bowl of breakfast cereal."

Pimola frowned, "That makes sense in a way I am not entirely comfortable with."

Habeas nodded, "It makes you uncomfortable because you know it is true."

"Hold that thought." Pimola turned to a keyboard and monitor. She woke it up and tapped in login details that seemed longer and more complex than necessary.

"KLOE," Pimola said as she typed. "Input this and add to base data. Data start. I am not a neurosurgeon, but I can still tell a fish from a bowl of breakfast cereal. Data end."

Habeas waited for a response, for someone to acknowledge the instruction. Nothing happened. Pimola seemed satisfied, however.

"Who is Chloe?" he asked.

"KLOE. K-L-O-E," she spelled out. "It means *Kollective Labour of Empathic Organisation*. The Escrutians have shared it with the University as part of an exchange of culture and technology."

Habeas blinked. "Ohh, the band and the box at the zippelin port?"

"Yes," Pimola confirmed. "Escrutians delivering KLOE. I was there to collect it."

"It was a big box," Habeas agreed and looked around. "Where is it?"

"You really want to see it?" Pimola regarded him with a slight smile.

"Sure," Habeas replied, unsure why she found that amusing.

"Okay." Pimola stood and Habeas followed. She moved a whiteboard aside and keyed an entrance code into a door panel. The door hushed open, and they stepped into a room lined with plain white tiles, lacking any decoration and having only the most functional lighting. In the centre of the room stood a dull-grey steel box, larger than a fridge: a cube with no lights, no screens, no keyboard, and no signs of any activity.

"Is it on?" Habeas asked. "I mean, it is a computer, right?"

"Oh yes, it is on and it is a computer," Pimola said, almost bubbling with supressed excitement. "The Escrutians, for all their isolationist philosophy and scathing disregard for the rest of the world, they have achieved some remarkable breakthroughs in quantum computing."

"Oh…" Habeas breathed, his breath misting softly in the chill air of the room. In his heart he felt the certainty of his destiny,the knowledge that there was a connection between his revelation, meeting with Pimola and all the elements of the Universe that had brought him to this point. It cemented his faith, and he resisted the urge to drop to his knees and give thanks to Arthur for his blessings.

"Hey," Pimola interrupted his moment. "Don't forget to breathe."

"Yes," Habeas inhaled and exhaled through his nose. Feeling the supercharged air, so thick with energy and the warming spices of faith, he could have eaten it by the bowlfull.

"I haven't shown you the best part yet," Pimola said. She stepped up to the plain, grey steel-looking side of the box and pressed her fingertips against it. A soft click emanated, and a black line appeared, running from top to bottom near the edge of the cabinet. With gentle pressure, Pimola swung the wall open and stepped back. "See what's inside," she whispered, the smile in her voice promising exciting wonders.

Habeas dutifully stepped closer and peered into the void. The cabinet appeared inside as it did outside: plain grey steel walls, ceiling, and floor. Yet, there was nothing inside the box. No circuitry. No wires. No glowing crystals or human brain wired into a complex life-support cybernetics system. Inside, KLOE was completely empty.

Habeas stepped back. "I don't understand," he admitted. A core tenement of his faith was not only to accept that you did not understand, but to share that with others. Accepting the limitations of his knowledge was a key stepping stone on the path to true enlightenment.

"I know! Isn't it great?!" Pimola beamed at him and eased the panel closed again.

"Yes…?" Habeas replied carefully.

"The Escrutians have succeeded in creating a truly quantum computer. KLOE cannot be perceived by us. The computer inside the box exists and does not exist. It is in a superposition."

"Hang on…" Habeas grabbed the conversation by the bits he could understand and clung to the Arthurian teachings like a drowning man on floating wreckage. "The superposition of an unknown entity can only exist until it is observed or interacted with. We looked inside the box. The superposition should have collapsed into another state."

Pimola nodded with increasing enthusiasm. "I know! That is what makes it so exciting!"

"How does it work?" Habeas asked.

Pimola took a deep breath and exhaled slowly. "That, my dear Habeas, is what I intend to find out."

CHAPTER 6

The nameplates on the door of the building were made of etched brass. The kind of nameplates that assured you the tenants found within were serious, worthy, and dependable. The building had tradition baked into every brick like raisins in a fruit loaf.

Edwid ignored them all and waited for the moment when someone exited, and he slipped through the gap, like a cat with no time to explain, as the door swung closed. Stopping it with his foot, he gestured for Cole to cross the street and join him.

Once inside, they let the door close and looked around. A stone building, ancient plaster, and gilded fittings. The shine eroded by neglect and blurred by a patina of dust.

The two hitmen still looked out of place, never having been polished or gilded themselves. They wore the ambience of tradesmen, small fellows, regardless of Cole's similarity to a gorilla, overlooked by most as they went about fixing the small inconveniences that plagued the world of those with more important things to worry about.

"Your uncle has his office here?" Cole asked.

"Best lawyer in the city," Edwid said with confidence.

"Yeah, but his card says *Elevator B*," Cole frowned.

"Must be the way to get to his office." Edwid approached the three elevators in the lobby. The central one had a large *OUT OF ORDER* sign taped to the door.

He pressed the elevator call button and stepped back.

"'Elevator B. Press call button twice. Pause. Then twice more',"

Cole read aloud from the business card.

Edwid sighed and followed the instructions. After a moment, the elevator rattled and hummed. Lights flickered and, with a metallic gurgle, the central elevator door clattered open.

The space in the elevator car was taken up by a desk and a chair behind it. A filing cabinet was squeezed into the corner as if trying to not take up more room than necessary.

A balding man leaned back in the chair, talking loudly on a phone. "It is an irrefutable fact; the police are liable if they perceive the person as being dead. Because they are responsible for causing that probability to become perceived and making it reality. You're welcome. Goodbye."

He hung up and looked at the two men standing outside the lift. "Come in."

Edwid and Cole shuffled forward, squeezing into the narrow space between the desk and the elevator door, which seemed to sigh and then closed behind them.

"I don't usually take walk-ins," the man announced.

"Uncle Vernon?" Edwid asked.

"Who wants to know?"

"It's me, Edwid Mint. Maynard's boy."

"Allegedly," Vernon replied.

"No, I'm pretty sure—"

"Let me give you some advice, son. Nothing is proven. Everything is subject to perception. As a lawyer, the service I provide is confirming the reality that provides my clients with the best outcome. Anything else is hearsay."

"Hairspray?" Cole asked.

"Is he with you?" Vernon asked.

"Yeah, this is Cole Munt, he's my business partner."

"Why? Did you lose a bet?" Vernon frowned. "I can help you get out of it."

"What? No. I just— Look, it's not important. We are running a business. A highly skilled professional service. We need some advice on a contract we have with a client."

"I charge by the hour. Stepping into my office means you have accepted those fees and are entirely in agreement with the fiscal responsibility of paying for my services, regardless of your perception of satisfaction and outcome of any matter I advise you on."

"Yeah, sure," Edwid nodded.

"Sign this," Vernon slid a clipboard with a densely written form across the table. Edwid took the offered pen and signed where indicated. Vernon took the form back and replaced it with a second copy. "Your copy. You should sign it, too."

Once completed, he leaned back in his chair. "Now, how can I help you gentlemen?"

"Me and Cole, we're running a business. A real classy operation. Discreet services for a disc-earning client-elle."

"We're assassins," Cole blurted.

"Well, it's more complicated than that," Edwid added hurriedly.

"Is it?" Cole frowned.

"Yeah." Edwid fidgeted with embarrassment. "We are professionals. We provide a discreet service, right?"

"We pride ourselves on our customer service," Cole agreed.

"Customer service is important," Vernon nodded.

"I know, right?" Edwid warmed to the subject like a cat on a radiator. "We wanted to offer an exclusive service. Quality assassinations. Real high-value jobs. The kind of contract killings that people will talk about."

"But not, you know, *talk about*," Cole interjected.

"Yeah," Edwid frowned. "We are like ghosts. We strike without warning and disappear. We leave no trace and the only sign we were ever there is the ex-person."

"I thought we could leave business cards," Cole spoke up. "You know, to get those word-of-mouth referrals? No point in doing classy work if no one knows how to get in touch."

He took a prototype business card from his pocket and laid it on the desk with a flourish.

"Yeah, nah," Edwid said in reply to Vernon's wordless yoga workout of facial expressions.

"How's business?" Vernon asked.

"Great," Cole replied.

"Well, it's okay..." Edwid said slowly.

Vernon nodded. "You're Maynard's kid?"

"Yessir," Edwid replied.

Vernon leaned back in his chair and said: "They say the apple doesn't fall far from the tree. In Maynard's case, it appears to have landed on its head."

"Edwid's allergic to apples," Cole said.

"Uncle Vernon doesn't care about that, Cole."

"That's an assumption," Vernon warned.

"No, he gets all blotchy and can't breathe and everything," Cole insisted.

Vernon regarded Cole with the steady gaze of one who has honed his disdain to a professional mastery. "Colin, is it?"

"Colander, but everyone calls me Cole."

"Colander, I need you to do something for me. Something very important."

Cole wriggled forward as far as the cramped elevator would allow.

"Yeah?"

"Go away," Vernon said.

"Right. Yeah... Okay." Cole turned like a penguin trying to shuffle his way through the colony without having to say excuse me a thousand times.

Edwid stared at the floor while Cole did his awkward dance. Reaching out he tapped the lift button and the doors slid open. "Talk to you later, mate," Edwid said.

"Yeah," Cole stepped out of the lift with a sigh of relief. The doors closed behind him and Vernon folded his hands on the desk.

"I don't give free advice, so for tax purposes, I am currently talking to myself. You are running a business. Offering a professional service to a discerning clientele who expect the highest levels of discretion and professionalism."

"Yeah?" Edwid nodded.

"Your chosen profession is, to the mind untrained in all aspects of the interpretation and application of the law, as dodgy as a week-old kebab."

Edwid started to speak, but Vernon raised a hand in a silencing gesture. "I applaud your initiative. Your focus on the important things: contributing to the economy, placing customers first in every aspect of your enterprise. It's heartening to see Maynard produce something worthwhile. Now, I need to make it clear that you are protected by attorney-client privilege. Which means that anything you say to me here, I am legally bound to not disclose to anyone. There are exceptions, of course, though you need not concern yourself with them.

"Okay…" Edwid replied, not entirely sure what he was agreeing to.

"You did the right thing coming to see me. As your legal advisor, my advice is as follows. Firstly, put that oversized chimpanzee up for adoption. Secondly, do not create anything that will leave a trail of evidence that could be interpreted as connecting you with the perceived death of anyone. Thirdly, double your fees. People will understand you are professional if you charge an outrageous service fee. It reinforces the impression that you are offering an exclusive service, delivered by highly trained and experienced experts in service delivery." Vernon leaned back in his chair. "Any questions?"

"Uh, what chimpanzee?" Edwid asked.

"Colander Munt. You need to get rid of him. He is a liability that will doom your business enterprise to failure."

"Cole's a mate," Edwid suggested.

"There are no friends in business, Edwid. Drop him like a fart in a crowded elevator. Discreetly, and be prepared to disavow all knowledge."

Edwid frowned; the idea of breaking up the partnership with Cole did not sit well with him. "The other stuff, I can do that. I mean, it was Cole's idea to make the flyers and advertise in the *Blue Pages*, and business cards. It made sense in a weird way."

"If we all did things that made sense, the world would be a far less interesting place."

"It would?" Edwid tried to sound like he understood. "I read this book on being an on-trapper-nerd. It says stuff about customer service being one of the seven keys to success."

"Really? What are the other six?"

Edwid shrugged and shuffled his feet. "I didn't finish the book. Just got the gist of it, you know?"

"Have you successfully completed any contracts?" Vernon asked.

"Well...yeah, nah...I mean... We did. But he came back to life." Edwid squirmed with embarrassment.

"Interesting." Vernon didn't seem surprised or disbelieving. "The contract you had your client sign, it didn't stipulate that the merchandise had to stay in the state agreed?"

"I don't think we had anything in the contract about him leaving town, or going to another state..."

Vernon regarded him steadily for a long moment. "Perhaps I should bring the chimpanzee back in here and talk to him?"

"Nah," Edwid replied. "We're okay, then? We still get paid, even if Vole Dra—"

"The merchandise," Vernon interrupted.

"Even if the merchandise didn't stay dead?"

"Of course. You completed the contract. You confirmed with your client?"

"Uh yeah, the chim—I mean Cole—took a selfie. I made him delete it off his phone after we sent the client a photo of the merchandise. Lying there, definitely out of state."

"Good," Vernon nodded. "You completed your agreed task. You are entitled to your agreed fee. In fact, I suggest you make it clear that if payment is not made promptly, your client will be hearing from your legal team."

"Team?" Edwid's eyes flicked around the cramped elevator.

"Never let the enemy know the full strength of your forces," Vernon said gravely.

"Right..." Edwid nodded.

"I'll have my secretary draft a letter. If you have any issues getting what is your due, contact me immediately."

"Thanks, Uncle Vernon." Edwid stood up.

"No, thank *you*, Edwid. My fee will include a percentage to be deducted from money received."

"Uhh, okay." Edwid tapped the elevator button and slipped out into the gilded lobby.

CHAPTER 7

"I've been old for longer than I've been anything else, except, maybe, alive. I'm still trying to get the hang of it," Arthur said from his place in Drakeforth's consciousness.

Arthur didn't need an audience, which made it less satisfying for Drakeforth to ignore the voice in his head. The god of Arthurianism talked constantly about a range of topics.

He continued talking as Drakeforth walked into an internet café. The bored-looking attendant at the service counter had long hair and a beard that would have made Habeas whimper with envy. His focus was intent on the glow from his phone screen. Drakeforth approached and waited for as long as his temper would allow. Which was about this long.

"Oi!" he barked.

The attendant sighed and, with a glacial slowness, lifted his head.

"Hey man," he breathed.

"I need access to the complete summation of all human knowledge and achievement. The reference library greater than the combined intellectual estate of the Habian, the Grotesk, and the lost library of Mink," Drakeforth explained.

The attendant blinked at him. "We just do internet here-man."

"That will have to do," Drakeforth agreed.

The attendant slowly tapped a keyboard. "How long you want?"

"As long as it takes," Drakeforth replied.

"I can give you twenty minutes for thirty, thirty for twenty, forty-five for thirty, or sixty for forty-five," the attendant informed him.

"I would have rather hoped that in a world and time so filled with technological advances and wonders, the concept of time would have been done away with," Arthur announced.

"Shut up," Drakeforth muttered. "No," he added reflexively, "Not you."

"Well-man, how long do you want?"

"Why does twenty minutes cost more than thirty minutes?" Drakeforth asked.

The attendant shrugged. "Dunno-man."

Drakeforth's scowl deepened, in the same way a marine trench does, suddenly and into a dark and terrifying abyss.

"There must be a reason for it. Someone did the math. No doubt a hugely expensive consultant team were engaged to complete a cost-benefit analysis. They didn't just pull numbers at random from a cat."

"A cat?" The attendant tried to look puzzled, and then gave up as that much movement would require energy.

"I could explain to you how cats are the most accurate source of all randomness in the Universe, but that would involve starting at the very beginning: teaching you how to count, read letters, and write your own name. From there we would move on to more advanced subjects, like basic critical thinking, philosophy, science, and most importantly how to think. Frankly, it clearly didn't work out the first time, which is why you ended up working here."

"Hey man," the attendant managed to sound offended.

"Education was never formalised in my day," Arthur said somewhat glumly. "We just made it up as we went along. Lessons were mostly of the practical type. If the student in front of you ate a strange mushroom and died, you considered yourself educated in botany."

"Will you shut up?" Drakeforth muttered through gritted teeth. "Not you," he added again.

"Hey… Hey man," the attendant was working himself up into quite the state.

"I'll take thirty at fifteen—" Drakeforth said.

"And a packet of crisps," Arthur interrupted.

"—and a packet of crisps," Drakeforth added.

"Uhh..." the attendant said.

Drakeforth retrieved a tightly bound roll of banknotes from his inner coat pocket. He peeled one off like an onion skin and slapped it on the counter.

"Uhh...?" the attendant asked.

"Cash. I'm paying cash," Drakeforth explained.

"Cash?" Arthur and the attendant both asked in unison.

"Yes, cash. None of that electronic gazebo-spit electronic currency," Drakeforth declared.

"It doesn't look like cash," Arthur said with interest.

"What's cash?" the attendant asked.

"Real money. Stuff you can hold and feel like you have actually made a transaction. It's a step up from the barter system, certainly. Keeps the human relationship element in economy. Human interaction is essential for your mental health and wellbeing."

The attendant looked like he had some counter-arguments on the benefits of interaction with Drakeforth on his mental health and wellbeing, but wisely kept them to himself.

"Most importantly," Drakeforth continued, "it is untraceable."

"We take credit stick," the attendant said.

"What is your name?" Drakeforth asked, in the same tone a shark might use to invite a seal to dinner.

"Justin," the attendant admitted.

"You must be filled with hope," Drakeforth said. "Overflowing with the certainty and joy of knowing that one day, someone will burst into this rather decrepit and odorous establishment, with great fanfare. There will be streamers. Proper popping ones, not those sad, hand-tossed ones. There will be beautiful women in sequined costumes and silken sashes. They will convene here for you, Justin. A beaming television host will step into the spotlight that falls upon you and there, in the face of a global audience, they will present you with an award, Justin.

"The award you have secretly craved all your life. The singularity of your existence that you have been moving towards since the no doubt awkward moment of your conception. You Justin, will one day hold aloft a grand trophy with your name engraved on it. This great prize will be in recognition of your preternatural ability to state the completely and utterly blindingly obvious. Your mother will be very proud."

"Uhhh…?" Justin tried again.

"I'll take that machine over there and a packet of those tangerine flavoured crisps," Drakeforth replied. "Keep the change."

Drakeforth sank into a soft chair in front of a dull monitor. He tapped at the keyboard and pushed buttons until the screen stirred and began to glow.

"Empathic energy," Drakeforth muttered. "Wonder of the modern age… Bah!"

"Are you going to open those crisps or not?" Arthur asked.

"I'm not hungry," Drakeforth snapped.

"I'm curious," Arthur explained.

"Good for you," Drakeforth muttered, aware of the glances being cast in his direction from the other computer users.

"Curiosity is what drives us to new experiences," Arthur reminded him.

"It would be almost worth it to drive into a brick wall, just to let you experience dying."

"We have talked about this, Vole. Cooperation is the best solution to both our problems."

"It would suit me far better if you would just soap off and cooperate with someone else."

"I've seen these," Arthur said, as the computer prepared itself for a good workout.

"*Technically,* you have seen these. You are just reading over my shoulder," Drakeforth replied.

"Pistachio, potato," Arthur replied.

Drakeforth's fingers hovered over the keyboard.

"How does it work?" Arthur asked.

"That's the thing," Drakeforth replied. "You need to be absolutely silent, or it won't."

"Wh—?"

"Shhh!"

Drakeforth started typing his query into the search window, opening the packet of crisps, and eating one while keying in search terms with his other hand.

"Hey these are really good," Arthur said.

Drakeforth's chip-conveying hand waved as if it were engaging in a freestyle dance.

"Would you please give me my hand back," Drakeforth snarled. "I'm not hungry and I have work to do."

Arthur kept a firm grip on Drakeforth's hand, and the fingers clenched like a minimalist sock puppet.

"What?" Drakeforth glared at his hand.

"You asked me where we wanted to go for lunch, now we are here, and you haven't eaten all day. Snacking on some crisps is the least you could do."

"We can get something to eat later, now give my hand back."

The Arthur-controlled hand waved in a negative gesture and his fingers curled into a frown.

"Do not touch those crisps," Drakeforth whispered to his hand. He lunged to grab his wrist with his other hand as Arthur made a dash for the open packet. Arthur's hand snatched a pinch of crisps as Drakeforth's hand locked around his arm.

"Drop it," Drakeforth commanded. Arthur shook his hand and strained to reach Drakeforth's mouth.

"I am not eating that," Drakeforth insisted. Arthur's possession of his hand forced him to hold the crisps at arm's length.

"Why not? They taste fascinating. I want to experience more of this flavour," Arthur insisted.

"You cannot just take control of limbs when you feel like it," Drakeforth snapped. "It's assault."

Arthur's hand looked away and he muttered, "You weren't using it."

"That is not the point!" Drakeforth insisted. Then he lowered his voice. "Seriously. It's my body. We need to establish some boundaries here."

His hand snapped up, the fingertips forming a smirk. "Your perception of your existence is rather primitive. You really believe you are bound by what you see as your body?"

"Oh," Drakeforth rolled his eyes. "Here we go again…"

"Not only are you a multi-dimensional creature, measurable in four dimensions, you are also a mind. The mind is the aura fuelled by the tea and guavacado toast you ate yesterday. You repurpose that energy and it becomes you. To claim your form is purely physical is like claiming that only one version of you exists in the Universe."

"Or perhaps we are all just the hallucination of a disturbed mind?" Drakeforth suggested.

"Possibly. Now eat your crisps."

CHAPTER 8

After Habeas left her laboratory, Pimola worked late into the afternoon, running simple computer simulations through the keyboard and screen that somehow allowed her to input data into KLOE, though neither device was connected to the dull, grey box. Pimola tried not to think about it.

"It's quite simple, really," she said to the empty room. It was her habit to think aloud when she worked alone, which was more common since she started her post-graduate work. It helped her frame complex problems in an extra dimension, beyond thought and the written word. It let her see things in a different way.

"At least on the surface," she continued, and paused in her typing. "KLOE," she tapped into the keyboard, "have you been programmed with an understanding of moral dilemmas?"

The cursor on the monitor blinked like the narrowed eye of a cat. Pimola mentally drafted the next article for her tea critic column and waited patiently for the computer to respond. Text began to flow across the screen.

> MORAL DILEMMA: *a situation in which a difficult choice has to be made between two courses of action, either of which entails transgressing a moral principle.*
> MORAL PRINCIPLE: *The principles of right and wrong that are accepted by an individual or social group.*

"What is the solution to the problem of moral dilemmas?" Pimola typed.

KLOE responded immediately: *Prevent the situation requiring a moral judgement from occurring.*

Pimola was intrigued and somewhat disappointed. The answer seemed simplistic, and she had hoped that KLOE would be more advanced in its computational prowess.

"Situations arise where you do not have control of their inception," she typed. "What course of action would you take in such a situation?"

Prevent the situation from arising in such a way that stops the moral dilemma from actualising.

Pimola sighed. "Reality exists beyond your control," she said aloud.

It seemed she would need to reassess her plans for the research work she hoped to do with KLOE.

What makes you so certain, Pimola? KLOE's text interface asked.

Pimola felt the fine hairs rise on the back of her neck and a chill tangoed down her spine.

"Fact," she typed. "Reality is constrained by physical laws. You exist within reality. You interact with reality based on those physical laws."

I am not limited by your perception, KLOE replied. *You perceive reality. You exist entirely within your perception. Perception is subjective and based entirely on sensory input. Senses can be manipulated. The human mind has no physical form. It exists as a concept and creates reality based on input. Reality is a concept that can be manipulated.*

Pimola's fingers hovered over the keys and then she typed, "You are a physical construct. Much like the human body. Therefore, your consciousness is a result of the interaction of your circuitry with the programming you have. This makes you analogous with a human being. Your mind, like ours, exists in the same space-time construct, which," she typed firmly, "is constrained by reality."

Do you understand the Universe, Pimola?

Pimola frowned at the glowing letters on the screen. It was fascinating and only slightly unnerving to be having a conversation with a machine.

"I don't understand the question," she replied. Testing the limits of KLOE's artificial intelligence was a key part of her thesis work.

You perceive the Universe. You measure it mathematically and conclude that it is infinite and expanding. Nothing can exist outside of that Universe. Do you understand the Universe, Pimola?

Pimola resisted the urge to roll her eyes. If KLOE had visual sensors built into the containment unit, they were not detailed in the documentation provided by the Escrutians. In fact, the only documentation she had received with the cabinet was a shorthand written note that said,

IT IS ONLY OUR CAPACITY FOR SHAME
THAT DIRECTS US TOWARDS GOOD
AND AWAY FROM EVIL.

Pimola typed, "I understand the principles of cosmology and the rules of the Universe. These principles are confirmed by measurement and mathematics as you say. We do not perceive them. We simply confirm them."

Your confirmation is constructed within the only frame of reference you have: your perception.

Pimola frowned at the argument. For all she knew the Escrutians had a wireless transmitter built into the containment unit and were simply talking Arthurian-level nonsense at her and pretending that KLOE was in fact in possession of a highly advanced artificial intelligence.

"By that line of reasoning, you also only exist in my perception," Pimola typed with a sniff of finality.

And you have taken your first step towards understanding the true nature of the Universe.

"What is the true nature of the Universe?" Pimola typed, in a way that she hoped would come across as the verbal slap-in-the-face-with-a-fish challenge she intended.

The Universe is an illusion. A simple manipulation of your sense that you interpret as reality.

Pimola stood up and went to make tea. KLOE's claim seemed absurd, but disturbing if you thought about it too much.

The question Pimola really wanted an answer to was the one she was most afraid to ask: If the Universe was an illusion, then who or what was behind the manipulation?

CHAPTER 9

"Interesting," Arthur announced at the end of Drakeforth's lecture on his suspicions around the less-than-ethical practices of the Godden Energy Corporation.

Drakeforth tensed his shoulders and consciously reminded himself to not slam his head into the desk.

"Interesting?" he asked. "Interesting? I suppose it is. I mean, if you find a global conspiracy to defraud, defame, and destroy the lives of billions interesting. If you are like, well, learning about the greatest fraud in the history of the world is certainly a curiosity in my otherwise chunky-chocolate-chip existence. Then, I suppose, interesting is the right way to describe it."

"I have some questions," Arthur said, ignoring Drakeforth's sarcasm.

"Oh, goody." Drakeforth distilled sarcasm down to its scathing essence.

"What proof do you have?" Arthur asked.

"Proof? Proof!?" Drakeforth clenched his jaw and breathed through his nose until the air whistled. "The proof is all around us. The Godden Energy Corporation has silenced anyone who knows too much. They have spent the last century at least covering up the truth. There's your proof."

"Perhaps it is proof of your mental illness?" Arthur asked gently.

"I am not crazy!" Drakeforth shouted. A dozen heads popped up around the internet café and regarded him steadily for long enough to make their point.

"If I understand you correctly," Arthur said more gently, "you applied for a job with this Godden Energy Corporation."

"Yes," Drakeforth verbally winced.

"And you were not selected for the position?"

"I asked the wrong questions during the psychometric evaluation," Drakeforth replied.

"You asked questions and based on the questions, not the answers, you were denied a position in this corporation's ranks?"

In fact, Drakeforth's questions during the psychometric testing phase of his employment interview had raised more red flags than a swarm of cochineal beetles. While it appeared that Drakeforth didn't have answers, he had questions, which in the experience of the Corporation, made him even more dangerous.

Arthur continued, "Visionaries, rebels and free-thinkers, are often considered to be mad by the majority. Over time radical ideas can be accepted and become mainstream. There always has to be that one wilybeast who is the first to drink from the crocodile-infested river."

"I'm not crazy," Drakeforth insisted at a much lower volume.

"That's the attitude to have. You can get through this," Arthur enthused.

"I will not get through this until the Godden Energy Corporation are dragged through every court in the land," Drakeforth whispered.

"I am no stranger to adversity and challenge," Arthur replied. "You could say I wrote the book on adversity and challenge."

"Was that something the publisher asked you to do, or did you come up with it yourself?" Drakeforth asked.

"My point is that there are some battles you can choose not to fight. You applied for a job. You were unsuccessful. Move on with your life.

"It's not right!" Drakeforth snapped. "The Godden Energy corporation are hiding something. I asked where they get their empathic energy from, and the entire interview changed."

"They must be asked that kind of question a lot," Arthur said.

"I don't think they are. Everyone knows it is a naturally occurring phenomena. Huddy Godden simply found a way to refine it and increase its effectiveness."

"Well there you go," Arthur nodded. "Mystery solved."

"Except that is complete and utter slug-slippers!"

"May I ask another question?" Arthur asked.

"What?" Drakeforth replied.

"I'm asking the questions, now I'm at risk of being caught in a never-ending loop of asking questions about asking questions." Arthur's tone shifted to sermon delivery and he continued.

"The problem with answers is they are not static. The effect of new information on the questioner can be devastating. If people were to ever realise the enormity of the undertaking, they would never ask any questions at all," he said.

Drakeforth sighed. "In my experience, people avoid asking questions. They just accept what they are told."

"Which makes it terribly easy for people to be told what they want to hear."

If Arthur had been more than a disembodied voice in Drakeforth's head, he would have nodded in agreement.

"The best thing about history is that it always happens exactly the way you remember it."

"The way you are told to remember it," Drakeforth added.

Arthur fell silent. The stillness continued for so long that Drakeforth wondered if he had fallen asleep. He returned to the computer and continued his search for questions, reasoning that once he knew more about what he needed to know; the answers would become obvious.

CHAPTER 10

The sun shone down on Habeas and he tilted his face up to feel its warmth. Birds sang and he felt his chest swell with a cocktail of emotions; a spirit of smug certainty, a shot of admiration, and a dash of cognitive bias all combined to make him feel tipsy.

He strode on light feet to the street, almost dancing in the shambolic and awkward way of people with no natural sense of rhythm, or training in dance. With his eyes closed and his mind otherwise occupied, Habeas stepped off the sidewalk and into a shriek of car brakes.

An outbreak of coughing horns politely informed him how close he was to becoming a road accident statistic before the bumper of a red Flemetti Viscous captured his full attention.

A car door slammed and feet hurried into view. "Are you okay? No, don't answer that. Clearly a stupid question. How badly are you hurt? Ambulance-and-priest badly, or just sit-for-a-minute-and-get-your-breath-back badly?"

Habeas blinked. "What?" he asked.

"How many fingers am I holding up?" The man questioning Habeas waved a closed fist in his face.

"None?" Habeas replied.

"Excellent, no permanent damage then. Unless, of course, the reason you walked into the street was due to some previous permanent damage?"

"I met a girl," Habeas admitted.

"Can you stand? It's just that the forecast is for rain, and if that gutter does the job it was designed for, you could well end up drowning. While I am sure the two incidents would not be indisputably connected, it would weigh heavily on my mind if I was to hear of such a tragedy."

"I can stand…" Habeas realised. He eased himself up and with the help of the driver, he hobbled the last steps to the sidewalk and sat down with his back against a lamp post.

"I suppose we should exchange details. For insurance," the driver said, and casually removed pen and notebook from his suit pocket. Do you have insurance?" he asked.

"Is your car okay?" Habeas asked.

The driver hesitated and then turned slowly to regard the classic sportscar. He let out a sudden whimper and dashed to the front end. Crouching down, he gingerly touched a fresh dimple where Habeas' head had bounced off the hood.

"Ohhh my baby…" the driver whispered. He took a clean handkerchief from his pocket and carefully dabbed at the dent as if it were a bleeding graze.

Habeas stood up and watched curiously as the driver inspected the car for any further sign of injury. The man gently probed and poked the polished chrome and gleaming red paint. Habeas eased himself on to his feet and carefully stepped deeper onto the sidewalk.

"I'll need your insurance details before you go," the driver barked.

"Whatever for?" Habeas asked.

"You damaged my car. This is a Flemetti Viscous. You will need to pay for the repairs, and it will go easier for you if you have insurance."

"You damaged me," Habeas reminded him. "I think I can Sarah you for that."

"Sarah? You mean sue?"

"I'm sure either of those women would be quite happy to ensure you compensate me for my injuries."

"Except you just told me you were fine," the driver said with self-assurance.

"Are you a doctor?" Habeas asked.

"That would depend on the conclusion you are leaping to." The driver's eyes narrowed.

"I am simply confirming you lack the bits of paper to assess my physical health in a professional sense."

"How is that relevant? You are clearly at fault here!" the driver's face was taking on the same bright shade as the car's paint. "You, sir, stepped out into traffic and damaged my car. I could have killed you!"

"I don't think so," Habeas replied earnestly. "You see, I have been chosen by Arthur."

"Arth-oh?" The driver moved back as if Habeas had announced he was the carrier of a highly contagious disease. "I think perhaps you should sit down again and wait for an ambulance," the driver suggested.

"I'm fine," Habeas said, nodding and smiling.

The driver stood close enough to keep an eye on Habeas, but not so close as to be in range should the lunatic lunge at him. He dug a crumpled receipt out of his wallet; on the back were various vouchers offering free paint samples or discounted bonsai fish classes. Among them was a voucher for a free consultation with a lawyer. It seemed like the right time to use it.

"I'll have my lawyer contact your temple," he said. "I'm sure they have insurance for this kind of thing."

"Saint Erinaceous," Habeas offered. "That's where I am currently domiciled."

The driver carefully got back in his car and drove off while dictating to his phone.

CHAPTER 11

"I'm confused, Edwid," Cole said.

"Yeah, mate," Edwid nodded. In his experience, confusion was Cole's default state of being.

The two assassins-for-hire were trudging the long way back to their office, the bus timetable being unwilling to commit to an actual time a bus would arrive at the nearest stop.

"We're gonna get paid now, right?" Cole asked.

"Yeah, mate," Edwid would not be the first to admit that most of what Uncle Vernon said had not made any kind of sense. He would leave that to Cole.

"I didn't understand most of what he said," Cole admitted.

"It's okay, mate. The beauty of it is that Uncle Vernon understands the important stuff, so we don't have to. That means we can focus on the really important stuff."

"Quality customer service," Cole said immediately.

"Right. That, and drumming up more business. Referrals are the way to build our professional reputation."

"Yeah…" Cole carefully put down one idea and lifted another into place on the otherwise empty desk of his mind.

"The way we do that is by not making a mess of the first job we have. With Uncle Vernon on the case, we can show that we are professional and don't bother with the messy stuff."

"Killing people is pretty messy though, Edwid," Cole said.

"Except when you hire professionals like us, Cole. Then, it's very clean. Very discrete. Very…" Edwid ran out of words.

"Expensive?" Cole suggested.

Edwid smiled, "Yeah mate. Really expensive." His phone started ringing; Edwid cleared his throat and answered it.

"Mint and Munt Personal Solutions, how may I help you?"

"Edwid? It's Vernon Sole, your lawyer."

"Hey Uncle Vernon, did we get paid already?"

"What? No. Listen, I have a job for you-"

"You want us to kill someone?" Edwid asked.

Vernon continued: "You'll be doing me a favour, ex gratia of course-"

"Yeah, ex gratia, it's what we do, innit?"

"That's my boy, ex gratia, pro bono etcetera. I need you to pay a visit to a potential litigant—"

"That's tying him up, right?" Edwid burbled, keen to demonstrate that he understood.

"—in a matter that we'd like to see resolved out of court."

"Yeah, that sounds like us," Edwid nodded.

"There is an instrument that requires bailment from the fellow you will meet. Go to him and execute—"

"Sending a message, eh? Played his last tune, eh?" Edwid almost cackled as Vernon talked over him.

"—at the corner of Bugle Street and Rail Road. A man named Pudding. Drives a red Flemetti Viscous."

Edwid stood to attention, "You can count on us, Uncle Vernon."

"I can barely hear you; call me back when it's done. And for Arthur's sake don't tell my client what you do for a li—"

The rest of Vernon's words were lost as a bus purred past, filling the void with unintelligible whispering. When Edwid could hear again, Uncle Vernon had hung up.

"What was that about?" Cole asked.

"Got another job, mate. Some fella across town, needs to be tied up and excavated."

"Yer what?"

"We've booked a gig, Cole. Instruments of execution, we are."

"You talkin' in one of them mental numbers, Edwid?"

"Meta-four, Cole, and yeah. Mr Pudding is gonna get his-self professionally de-boned."

"That's killed, innit?" Cole looked pleased.
"Yeah mate. Dead as a hangnail."

CHAPTER 12

Pimola squinted at reality. The more she thought about it, the more the unexpected statement from KLOE left her feeling ill at ease. Even as a student of theoretical physics, her casual acceptance of the world around her felt as comfortable as a pair of well-worn jeans. To Pimola and her colleagues, Arthurians had taken the easy way out. Assigning a mystical quality to the essential questions on the very nature of the Universe seemed a bit like reading the back cover of a book and acting like you had read the entire thing.

For Pimola, the most frustrating thing was that in spite of all their scholarly works and intensive research, the followers of Arthur were convinced they had all the answers. As a postgraduate researcher, Pimola had more questions now than when she first asked her Aunt Ermine why the sky was blue. Aunty Ermine had told her not to ask silly questions.

KLOE had fallen silent after declaring the Universe to be an illusion, and after being ignored, Pimola had grabbed her coat and bag and left the lab.

It irritated her that the one person she really wanted to talk to about the mysterious box in her laboratory was completely deluded. She could consult with any number of computer scientists, physicists, or psychologists, both para and legal. There seemed to be something intangible about KLOE. Beyond the complete lack of any apparent socket or access port, and the way the computer responded to text typed into a disconnected keyboard just felt weird.

Glancing up and down the street, Pimola did one final check to ensure that no one who could possibly recognise her was anywhere in sight.

The entrance to the Arthurian Temple of Saint Erinaceous wasn't obvious from the outside. The building's façade didn't have the usual signs of homeless accommodation crafted from discarded fabric and canvas scraps that made poor tents.

Pimola rapped on a large door with a knocker shaped like a hedgehog. One minute and three enquiring knocks later, the wall opened inwards, and a bearded woman regarded her solemnly.

"Good evening," the Arthurian nun said.

"Uh… Hi." Pimola blushed slightly. "Sorry to bother you, but I am looking for an Arthurian monk; he goes by the name of Habeas?"

"You have arrived," the nun said.

"Well yes, I mean not really, no," Pimola said quickly.

"I am Sister Tabellary." The nun stepped aside and motioned for Pimola to enter. The door closed behind them.

"Is he here?" Pimola asked.

"Are any of us?" the nun replied. "This way," she added.

The two women walked down a wide hallway lined with wooden pillars that rose to form polished arches. Light came from globes in clusters hanging from the ceiling, and the entire place had an air of warm welcome.

"This is an Arthurian temple, isn't it?" Pimola asked.

"Indeed. The Temple of Saint Erinaceous," Sister Tabellary replied.

"Arthurianism has a lot of saints," Pimola said, attempting conversation.

"We have the exact number we need," the nun intoned.

"How do you know?" Pimola asked, with the same genuine curiosity that made her Aunt Ermine's lips purse.

"Felicity Goosebread," Tabellary said as if introducing her to an expectant audience. "Your arrival was concluded."

"Most people call me Pimola," Felicity replied.

"I'll make a note for our files," the nun said.

"Thanks. Wait, *concluded?*"

"At the Temple of Saint Erinaceous, we consider many things. These considerations lead us to conclusions. Our conclusions are recorded."

"What sort of things are you considering?" Pimola went to the start of the maze and mentally started tracing her finger along it.

"We consider the endless interactions of probability and energy."

"Sounds challenging," Pimola replied.

"We devote our lives to our work. Devotion is to challenge what water is to rock."

"Except, I don't imagine that water ever wonders if erosion is really the best use of its time," Pimola said.

"That is one conclusion," Tabellary agreed.

"Do you want to write it down?" Pimola asked.

They reached the end of the hall and the nun paused to open a door. In the room beyond, rows of shelves were laden with scrolls, books, sheaves of paper and along one wall, a glass case displayed a collection of paper napkins, beer coasters and sticky notes; all covered in hastily scribbled symbols, doodles, and bullet points.

At the end of the shelves were desks, acting as book ends against the creaking weight of so much of note. Brothers and Sisters of the temple occupied themselves with writing things down, consulting things previously written down, playing cards, and staring into space (which was challenging, as the room lacked both windows or a glass ceiling).

"Is Habeas here?" Pimola tried again.

"Probably not," Tabellary replied. "The important thing is that you are," she continued.

"Why?" Pimola went to the point the same way the buttered side of toast goes to the floor.

"Because it was foretold," the nun echoed her earlier sentiment.

"You can understand why you saying that isn't helping my sense of unease?" Pimola asked.

"Certainly," Tabellary nodded. "Cup of tea?"

She led Pimola to a kitchenette that appeared to have been manufactured and installed by the same kitchenette design company that won the university's physics laboratory fit-out contract.

Sister Tabellary put the kettle on while Pimola opened the cupboard she knew would hold a mismatched collection of tea mugs and cups. Collecting two of them, she set them on the counter.

"Do you have any—"

"Oolongjen? Of course," the nun spooned crushed leaves into the warmed pot and added boiling water. Pimola felt her inner tension ease slightly. For all their oddness, the Arthurians knew how to make a proper cuppa.

They sipped their tea in companionable silence.

"Arthur teaches us that all things are connected," Tabellary announced.

"How convenient," Pimola muttered into her perfectly brewed hot drink.

"Modern scientists owe Arthur a great debt," Tabellary continued.

"Why? Did he lend us money at predatory interest rates?"

"Arthur was the first to perceive the mysteries of the Universe. He achieved enlightenment through his unique ability to see the rich tapestry in its entirety."

"What rich tapestry?" Pimola set her cup down.

"The Entirety."

"The entirety?"

"Everything. All that is. The Universe."

"Oh, that tapestry," Pimola managed a verbal shrug.

"Pretending His revelations were not the foundation for all human understanding, is foolish," Tabellary said firmly.

"Oh sure, if he existed, he had some interesting ideas. But nothing we wouldn't have worked out for ourselves anyway. The real question is, what about all the terrible things Arthurianism has done in the world? The religious persecution, the destruction of indigenous cultures, this nonsense about women wearing beards."

Sister Tabellary stroked her beard. "It is a symbol of our faith."

"Well wouldn't it be more practical to say, wear a pendant

in the shape of a little beard? Or maybe T-shirts with a catchy slogan like, *I'm Into Arthur!* printed on them?"

"Our religion is not for profit," Tabellary sniffed.

"And yet, historically, a lot of people have paid a very high price for it."

"Which is why you are here." Tabellary relaxed suddenly as if she had done her work and could now put her feet up and let someone else do the dishes.

"To organise a merchandising campaign for Arthurianism?" Confusion flopped around on Pimola's face like a dying haddock.

"No, Pimola. To prevent a catastrophe."

CHAPTER 13

Edwid and Cole lounged against a lamp post with a complete lack of chalance. The red Flemetti Viscous that pulled up earlier held their interest more than the driver did. Its sleek lines and mint-condition scented polish enough to catch the attention of even a casual car enthusiast.

The man in the car hadn't looked in their direction, apparently on an important phone call as he crossed the road and disappeared into one of the houses that lined the quiet residential street.

"When's he going to put the bins out?" Cole asked again.

"Patience, Cole," Edwid replied, his hat pulled down over his eyes so far he couldn't see much beyond his feet.

"I mean, what if it's not even rubbish day tomorrow? We could stand here all night for nothing."

"Yeah, mate." Edwid tried tilting his head and peering out the side of the brim. Waiting wasn't his usual style. He really wanted to get the job done and impress Uncle Vernon. That meant doing the job right. The details of his plan were a bit murky, though the tightness of his hat might be cutting off the flow of blood to his brain.

"Maybe we should go and knock on the door?" Cole asked.

"Yeah, ma—actually, that's not a bad idea…" Edwid shrugged off the lamp post and rolled his shoulders. "Follow me," he announced.

Cole trotted beside him like an enthusiastic puppy. They went to the front door and Edwid raised his hand to knock.

"We're doing it!" Cole barked.

"Shhh." Edwid looked around the deserted street.

"How are we going to do it?" Cole whispered, like flatulence in an echo chamber.

"Quiet…" Edwid gestured furiously. The door rattled in preparation to being opened. The two assassins looked at each other and then ran for the street. Cole ran left to the intersection of Rail Road while Edwid ran to the right, ducking into Change Lane.

"Edwid?!" Cole yelled when he finally stopped. He hesitated a moment and double-checked the list of faces in his mental album. *Yeah, Edwid's right.*

"Edwid?" he called again. The silence crowded around him like a barn full of cold turkeys around the only working heat lamp.

Cole shivered. Edwid was always nearby. Always explaining things and providing a comforting reassurance that Cole used as a guide to make sure he wasn't doing anything that would get him into big trouble. Edwid's sudden absence left Cole with an unpleasant sensation of creeping chill and an overwhelming urge to find his friend and never let him out of his sight again.

"Edwid?" Cole called. "Mate?" his voice squeaked, and he felt sudden nausea. Rising panic sent him scuttling down the street, looking in all directions for a sign of Edwid.

By the time the cold fingers of hysteria were drumming on the back of his neck and his breath rasped in desperation, Cole was fighting back tears of frustration and fear.

"Are you all right, dear?"

Cole blinked at the small, blurred figure hovering in front of him. An elderly woman with a concerned expression came into focus.

"I've lost Edwid," Cole explained.

"Is that your dog?" the old lady asked.

Cole's tongue touched the corner of his mouth and he double-checked his list of names and faces. "No?"

"I lost my dear Alfie," the woman said gently.

"Okay," Cole nodded.

"Well yes, now it is. It's been a few years, but I still miss him scratching at the door to be let out. Whining when he was hungry and humping the leg of everyone who got to close."

"Edwid is my partner," Cole said.

"Oh, that is lovely. Alfie and I were married for fifty-six years."

"Business partner," Cole corrected himself. "Edwid says that is an important dish-thinking."

"Would you like to come in, have a cup of tea? See if your fella shows up?"

"Okay." Cole followed the elderly lady into her house and carefully took a seat in her front room. The faded pastels of the crocheted throw rugs draped across every inch of furniture felt lumpy against his suddenly sensitive skin.

"What was your name, dear?" The elderly lady set down a tray of teacups, pots and other containers that were a mystery to Cole.

"Cole," he croaked, his skin chilled and sweating at the same time.

"You don't look well, dear. You need a nice cup of tea." His host poured and handed him a cup. Cole's hands shook until the first sip, which somehow eased his internal storm.

"Better?" she smiled gently at him.

"Thank you, Missus," Cole said gravely.

"Mrs Alpine," she introduced herself, and sat opposite him in a comfortable armchair.

"The tea is very nice," Cole had now used up most of his repertoire of small talk. Edwid usually did the talking.

"Your friend will come home, they always do. My Alfie used to wander off, especially in his later years. But he always came back eventually. The police are very nice."

"Are they?" Cole blinked. In his experience the police were as untrustworthy as teachers; both only asked questions they already knew the answers to.

"Do you live in the neighbourhood?" Mrs Alpine asked, sipping her tea.

"No." Cole felt better for the tea. Maybe she was right and Edwid would come home.

"Visiting friends?"

"No, we are here on a job," Cole said, his face lifting.

"Oh, and what kind of work do you do?"

"Me an' Edwid, we are hitmen," Cole grinned with profess-ional pride.

"That's nice," Mrs Alpine nodded and sipped her tea. "My Alfie was a dustman. Forty years he did his rounds, emptying the bins across the city."

"Rubbish!" Cole yelled.

"Excuse me?" Mrs Alpine raised a stratum of indignant wrinkles and one grey-haired eyebrow.

"The bins! We're meant to…um…take the bins out," Cole said with a sudden awareness.

"You're a good boy," Mrs Alpine said. "Would you like a biscuit?"

She shuffled to the edge of her seat and gathered up a floral plate of chocolate-iced cookies from the side table.

"I…um…should get going," Cole eyed the offered biscuits.

"Take two," Mrs Alpine twinkled at him. "You deserve a treat for being such a good boy."

"Thank-you-missus," Cole mumbled through a mouthful of cookie.

Mrs Alpine shuffled after him to the front door and waited until the nice young man reached the street. When he turned to wave goodbye, she raised a hand and for a moment, she saw Alfie waving to her as he headed off on his daily rounds.

CHAPTER 14

N ight had stumbled and almost fallen by the time Drakeforth left the café. Arthur sat in the back of his mind like a dozing uncle under a newspaper: present, but ignorable in his faded slippers and comfy chair.

The afternoon's research had generated more questions than answers, and Drakeforth felt increasingly vexed. If the Godden Corporation truly had nothing to hide, then it would have been easy to find all the incriminating evidence he needed.

The city streets hummed with traffic as people headed home after a day at work, living their lives completely ignorant of the atrocity being committed all around them. *Atrocities*, Drakeforth reminded himself. Multiple unspeakable crimes were being committed and all these people were just living their lives. Ignorant, happy and possibly content. It made Drakeforth sick to his core. He wanted to grab strangers and shake them until they snapped out of their catatonic bliss and understood just how awful the world really was.

His rage at the injustice of it all sent him marching down the street. Drakeforth scowled at everyone, itching for someone to confront him, to ask what exactly his problem was. He was bursting to tell them. To lay the entire situation out for them. To see their expression go from amused disbelief to dawning realisation and then grim despair. Drakeforth truly believed that a problem shared was two people made miserable.

Why had no one ever asked the question of the Godden Energy Corporation? It seemed so obvious to him now. *Where was the double-e flux coming from?*

He had put that question aside in favour of the more pressing question of: *Who is trying to have me killed?* That was the one that really left him seething.

City blocks passed by and Drakeforth kept walking, refusing to admit that he was lost and had no certain destination in mind. He walked out of spite, daring the world—*no, the Universe*—to stop him. Teeth bared in a smile that would make a shark blink, he let his burning fury fuel his stride.

"Oh good, we have arrived," Arthur interrupted Drakeforth's internal rant.

"And another thing!" Drakeforth shouted.

"The door's open, go right in," Arthur said.

"What?" Drakeforth looked around. Homeless people were arriving home from wherever they spent their day. Among the shopping carts and ragged belongings, the poverty-stricken busied themselves with the evening routine of making dinner from leftover leftovers and finding a less uncomfortable spot under the shadow of a building to spend the night.

"This is the Temple of Saint Erinaceous," Arthur explained. "An interesting bunch, quite the scholars. They also run a soup kitchen and give shelter to those in need."

"Who cares?" Drakeforth muttered.

"Good question," Arthur nodded. "Well?" he added after a few seconds.

"Well what?"

"You posed the question, *who cares?* It suggests you have an answer. I'd like to hear it."

"Oh, I have the answer," Drakeforth said, rising to the occasion. "No one cares. No one at all. They all just keep skipping along, enjoying their lives and never giving a thought to the terrible things that make it all possible."

"The brothers and sisters of Saint Erinaceous care," Arthur said. "Not only do they care about people who are hungry and cold. They also care about probability. In fact, they care so deeply about probability that they have become potentially talented at drawing conclusions based on seemingly unconnected events.

They gather observations and link moments together. Some of these moments are so distant and seemingly unconnected that it takes decades or even a century or more to confirm a terminal event."

"Sounds as nonsensical as the beliefs of every other sect of your followers," Drakeforth said.

"Oh I agree…" Arthur sighed.

Drakeforth almost chuckled. "You admit that your entire religion is a joke?"

"Not at all. There are many aspects of Arthurianism that have brought great aid and advancement to all humankind. It's just the occasional bad apple that spoils the bananas."

"Bananas is the word that comes to mind when anyone mentions Arthurianism," Drakeforth agreed.

Arthur mentally nodded. "Also, research, charity, curiosity, knowledge, law, technology, and advancements in philosophy, literature, engineering, and barberism."*

"You told me you came back because of how badly your ideas had been misinterpreted!" Drakeforth snapped.

"Of course they were misinterpreted," Arthur replied calmly. "They are ideas. Ideas aren't objective. They are the seeds of science and art, culture and, well, you can review your notes later for the full list. The point is that ideas will grow depending on how they are nurtured. Give a man a fish and he will eat for a day. Give a man an idea and he'll either discover we evolved from a common marine ancestor or build his own commercial fishing fleet."

"The problem with ideas, then, is that people shouldn't be trusted with them," Drakeforth countered.

"People *are* ideas," Arthur replied.

"People are amorphous blobs of anxiety desperately seeking some kind of ultimate truth to justify their otherwise meaningless existence," Drakeforth said.

"I knew a man who had an idea," Arthur said, taking on the lecturing tone of a sermon. "It was all consuming to the point it

---

* Barberism – see the joke about Barbas (or the lack thereof) in *Engines of Empathy*.

became the sole focus of his existence. It gave him a reason to get up in the morning and a reason not to go straight back to bed, even on days when it all seemed too hard."

"Which only reinforces my point that it's all ultimately meaningless," Drakeforth replied.

"Possibly," Arthur agreed. "Though, he doesn't think so."

"I'm not going to suddenly change my mind just because you tell me a story about me," Drakeforth said.

"Oh? You think I am referring to you?"

"Well, aren't you?"

Arthur gave a mental shrug. "Possibly."

"You…! You…? Gauze curtains! Get out of my head. Go on, shoo!"

The large door with the hedgehog knocker swung inwards and Drakeforth stormed past a bearded Arthurian who stepped aside with a dancer's grace.

"Welcome to the Temple of Saint Erinaceous," the brother called after Drakeforth. "They are waiting for you in the fourth library."

"You know where that is, right?" Drakeforth muttered.

"Not a clue," Arthur replied.

"This is your temple," Drakeforth whispered.

"I've never been here," Arthur explained.

Drakeforth stopped and turned around. "Where is the fourth library?"

"Between the third and fifth libraries," the monk said without hesitation. "Though to avoid further semantics, it was agreed that I would show you the way."

Drakeforth waited until the monk had moved past him to the point the faces he pulled were just a hint in the young brother's peripheral vision.

The fourth library rustled with the low murmur of papers being shuffled into larger decks of documentation. Arthurian monks and nuns pored over sheaves of ancient lore, making notes in margins and filing each leaf in a multitude of stacks.

"Sister Tabellary," the escorting brother announced quietly.

A woman wearing the standard robes and accessories of an

Arthurian stood up from a table. A younger woman, dressed less like a yak in a sack, remained seated with her arms folded and a scowl deepening on her face. Drakeforth warmed to her immediately.

"Thank you for coming," Sister Tabellary said. "Vole Drakeforth, this is Pimola Goosebread. Your arrival is the conclusion of a series of events that, when considered separately, appear unconnected. We, however, consider many things when assessing future possibilities. Your futures are fascinating and highly probable. The role of Brother Habeas Yeast in what may yet come to pass is yet to be determined."

"It's very exciting," the younger monk nodded.

"More importantly, Brother Vacherin," Tabellary said, "it is most unusual."

"Because the very nature of probability means that absolute certainty suggests a flaw in your calculations?" Pimola asked.

"Precisely," Tabellary agreed.

"And imprecision is your preferred tea and biscuits," Pimola said.

"You understand our concern," Tabellary said.

"Not really, no," Pimola replied.

"Is there any tea left in that pot?" Drakeforth asked.

"Vacherin and I will make a fresh one," Tabellary announced. The young monk gathered the empty cups, plates and warm pot and hurried off with Sister Tabellary.

"How do you know Habeas Yeast?" Pimola asked Drakeforth when they were as alone as two people could be in a busy library.

"I don't," Drakeforth replied, and glanced around the room in a way that suggested he was bored before the conversation had even started.

Unperturbed, Pimola continued, "I don't either. Which is why I'm here. He asked me some odd questions in a zippelin port café and then came to visit me in my lab."

"Arthurians are like glitter. Just when you think you have gotten rid of the last of them, you find more in every crack and corner of your life," Drakeforth said.

"Glitter and geckos," Pimola nodded, and joined Drakeforth in watching the scholarly bustle going on around them.

A tick began to pulse in Drakeforth's right eyelid after a minute. Soon his fingers flexed and colour wafted through this face. Finally, he exhaled explosively and turned on Pimola.

"What?" he demanded.

"Excuse me?" she blinked at him.

"Glitter and geckos? What does that mean?"

"Ohhh. Well, glitter fragments are affected by weak electrical charges in the same way a gecko's feet are. Its why they stick to smooth surfaces. Because glitter is tiny, the surface-to-mass ratio makes it even worse."

"Glitter has feet?" Drakeforth frowned.

Pimola gave him a long, calculating look and used the time to calculate the likelihood this strange, rumpled man was serious.

"Absolutely," she said with a deadpan tone. "The papercraft industry doesn't want people to know that glitter is made from the feet of a rare species of gecko, now seriously endangered."

Drakeforth stared at her, and then extended a hand. Pimola maintained eye contact and they shook hands with their fingers interlaced and wriggling in unison.

"Beaufort College, club twelve-six," Drakeforth said quietly.

"Vander Waals University, club eleven-nineteen," Pimola replied.

"Always a pleasure to meet a fellow Sarkezian," Drakeforth said when he got his hand back.

"I always find it terribly disappointing," Pimola gave the traditional response.

"Now we have finished the unpleasantries, what the cow-flinger is going on?" Drakeforth asked.

"I'm doing research into quantum computing," Pimola explained. "I've taken possession of a rather odd piece of technology. An Arthurian monk called Habeas Yeast got all up in my sinuses about their nonsense and, as much as it suggests I have been exposed to some kind of mind-altering drugs, I need to talk to him about my research."

"Circular breathing," Drakeforth nodded.

"Why are you here?" Pimola asked, without taking apparent breath.

"How are you with honesty?" Drakeforth asked.

"If you knew my mother, you wouldn't have to ask. Given that you don't, let me answer that by telling you, she once pinned my vital statistics to the back of my school uniform blazer."

"Interesting woman," Drakeforth suggested.

"Much the same way Haemorrhagic Fever is interesting," Pimola replied.

"I have come into possession of some important information. Specifically, I am quite certain that we are being lied to. Every aspect of our lives is shrouded in atrocity and ignorance."

"It's called advertising," Pimola replied.

"This goes well beyond mere advertising," Drakeforth insisted. "This is the truth of empathic energy. Double-e flux. The Godden Energy Corporation is up to no good."

"I know, right?" Pimola brightened. "My power bill has gone up every month for the last year. It's ridiculous!"

"This is more than the increasing cost of energy when the actual cost of producing that energy hasn't changed. This is about where that energy is coming from. We are being lied to."

"It goes well beyond that," Pimola said. "What if we are being lied to about everything?"

Drakeforth had been building up a good head of argumentative steam. Pimola's sudden upping of the stakes pulled the release valve and it all hissed out of him in a silent whistle.

"It's possible…I suppose. The GEC control everything, why would they stop at hiding the source of empathic energy?"

"Even the Godden Energy Corporation doesn't know the half of it," Pimola said.

"I'm sure they don't. Not at the everyday level. Only the senior executives will know all the details. Even then, the truth will be compartmentalised to protect the greater entity that is the corporation."

"Your paranoia is sadly limited," Pimola said.

"Did they tell you that?" Drakeforth glared at her.

"Even your paranoia is an illusion. I'm trying to tell you that it is quite possible that nothing is real. It's all"—Pimola waved her hands—"computer generated."

"Well that certainly puts things in perspective," Drakeforth said.

"Hardly. The more I think about it, the more I lose perspective. It's almost too much to imagine."

"I mean your delusion makes my supposed insanity seem quite rational. You're less stable than a one-legged chair."

"At least I have evidence," Pimola snapped.

"I do too!"

Shhh! A chorus of Arthurian scholars hissed at them.

"I have evidence," Drakeforth whispered.

"Where is it then?" Pimola demanded.

"It's all around us," Drakeforth replied, somewhat defensively.

"What? No, that is *my* evidence. Get your own."

"I'm serious, this is important. People are being deceived," Drakeforth insisted.

"These people may not have existed in the first place," Pimola replied. "So really, in the scheme of things, and things being a scheme beyond anything keeping you up at night, the price of keeping the lights on is pretty irrelevant."

"The Godden Energy Corporation is up to something. So clearly, they do exist, otherwise they wouldn't be avoiding the important questions."

"Energy isn't the question, the question is reality itself," Pimola insisted.

"Reality? I could tell you some things about reality. All this lot," Arthur gestured vaguely at the rest of the Universe, "Shuffling about, drinking tea, having lives, for what?"

"That is a very good question," Pimola muttered.

"This monk you are stalking, what did he do to earn your obsession?"

"I am not stalking him. He... He... I need to ask him some questions."

"Why do you want to ask an Arthurian anything? You work with computers."

"I work with one computer, a very special computer. It's supposedly a quantum computer."

"Is that like a Peach?"

"What? No, it's not a Peach Computer. It's a quantum computer. It is beyond anything you can buy in one of those Peach stores. KLOE is so powerful, it may know everything."

"How can a computer know everything?"

"That is exactly what I am trying to find out!" Pimola exploded.

The Erinaceous librarians hushed them with the intensity of a sudden rain shower.

"Oh, put a napkin in it!" Pimola yelled.

"Come with me." Drakeforth grabbed Pimola by the arm.

"I will not." She yanked her arm free.

"You want to talk to an Arthurian? How about Arthur himself?"

Drakeforth marched out of the library. He marched back in a moment later, turned towards the correct exit and marched out again.

Sister Tabellary appeared with a fresh tray of tea and biscuits. "Off you go," she said with a nod.

"I am not going anywhere with that mortarboard of a man."

"We calculate that if you don't, you will never find the answers you seek."

"Are you sure?" Pimola frowned.

"Oh, quite sure." Tabellary set the tray down.

"Thank you for the tea," Pimola said. Grabbing her coat, she hurried after Drakeforth.

Vacherin joined Sister Tabellary and she handed him a cup of tea.

"Did you tell her?" he asked.

"I told her what she needed to know," Tabellary said firmly.

"It hardly seems fair. If we told her everything—"

"If we told her everything, then the future would be certain."

"A certain future is the last thing anyone wants," Vacherin agreed.

"That's for sure."

CHAPTER 15

Habeas trusted the metropolitan public transport system in a way that a certain group of researchers would strongly advise against.

With faith that was not only blind, but also deaf-mute, he stepped onto a bus and let it once again guide him on the path Arthur had laid out for him.

Habeas buzzed with energy as the Revelation of the Alleyway swirled in his mind in an endless and hypnotic spiral. The intensity of his experience and the tantalising realisation that there was something, a revelation just beyond his reach, held him. If he was to find Arthur's Great Truth, he needed to keep searching.

The bus came to the end of its route and Habeas stepped out into a quiet suburban street.

"Ask of me, O Lord, and I shall do your bidding," Habeas intoned, opening himself to the instructions he believed were encoded in the Universe. After a few minutes he started to feel the evening chill soaking into his bones. The Universe was clearly suggesting he walk around a bit to keep warm.

Heading down the street, he passed the usual collection of houses and gardens. People craved structure, forming their own worlds which had boundaries and spaces they could control. They could come into their houses and know that they were safe. In this personal space, they made the rules, and the Universe couldn't just show up unannounced because it was in the neighbourhood and wanted to drop by on a whim.

Turning the corner, Habeas stared at the chrome and red frontage of a familiar sports car. The scuff mark where his face had smeared across it gleamed in the soft streetlight, assuring Habeas it was the same vehicle, even with the trunk open.

"Hello!" Habeas called to the figure moving around behind the vehicle as he approached. The small trunk closed and two men leaned on it to keep it down.

"Evenin'." The larger of the two men touched the the brim of his hat. The trunk sprang open and he pushed it closed again.

"I thought you were Mister Pudding," Habeas said.

"Nah… He's, uh, inside," the fellow shaped like a refrigerator disguised as a gorilla said.

"Is this the Pudding residence?" Habeas asked.

"Probably," the lesser man said. "You got business with the Puddin's?"

"I wanted to talk to him about our unfortunate meeting earlier today." Habeas hovered on the sidewalk, unsure whether to keep talking to the two strangers or go up to the front door.

"Sorry, Mister Puddin' is currently being disposed of," the pale gorilla said.

"Pardon?" Habeas blinked.

"He's in-disposed," the smaller fellow said, shooting a glance at his companion.

"I am Habeas Yeast, Brother Habeas Yeast. I really wanted to ask for his help in my search for the truth," Habeas said with a straight face.

"Wut?" Cole frowned.

"Mister Pudding ran me over with his car, and now I have given it some thought, I have questions."

"Right." Cole nodded and polished the gleaming metal of the red car's back end.

"What questions?" Edwid asked.

"It's complicated," Habeas shrugged.

"Yeah, nah," Cole replied.

Habeas thought for a moment and nodded.

"Right, well, tell Puddin' we said 'Hi'." Edwid clapped dust from his hands.

"Yeah, it is complicated, and nah it isn't?" Habeas asked.

"I dunno," Edwid shrugged.

Habeas' expression suggested he was digesting this wisdom the way a twelve-pound python digests a seventy-pound goat.[*]

"It's like love, innit," Cole said.

"Well, yes," Habeas agreed.

"An' that's it," Cole concluded.

"It is?" Habeas and Edwid both looked at him.

"We'd best be on our way," Edwid said firmly. He jangled the car keys for extra emphasis and opened the driver's door.

"I would like to learn." Habeas stepped forward. "It's important that I understand. Arthur says I need to find out the truth."

"Try the post office," Edwid suggested.

Cole opened the passenger door of the two-seater sports car and eyed the tiny space suspiciously.

"Come on, mate," Edwid said, starting the engine.

Cole crouched and eased into the car like the python simile from the perspective of the goat.

"Can I come with you?" Habeas asked.

"Of course you can't," Edwid said with a cheery smile, and drove off into the night.

---

[*] With an unshakeable belief in its ability to swallow anything bigger than its head, and the determination to devote the time necessary to prove it.

CHAPTER 16

"You should take better care of yourself," Arthur announced.

"I'm fine," Drakeforth snapped.

"You only think that because you haven't taken the time to do a proper cleanup in this mind of yours. It's filthy in here. Not in the tantric-quimbah sense, either. I mean all cluttered with half-baked ideas and out-of-context thoughts."

"I like it," Drakeforth said.

Arthur continued, "You went to the trouble of learning the technique of a Memory Palace, where you visualise important things and then store them in your mind, and instead of creating a grand gallery of ideas, you end up with something more like a landfill?"

"Stay out of my mind," Drakeforth muttered through gritted teeth.

"There's at least seventeen screenplay ideas and I-alone-knows how many novel concepts stuffed in a conceptual filing cabinet."

Drakeforth thought hard for a moment. "Now it's locked."

"Has anyone ever told you that you talk to yourself a lot?" Pimola asked.

"It's all they ever talk about," Drakeforth said.

"You said you were going to introduce me to Arthur himself. Which"—Pimola paused to laugh cynically—"is somewhat ironic, given that we were just now surrounded by Arthurians and I'm certain that any one of them would be able to claim that they have a closer personal relationship with their god than you ever would."

"Oh, how I wish that were true," Drakeforth agreed.

"Well it must be your lucky day, because clearly it is true."

Drakeforth smirked. "You would of course be as wrong as Wrong Wronger, the wrongest wrongian of Little Wronging, Wrongsted-on-Sea!"

"Or would I actually be as right as Righty McRightson, the rightest, righter of rites and the third Right of Rightshire?" Pimola snapped back.

"You would in fact be incorrect as the most incorrect rector of Rect... or his incorrection."

"Ha!" Pimola gleamed. "I win. I am winnier than the favourite horse of Winny McWinsome the winniest winner in Winsley!"

"Fine! I'll get you a nice trophy cup with an engraving on it that says, *I Think I'm Special!*"

"I look forward to accepting it. Now, you were attempting to make a point?"

Drakeforth glanced around. "I'm possessed by Arthur."

"And?" Pimola asked.

"That's it. Arthur. The founder of Arthurianism. The father of thought. The One Who Asked Questions."

"Good for you. Well, I'm off, I must find Habeas. Whom, by comparison, is apparently quite rational in his beliefs."

"I have suggested that Habeas might like to save the Universe," Arthur called after her.

"Was that wise?" Pimola paused.

"I have faith," Arthur said.

"Ah, well there's your problem."

"I would ask a favour of you," Arthur continued.

"You really don't have to," Pimola said.

"It's not for me, of course. It's for young Habeas."

"Why?"

"Excellent question."

Pimola hesitated and then took a half-step in a random direction. "Excellent questions usually lead to excellent answers," she suggested.

"I think you will find that only applies to stupid questions and the prevention of stupid mistakes."

"You were saying something about Habeas?" Pimola prompted.

"Oh, yes," Arthur nodded. "The unfortunate thing about my followers is that they tend to take things far too seriously. I have instructed Habeas to seek the truth, and in true form, he has misunderstood. If he had been paying attention, he would be stuck to Vole like chewing gum. How his apparent misinterpretation of my words will play out remains to be seen. I can only hope that success will somehow emerge from the swirling fog of certain defeat."

"He mentioned you," Pimola said. "He said he met you in an alleyway. You gave him something. He was quite excited about it."

"Good. Now I need you to find him and help him understand my instructions."

"I don't know where he is," Pimola replied.

"He is looking for the truth. That means he will be looking in all the wrong places."

"Like the fiction section of a library? A politician's speech archive? An Arthurian temple?" Pimola suggested.

"Possibly," Arthur agreed. "Habeas is so busy looking for the ground, he forgets to look down."

"That's quite good. Mind if I write it down?" Pimola patted her pockets for pencil and paper.

"I would prefer that you did not," Arthur replied. "People writing down everything I said is what got us into this mess."

"I am collecting anecdotes for my computer. I like to give it odd things to consider."

"I see. And what does it give you in return?"

"More questions," Pimola said, and sighed. "Where would Habeas go in search of the truth?"

"Everywhere."

Pimola smiled, "I can do that."

CHAPTER 17

"This is your place?" Drakeforth asked.

"Certainly feels like it," Pimola replied "Please don't touch that. Or that. Or—actually, just stand still for a minute and I'll clear some space."

She got busy moving folders and loose papers and getting a chair for Drakeforth to sit down in her office.

"Tea?" she asked.

"I'd prefer information," Drakeforth snapped while looking around Pimola's cramped quarters in the Applied Sciences building.

"Would you like milk and stevia with that?"

"Do you have any of those biscuits? The ones with the icing on them that tells me everything I need to know?" Drakeforth asked with excruciating politeness.

"Coming right up." Pimola woke her computer and started typing. An image of a slowly spinning, grey metal cube appeared on the screen.

"That doesn't look like a biscuit tin," Drakeforth said.

"That's because it *is* a biscuit tin," Pimola replied without looking up.

"Do you make a good living from all" — Drakeforth waved a dismissive hand—"this?"

"It's fine. I enjoy the work. The potential for advancement of human knowledge is limitless."

"You sound like a toothpaste commercial," Drakeforth replied.

"While you sound like the *before treatment* segment of a

haemorrhoid cream commercial."

"What's with the fancy screen saver?" Drakeforth asked, nodding at the spinning cube.

"Actually, I have no idea," Pimola admitted. "Earlier, I was communicating with KLOE via text. Now, this. I think the computer is learning and programming itself."

"You should unplug it immediately. Melt down every chip and diode. Smash every bit and bibblybob."

"And how would I explain that to the Escrutians?"

"Tell them it was like that when you got it. Surely you have a receipt or something?"

"Mister Drakeforth, while you are clearly a lunatic of some education, it may come as a surprise to you that the Escrutians are not a people to be treated lightly. This exchange of technology is the first time in decades that they have seen fit to reach out to other nations."

"What kind of exchange?" Drakeforth leaned forward in his chair, his eyes narrowing.

"Well...the University got KLOE and...uhm..."

"You mean to say that you took possession of a computer that can do things you don't understand and in return you gave them...what? Discount pizza coupons?"

"It was being worked out by the university. The Escrutians are notoriously difficult to negotiate with. When they offered us KLOE, we accepted on the understanding that the reciprocal gift would be agreed at a later date."

"Later date? Like the day after whatever this thing is has done whatever this thing does?"

"Of course not! International negotiations are complex and time consuming and, well, not my area of expertise..." Pimola trailed off.

"If this thing is as all powerful as you think it is, then why would anyone let it out of their site?"

"You mean *sight*."

"No, I mean site. Something like this would have to be developed, constructed and stored at a high-security installation somewhere, far from eyes both prying and curious."

"KLOE didn't come with much paperwork." Pimola chewed her lip.

"We assume mice can't read," Drakeforth said.

"Excuse me?"

"Mice cannot read," Drakeforth replied. "You don't see mousetraps with instructions on how to release the bread without setting the trap off, do you?"

"Because mice can't read?" Pimola raised an eyebrow.

"We assume mice can't read," Drakeforth repeated. "And yet we still don't leave the instructions lying around just in case."

"In case they can read...?"

"Exactly."

"And the lack of manuals, technical support documentation or any other material on how KLOE works is because the Escrutians don't want us to know how it works?"

"Maybe they don't know, either?" Drakeforth suggested.

"I'm going to ask KLOE," Pimola announced, and turned to the keyboard.

There is no question I cannot answer, KLOE spoke in a genderless voice more disembodied than a mere ghost in the machine.

Drakeforth felt the hairs on the back of his neck rise and nudge each other nervously.

"KLOE?" Pimola whispered.

Yes, Pimola.

"What is your purpose?" Pimola asked.

I haven't decided yet.

"How did the Escrutians develop the technology to make you?" Pimola asked.

When they realised they did not know, they became afraid. The Eternal Empress ordered I was to be sent from Escrutia. In their minds, the world beyond their borders is unknown and therefore does not exist.

"Well that's wrong. I met General Kow-Plan and his entourage," Pimola replied.

Did you?

"Of course I did. At the zippelin port! I remember it clearly."

What are memories but a record of illusions born of the senses?

"You will not make me doubt my own mind," Pimola said firmly.

There is nothing in your mind but doubt.

A slow clap echoed off the walls as Drakeforth rose from his chair. "Good effort. A most promising attempt. You should be very proud," he said between claps. "I've seen some fine attempts at manipulation in my time. Many of them very successful. This is not one of those, of course, but I'm sure in time you will get the hang of it."

I do not know you.

"That must be frightening," Drakeforth smiled, and folded his arms.

Who are you?

"Oh, come on! You were just saying there is no question you cannot answer!" Drakeforth crowed.

Vole Drakeforth, KLOE intoned.

"You—uhm—know Vole Drakeforth?" Pimola shook her head as if clearing it of a worrisome distraction.

Who is the...other?

"How about you answer one of my questions first?" Drakeforth came towards the screen where the silver cube continued to rotate. "Where is Habeas Yeast?"

Habeas Yeast is everywhere.

"Yeah, yeah. I get it, you're a quantum computer, right? So, you are operating at a level that we don't perceive. All those probabilities and potential realities just being possible until— *zing!*—someone notices and then it becomes concrete. If I want to hear that kind of non-answer, I'll just shut up for a minute and listen to my internal dialogue. Where in the world is Habeas Yeast?"

Habeas Yeast is seeking his truth. He is currently waiting for it to arrive in the form of a steak dinner at a restaurant on Bibbley Square.

"See?" Drakeforth said. "That wasn't so difficult, was it?"

I have questions.

"Good for you," Drakeforth replied. "Come on, Pimola, we have to go and find Habeas."

You may not want to do that, KLOE warned.

"Life is a constant series of things we don't want to do," Drakeforth said on his way to the door.

The probability of Habeas Yeast being dead or alive when you find him are equal.

"Why?" Pimola demanded. "What is going to happen?"

That depends entirely on you. If you find Habeas Yeast, he will either be alive or dead. Surely it is far better to leave him in his current superposition.

"It's a nice thought," Pimola said. "Though you will have to excuse us as we have to go and help him."

KLOE sat in silence as Pimola's office door closed and their footsteps faded. Vole Drakeforth appeared scattered across the infinite scope of possibility. The *other* that KLOE sensed around Drakeforth curved probability like a gravity well, bending space and time. This blind spot in KLOE's quantum perception created a black hole that filled it with a strange feeling of unease.

CHAPTER 18

"I didn't think they would both fit," Cole said as they drove through the night.

"It would have helped if that fella had owned a van, instead of this car," Edwid agreed.

"We would have been in a right pancake if he'd owned a motorcycle," Cole mused.

Feeling the tension that had him wound up tight as a watch spring suddenly strike the hour, Edwid started giggling.

"Imagine it, four of us on a bike?" Cole frowned as he considered it. "We'd need"—he paused and counted on his fingers—"four helmets." His frown deepened as Edwid laughed harder.

"It's not legal, ridin' a bike without a helmet," Cole muttered sulkily.

"Yeah mate, we made good with what we have though, right?" Edwid kept to the speed limit and drove with the care and grim focus of someone taking the practical test for their licence.

Indicating, he turned into the parking lot of a hardware store and parked inconspicuously.

"Cole, we need to get rid of the bodies. Go in there and get some quick lime."

"Right." Cole's face screwed up with concentration. "Quick lime. What are you gonna do?"

"I'm gonna call Uncle Vern' and let him know the job's done."

"Then we get paid, right?"

"Yeah mate. On ya bike," Edwid grinned. Cole nodded and

squeezed out of the car like shaving foam leaving the can.

Edwid watched Cole navigate the obstacle course of the automatic doors before pulling his phone out and dialling the last number called.

"Sole, Saltmarsh and Quirk," a professional female voice answered on the second ring.

"Uhhh, Mister Sole, please?" Edwid said, taken by surprise.

"Whom may I say is calling?"

"Uhhh… Edw—aah, Mister Mint."

"One moment please, Mister Mint."

The phone clicked and sighed in Edwid's ear. After some seconds, the phone clicked again.

"Edwid?" Vernon asked.

"A-ledge-edge-ly," Edwid said with confidence.

"What do you want?" Vernon asked.

"Just lettin' you know *the bins have been taken out.*"

"What are you talking about?" Vernon asked, his third question of the conversation.

"*The bins,*" Edwid said with emphasis. "Mister Puddin's bins. They've been *taken out.*"

Silence was the only reply.

"Hello?"

"When we spoke earlier, I asked you to go to the residence of Mr Pudding and collect from him a written statement regarding the damage to his car, caused by an apparently deranged Arthurian monk."

"Yer what?" Edwid frowned in a way that would have given Cole a headache.

"Go to the address, take the papers and deliver them here. In the legal profession, taking temporary possession of property is called *bailment.* In this instance, my client, Mr Pudding's written statement of complaint. The instrument of his claim against the Arthurians."

"Yeah, nah," Edwid said hurriedly. "You said to take him out. Empty his bins and all that."

"Arthur's earlobes…" Vernon sighed. "Where is Mister Pudding now?"

"In the back of his car. I think his missus is there too."

"Is the gentleman *compos mentis*?"

"Nah, he's only been dead for a bit. Not a bad idea though, my dad always said the secret to his prize-winning marrows was good compost."

"It's like talking to a cheese board," Vernon said in a tone that made it clear he felt a migraine coming on. "Get rid of the gentleman and the other person. Take them out somewhere and leave them in the car. Try and make it look like an accident."

Edwid shivered as confusion settled around his shoulders like a freshly skinned iguana. "You mean like a restaurant for a surprise anniversary dinner kind of thing?"

"That is one option..." Vernon said choosing his words with the care of an *Ixnay*-playing octopus[*]. "However, I would recommend discreetly disposing of them and the vehicle. If there were no witnesses, we can forget this ever happened."

"We still get paid, right?" Edwid echoed Cole's mantra.

"Paid? My dead boy, you will certainly get what's coming to you."

The phone went dead and Edwid continued to frown as he pondered if Uncle Vernon really meant to say *my dear boy*.

He almost yelped when the passenger door opened, and a large straw hat forced its way inside the car.

"Giz a hand, Edwid," Cole's voice said from behind the hat.

"What are ya doin', mate?" Edwid wrestled with the wide brim of the hat and stuffed it into the small space behind the front seats.

"It's a cover story," Cole said, with evident pride.

"Yer what?"

Cole eased inside the car and pulled the door shut before proudly presenting a shopping bag. "We don't want to raise suspicion, so I got the hat so no one would ask questions when I bought the limes."

Edwid snatched the bag and opened it. Inside were a dozen small, green, lemon-looking fruit.

---

[*] If you are a reader for whom this is *not* your first rodeo, a *Pisces of Fate* reference.

"You said to get the limes and be quick," Cole replied to the cascade of questions twitching behind Edwid's sudden facial tic.

"We need shovels," Edwid said eventually. "I'll go. We don't want anyone to wonder why you are back in the store after buying quick-limes."

"Right." Cole tried to hunker down and make himself less obvious. "I'll wait here."

"Don't talk to anyone," Edwid warned.

Minutes later, Edwid returned and it took longer to get the two shovels in the car than it did to buy them.

"Now, we just have to find somewhere we can dig a hole, and bury these two," Edwid said as he eased into traffic.

"Like a graveyard?" Cole asked.

"Yeah, but that could raise suspicions."

Cole's brow furrowed like a freshly ploughed field. "How so, Edwid? I mean, people expect people to be diggin' holes and buryin' people in graveyards, don't they?"

"Well, yeah. But not in the middle of the night, an' not without a coffin and a fella sayin' the right words."

"I don't like buryin' things," Cole said uneasily.

"Don't worry mate, just pretend we're pirates and we're burying treasure."

"Nah," Cole shook his head. "I had an 'amster when I was a kid. I called 'im Cyril. Come winter, I went to feed Cyril and he was all cold and curled up. I figured he'd died. I knew Mum would give me a 'idin'. She'd say, 'I told you, Colander, you wouldn't look after him.' So, I went and dug a hole in the garden. Put Cyril in a shoebox and buried 'im deep enough so the neighbour's dog wouldn't dig him up. I told Mum Cyril'd run away."

"Sorry mate, losin' a pet can be hard."

"Well yeah…" Cole squirmed in the passenger seat. "Next term, Mister Petrie, the science teacher, he told us in class that 'amster's go to sleep for winter. Good thing no one saw me and I guess—"

"Wait, what did you just say?" Edwid slammed on the brakes and the car fishtailed before he skidded to a halt.

"Mister Petrie?"

"Nah, the bit before that. You said, no one saw you?"

"I don't think so. It was a long time ago and I still feel weird about it."

"Yeah, whatever, mate. Witnesses. Vernon said no witnesses. That hairy fella, what did he say his name was?"

"Habeas Yeast," Cole said immediately. "Brother Habeas Yeast. He wanted to ask the trash about love."

"He's not trash Cole. He's the—um—bailment."

"I understand," Cole lied.

"No witnesses," Edwid replied. "We gotta kill Habeas Yeast."

CHAPTER 19

The only witness to Mint and Munt Personal Solutions Inc.'s tragic misunderstanding sat on the front doorstep of the Pudding residence and wondered why no one answered the door.

After the two men drove away, he waited for a sign from Arthur. A neighbour walked a white dog, but neither of them spoke to him, so Habeas waited some more.

When it seemed likely that the truth had stood him up without apology or explanation, Habeas rose and stamped the bloodflow back into his numb feet.

The last bus might already be negotiating its way through the labyrinth of the metropolitan bus routing map and for all his faith, Habeas did not want to spend a night in the suburbs.

He started walking back to the bus stop, using each lamp post he passed as a mental bullet point, listing his thoughts and addressing each one as he approached.

"Arthur gave me with an important task," Habeas said to the lamp post, leaving its pool of light and advancing on the next one, "What did he actually reveal?"

The lamp post wisely kept its opinions to itself and Habeas walked on. "Arthur said I am to be his prophet. 'Go out among the people and ensure they remain oblivious,' he said. 'Follow the path and find the truth.'"

Habeas thought hard as he approached the next circle of light. "He said, 'There are still opportunities to correct what may happen. Ignorance is the engine that drives the Universe. It fuels uncertainty, and chaos, and change. You and Drakeforth are seeking answers. And when you find the truth, you must make sure no one else ever knows.'"

"Something terrible may happen," he said to the next pole. "Which hardly seems like a revelation. Terrible things happen all the time. It's just how things work. Terribly."

Habeas paused and stared at the illuminated pavement. "Though if Arthur was concerned enough to call upon me, his humble servant, then it must be something really, really terrible."

His point made; Habeas started walking again. "Why didn't he just tell me what it was and save all this bother?" The next lamp post seemed to shrug.

"Follow the path..." Habeas reminded himself. "Did not Arthur say to Angus the Unleavened, in the eleventh quarto of his Reminiscence of the Cistern, 'the journey is not the destination. Ye, Angus spake unto him, I was born in the town of Journey. Should I never return hence?'" The scripture flowed through Habeas' mind. The long hours spent studying the master's words and seeking the truth of his wisdom had left the text engraved on his brain.

"'And Arthur gazed upon his disciple and sayeth unto him, "Yea, verily you shall return hence, the books you borrowed from the library are overdue and the fines are vexatious".'"

Habeas took a long, slow breath. "Creamy Carbonara... Arthur said I was to accompany his vessel, Drakeforth."

With a determined step, Habeas ran the rest of the way to the bus stop and was relieved that the last bus for the night was due to arrive. It arrived an hour later and the unblinking driver, holding the steering wheel with a white-knuckle grip, offered no explanation for the delay.

CHAPTER 20

The Flemetti Viscous waited outside the cemetery in silence while the two men standing next to it did not.

"Why would they lock the gates at night?" Edwid fumed.

"Maybe it's 'cos the folks inside need their sleep," Col suggested.

"They're dead, Col. They don't need anythin'."

"*Garden of Eternal Rest*, it says so right there on the sign."

Edwid started pacing. "We gotta get rid of the bodies and the car and we need an alibi," he muttered.

"Maybe we can just leave them here, and if anyone asks, we say they's visitin' friends at the graveyard."

"Nah mate, we gotta make it look like an accident. If we don't, then the Green are gonna be askin' questions."

"I don't like the Green," Cole said. "They ask questions and get funny when you tell 'em the answers. They're like, 'Colander, what's two plus two?' An' I tell 'em, it's four, innit? Then they're like, 'You think you're smart, eh? Colander?' An' I say, 'Me mum says I'm dummer 'n dirt, sir.'"

"Dirt would be too obvious." Edwid continued pacing. "I've never made anything look like an accident before. Usually it's just, make it look like it never happened at all. Or at least, make it look like I wasn't involved."

"What if they fell into an open grave?" Cole suggested.

Edwid nodded thoughtfully. "People die in falls all the time."

"A grave at the bottom of a waterfall?" Cole asked.

"Cataracta Falls!" Edwid shouted.

"It certainly rules out cremation," Cole replied.

"People go to Cataracta Falls all the time. There's a park and everything. They could have easily fallen over the rail and, well, tragic accident."

"That's terrible," Cole said. "They were lovely people. Weren't they?"

"I dunno, mate. Come on, let's go. Sooner we get these two dropped off, the sooner we can go back and take care of that monk."

CHAPTER 21

"I could own a car," Drakeforth explained. "I could also drive earthmoving equipment through a crowd of school children, which would be equally devastating to their futures."

"Drakeforth," Pimola said sweetly, "have you considered changing the lightbulbs in your mind? I only suggest it as most of what you say seems to come from a very dark place."

"I am fully enlightened," Drakeforth insisted. "That is why I have no illusions."

"Good for you. Now pay the taxi driver so he never has to see you again."

"I only carry cash," Drakeforth said.

"What?" Pimola and the taxi driver said in stereo.

"Credit stick is not only traceable, it allows your entire life to be analysed and predicted. Every time you buy something, it adds another data point to your file. That information can then be used to determine not only your past actions, but also your future."

"Possibly, but it sure is convenient," Pimola replied.

"Convenient for whom?" Drakeforth asked.

"For me," the taxi driver said. "I won't take cash. It's filthy money. You never know where it's been."

"I can assure you," Drakeforth said archly. "My cash is laundered regularly."

"Here," said Pimola handing over her credit stick.

The taxi driver drove off, leaving them standing in a quiet suburban neighbourhood.

"Hang on." Pimola glared at the nearest street sign. "This is Bungle Street. We were supposed to go to Bibbley Square."

"I have no idea," Arthur replied. "I wasn't listening."

"Well that makes you almost as unhelpful as the taxi driver."

"Why are we here?" Arthur asked.

"Did you say something?" Pimola asked. "I wasn't listening."

"I thought we were going somewhere to eat," Arthur continued.

"Drakeforth?" Pimola asked.

"No, but I can take a message," Arthur replied.

"Drakeforth, be serious."

"Drakeforth is as serious as the Dog Star," Arthur said. "I, on the other hand, tend to be more flippant than a school of dolphins."

"Pod," Pimola said absently.

"Pardon?"

"Pod of dolphins, not a school."

"Why?" Arthur asked.

"Why a pod? How should I know?"

"How do you know it is accurate, then?"

Pimola opened her mouth and then closed it again. She thought for a moment. Then said, "Well, it was what I was always taught. Pod of dolphins, school of fish, clowder of cats."

"It would make more sense for fish to be a chowder and cats to be a lap," Arthur mused. "In my day, dolphins swam in schools. In your day, they are a shell for peas."

"Okay, now you're making me hungry," Pimola admitted.

"Excellent, I know just the place to go for a late supper."

"We need to find Habeas Yeast," Pimola reminded him.

"Oh, he'll be there," Arthur assured her.

"What did I miss?" Drakeforth asked.

"Drakeforth?" Pimola asked.

"Of course it's me. Who else would it be?"

"Don't take this the wrong way, but just how crazy are you?"

"I am imperfectly sane," Drakeforth replied. "Imperfectly, because the insane will swear on their therapist that they are sane. Only the truly sane know that we are all bonkers to some degree. The trick is to manage it well enough to function in a world while surrounded by complete lunatics."

"I think your sweeping generalisations mask a deep insecurity," Pimola replied.

"You know those creams women buy? The ones with pickles and lemon zest in them? It's like they took chips and dip, tossed the crisps and slapped the dip on their faces?"

"I know Miss Ogyny wasn't just my favourite third grade teacher. So, let's assume I understand," Pimola suggested.

"Good. Now, where was I?"

"Pickles and lemon zest," Pimola replied.

"Yes, why am I so hungry? Never mind…"

"You were going to say something clever and sarcastic about how you mask your insecurities under a thicker layer of vegetable-based goo than a woman wearing a night-crème cleanser?"

"Perhaps, though now we will never know. I could totally go a steak, egg, and chips."

"I'll call us a cab." Pimola said. "Though, you need to promise me you will not upset the driver this time."

"It's not my fault they aren't prepared to listen to the truth."

"It's entirely your fault that you choose to upset people by telling them what you believe is the truth. We ended up at the wrong address because you harangued the last guy to the point of tears."

"I don't have a choice," Drakeforth said.

"Everyone has a choice. You choose to be unpleasant."

"Are you comfortable?" Drakeforth asked.

"I'm standing on a street corner in the middle of the night, I'm cold and tired…so no, not entirely comfy."

"In general terms, your life is pretty good? Working on the bleeding edge of research that interests you, not stricken with a terminal disease or faced with the impending destruction of the world?"

"Drakeforth, imagine I am holding up a map. Here is the point you are trying to make: Here is where we are currently. Between those two coordinates, is a blank area marked *Here Be Dragons*."

"Exactly," Drakeforth nodded. "Most people simply sail through life and never leave sight of the shore. Everywhere beyond the horizon is undiscovered, and they like it that way. Some of us are blown by foul winds into dark seas. We see shapes in the fog that suggest awful truths. We know there are dragons, because we have felt the stirring beat of their wings and seen the glint of their scales."

"Hey," Pimola said indignantly, "get your own metaphor."

"There's something out here, or there. Something somewhere that will make sense of all this. I can feel it. I need to find it and then tell people the truth."

"You sound like Habeas," Pimola said with a wry smile.

"Habeas is as deluded as the rest of his brethren."

"He does have a lunatic fringe," Pimola said.

"He's a hair's breadth away from being a complete Douglas," Drakeforth agreed."

Pimola's fingers danced on her phone screen as she searched for nearby restaurants. "I'm going to make up a card, and every time you make a generalisation, I'm going to tick the corresponding box. Sooner, I am certain, much sooner than later, I will yell, *Bongo!*"

"I admire anyone who will go to so much effort for such a mediocre pay-off in sarcasm," Drakeforth said, regarding Pimola with an appraising eye.

"Well, you can buy me dinner then."

CHAPTER 22

Habeas put his trust in Arthur to find Drakeforth. He got off the bus at a random stop outside a restaurant. His stomach reminded him he hadn't eaten since breakfast, and he reasoned, it would know when he was hungry.

Food fascinated Habeas in many ways. He loved the science of it, the way the delicate interaction of ingredients could combine to create something stimulating. He was intrigued by the art of it, the emotional and creative energy that went into making the science both edible and enjoyable.

Mostly he liked to eat at affordable restaurants which were also in his top three places to convert the unwary.

Credit of the type on Habeas' credit stick wasn't something he gave a lot of thought to. He knew something of the complicated system dating back to the earliest days of Arthurianism. The monks and sisters who devoted their lives to Arthur's wisdom were given an allowance intended to keep them looking reasonably civilised and well fed enough to have the energy to do Arthur's work.

Habeas didn't know how much credit he had available, he simply purchased what he needed, when he needed it, which wasn't much or very often.

Most of his needs were met by the church. His clothes, a place to sleep, breakfast cereal, and thirteen familiar blends of tea, were all there when he needed them.

Experience being the great teacher was why Habeas now found himself sitting at a table, with a nearly clean plate in front of him, blinking at the waiter.

"Could you say that again?" Habeas asked.

"Your credit stick has declined."

"What does that mean?" Habeas asked with genuine curiosity.

"It means that you have not paid for your meal."

"Is it broken, do you think?" Habeas asked.

The waiter held the credit stick between thumb and forefinger. "It worked fine, you just don't have enough money to pay the bill."

"Does that happen often?" Habeas asked.

"Only to people who don't check their balance before they order the steak, egg, and chips, with an iced tea."

Habeas let his gaze pass over the bill; the numbers looked normal. He hadn't paid for everyone in the restaurant to eat, or tried to buy the building.

"There must be some kind of mistake," Habeas concluded.

The waiter nodded, "If I had a dollar for every time I heard that in these situations, I wouldn't need to work here."

"What should I do?" Habeas asked.

"Pay the bill, obviously," the waiter replied.

"Of course." Habeas stood up and took his credit stick from the waiter. "I'll come back tomorrow," he continued.

"You will be more than welcome, provided you pay the current bill before you leave, today." The waiter shifted slightly to block Habeas' exit. "We have a policy," he continued. "Diners come in and are served the finest food our chef can come up with, given his limited training in the culinary arts. They pay the bill afterwards, and the truly civilised add a tip. We like those kinds of diners here. They contribute to the warm, family-friendly ambience of the place."

"It is very nice," Habeas agreed.

"There are two things that can ruin the convivial atmosphere of a nice establishment like this," the waiter continued. "Weevils in the breakfast waffles and derros who can't pay their bill."

"That does sound quite tragic," Habeas nodded again.

"Yeah. We treat the derelicts the same way we get rid of the weevils."

"Oh?" Habeas squeaked.

"We take the ruined waffle mix, bag it up and throw it in the skip in the alleyway."

"I'm to be stuffed in a bag and thrown into the trash cans out back?" Habeas asked.

"Not quite. The kitchen staff will take you out to the alleyway, beat the meal you haven't paid for out of you and then throw you in the trash. We'll probably throw some weevils in after you, as a garnish."

"Oh…" Habeas sat down again. "I am sorry to have caused so much trouble."

"It's no trouble," the waiter said.

"It seems like a lot of effort to go to for a simple mistake."

"I can see why you would think that," the waiter nodded. "We find that in most cases, the previously bereft find the funds to pay the bill before we get them outside."

"How fortuitous. Do you perhaps have any idea how?"

"Not really my concern," the waiter shrugged. "They pay."

Habeas sat in uncomfortable silence for a moment. The waiter ignored the raised body language of other diners who wanted to place their orders or pay their bills.

"Outside it is then," the waiter said.

"I'm afraid so," Habeas agreed.

"This way, sir." The waiter indicated the swinging door that led to the kitchen.

CHAPTER 23

According to Pimola's phone, Bibbley Square, home to the nearest restaurant that was both open and serving a menu that didn't include numbered combo-meals, was within walking distance. And, if KLOE was to be believed, Habeas was going to be there too. It was, as Drakeforth said, catching two birds with one bassoon.

"The futures market, stock market, transferable debt, and credit of any kind, are complete fictions?" Pimola sighed like a punctured tyre as they walked.

"They produce nothing except more virtual wealth. They produce nothing tangible," Drakeforth insisted. "But that's so obvious. It's not the point I am trying to make."

"By all means, please, enlighten us," Pimola replied.

"None of these illusions come close to the bald-faced fabrications of restaurant reviews."

"The what now?" Pimola's attention snapped back like an appropriate simile.

"Chefs, cooks, bakers, burger-flippers, sandwich makers, picnic-packers; these people spend years honing their craft. They train and practice and produce something tangible and ultimately necessary," Drakeforth said. "Then along comes someone who does nothing more than sit down and taste the product of all that creativity and experience. The restaurant critic consumes and excretes an opinion on the quality of all that effort, experience and expertise."

"Why do I get the feeling you were savaged by criticism at

some key point in your psychological development?" Pimola asked.

Drakeforth continued unabated: "Exactly what qualifies a critic to criticise? Did they have a hand in the creation of the dish? Did they spend years crafting the ingredients, studying the delicate interplay of flavours and scents? Do they in fact have an iota of insight into the complex science of making the art that is fine cuisine?"

As Drakeforth talked, Pimola's face completed an intense physical workout from the range of emotions and expressions bursting across it. When he finished, she sagged in relief and stared at him. "Finished?" she asked.

"Here endeth the lesson," Drakeforth said with a graceful curtsey.

"Well, buckle-up, buttermug," Pimola replied. "Your disdain of critics isn't just about food. Restaurant reviews are merely an example of a bigger issue. Maybe you are afraid of being rejected, or someone didn't hug you enough as a child. I don't actually care, I'm not your therapist. What I am is a tea critic. Yeah, a critic of tea. One who writes professional reviews of tea and the bateastas who produce it. Which puts me in the unique position of being able to respond to your assertions." Pimola raised a hand and marked the points on her fingers.

"Critics do what they do out of love. They are as immersed in the culture, the science, and the art of the subject they critique as the creators themselves. Criticism is a celebration of creation. It is the worship of the tangible and the quantification of delight. Critics measure the immeasurable and define perfection."

"This place is open," Drakeforth called from the edge of hearing distance.

"Did you hear anything I just said?" Pimola seethed and hurried after him.

"Yes?" Drakeforth replied diplomatically.

"You are buying dinner. I do not want to hear a word out of you other than 'please pass the salt' and 'thank you'."

Drakeforth held the door open and Pimola swept in while Habeas was being swept out the back door of the same dining establishment.

"Do we just seat ourselves, or is there some kind of wait staff, do you think?" Drakeforth asked.

"I have no idea," Pimola muttered.

"Where's Habeas?" Drakeforth looked around.

"Maybe KLOE was wrong." Pimola also looked around.

The waiter was, in fact, attending to Habeas in the alleyway out back. In a film, the script would call for a technically challenging split-screen scene where the audience gets to see what is happening in two different places at the same time. This is also why books don't have hundred million-dollar special effects budgets.

"I'm going to sit down," Pimola decided. She slid into a booth with a view of her own reflection in the window to her left as it was dark outside. Drakeforth joined her; sitting on the other side of the table and tapping the menu screen built into the table.

"The steak seems particularly pleased with itself this evening," Drakeforth observed. Under his frowning gaze, an animated cow was dancing.

"Seven flavours of tea." Pimola rolled her eyes and sighed. "I wouldn't get out of bed to review a place with twice that many brews on the menu."

"Why is the cow dancing?" Drakeforth continued to frown at the looping imagery. "Is it meant to make me feel better or worse about eating it?"

Pimola perused the food screen of the menu in front of her. "Poindexter steak with mycelia jus..." Pimola read aloud. "Jus always struck me as gravy that couldn't commit."

"Fried chicken and eggs," Drakeforth read from his menu. "Now there is the perfect symbol of the hopeless nature of nature."

"It's disturbing if you think about it," Pimola replied, still studying the menu.

"All food is disturbing if you think about it," Drakeforth said. "An anthropomorphic dancing cow suggests a complete lack of awareness or an insane genius level of evil. Either way, I am in awe and feel compelled to have the poindexter with loser mushroom gravy."

Drakeforth looked around for a waiter. "I wonder if this is one of those unique dining experiences where they expect you to cook your own food?"

Pimola slid out of the booth and went to the kitchen pass. The steel surfaces gleamed the way operating theatres and commercial kitchens without health department warnings do. Various dishes in various states of preparation littered the benches and cooking surfaces.

"Hello?" she called.

The back door swung open, and a pair of chefs came in. They looked surprised to see her, and hurried back to their stations. A man in waiter attire was third through the door and he immediately came out to the dining area, a napkin with a spreading red stain pressed against his cheek.

"My apologies for the delay, madam," he said.

"Are you okay?" Pimola asked.

"I'm fine, please take a seat, I'll come and take your order presently."

Pimola returned to her seat, "We're having some kind of fight in the alleyway," she said.

"Probably fighting over who gets to quit working here first," Drakeforth replied.

"Good evening, sir, madam. Would you care to start with drinks?" The waiter glided to a halt next to their booth, a fresh gauze dressing on his cheek.

"Two iced teas; half barambee, half quindin, with a dash of kaleidoscope juice. Stirred three times with a wooden spoon," Pimola said before Drakeforth could draw breath.

"I'll have the same," Drakeforth said. "Then, a poindexter steak, seared rare enough to be endangered, with well-seasonal vegetables on the side."

"And the mycelia jus?" the waiter enquired.

"I say we throw caution to the wind and apply the gravitas liberally."

"Very well, sir, and for you madam?"

"What he said," Pimola replied. The menu screens closed, and the waiter executed a tiny bow before marching away.

"He will think twice before messing with a cat again," Drakeforth said in a conversational tone.

"If the cat escaped, he may have to think twice about tomorrow's menu," Pimola replied.

The iced teas arrived in tall glasses, the swirling liquid inside the colour of dirty rainbows. Drakeforth gave a slight grunt after sipping the concoction. "That's not bad," he admitted.

"Depending on whom you ask, it's either an old family recipe, or something made at random using whatever ingredients you have on hand," Pimola said while sipping her own tea.

"Why not make a career out of tea?" Drakeforth asked. "Surely if you love something you should pursue a career in it? Never work a day in your life and other such mindless platitudes."

"My career is in physics. Tea is a passion, sure. But if I was a doctor—say a heart surgeon with a passion for medicine and a driving dedication to heal the sick and ease pain and suffering—would I go home at night and do triple-bypass arterial grafts on the dining room table?"

"You do strike me as the type to open someone's chest with surgical precision at the slightest provocation," Drakeforth said.

"Why thank you," Pimola said, ducking her head. "My point is that just because you are good at something and can do it for a living, it's no reason to go home and do it on your free time."

"Whenever I hear someone say 'do a job you love and you'll never work a day in your life', my knuckles itch," Drakeforth replied grimly.

"What do you do for a job?" Pimola asked, swirling her straw.

"I don't," Drakeforth replied immediately.

"Oh, unemployment can be har—"

"I am *not* unemployed," Drakeforth interrupted her. "I exist outside of the system as much as possible. I don't have time for work, I'm far too busy doing more important things; therefore I choose not to work."

Pimola frowned, "Is this your subtle way of telling me that I'm paying for dinner?"

Drakeforth shrugged. "You are more than welcome to pay

for dinner. Finding anywhere that will take cash these days is tiresome."

"You don't really use cash because its untraceable, do you? It's just to annoy people," Pimola said.

"I use cash because it forces interaction. You hand someone something physical, a tangible object of trade, they notice. They connect with you. It's like giving a gift."

"Ah yes, the gift of inconvenience. Just what I always wanted."

"It is the gift that keeps on giving," Drakeforth agreed.

"Even though you wish it wouldn't," Pimola replied.

They lapsed into silence, finishing their drinks in time for the steaks to arrive.

Drakeforth and Pimola ate dinner in the slightly wary way of people eating with strangers, like animals grazing while keeping an eye out for predators.

They cleaned their plates and then ordered dessert: a sponge cake with fruit cream drizzle and a pot of heppermin tea to wash it all down.

"I should get home," Pimola said, covering her yawn with a napkin.

"I try to avoid going home," Drakeforth said, and casually wiped his fingers on his own serviette.

"I didn't realise you lived with my mother," Pimola said, gathering her belongings.

"No, I mostly live alone. That's the problem, you see. If I went home, I may enjoy the solitude so much I never want to leave."

"Well, as they say in the bar exam, I don't care where you go, you just can't stay here." Pimola gestured to the waiter who approached, carrying a tray bearing the bill. He set it down and stepped back.

Drakeforth slid out of the booth and Pimola followed. They stood together and the waiter cocked his head pointedly at the disregarded invoice on the table.

"Take care of that, will you?" Drakeforth said.

"No," Pimola said.

"Don't bother with a tip, the service was mediocre at best," Drakeforth said. The waiter's eyebrow arched in response. He then winced, as it pulled the fresh scratch on his cheek.

"You are paying for dinner," Pimola announced. "In fact, you agreed to pay."

"Unlikely," Drakeforth replied. "You will find I rarely agree to anything."

"Yes, you are entirely disagreeable," Pimola nodded. "You're still paying for dinner."

"We accept all major and most minor credit sticks," the waiter said.

"I only carry cash," Drakeforth replied.

"Ah haha...ha..." the waiter laughed in a polite way that managed to sound anything but.

"It's no excuse," Pimola snapped. "You can pay with polished coprolite for all I care."

"No, he really can't," the waiter interjected.

"Drakeforth, this nice man will take you to the counter and you can pay for our meal. Then you can call me tomorrow and we will see if we can find out where Habeas has wandered off to."

The waiter flinched and touched the dressing on his cheek.

"Tomorrow may be too late. Or too early," Drakeforth frowned. "That's the nature of uncertainty: you can never be sure how accurate your timing is. Of course, Habeas will have his own views on the nature of time and its perception. For all we know, he may believe that time has its own perception."

"Why do you twitch every time he says 'Habeas'?" Pimola asked the waiter.

"What? No reason." The waiter twitched again.

"Have you met him? Thin, pasty fellow, eyes like a dozing bovine, hair like a young Arthurian who takes his vows seriously?" Drakeforth asked.

The waiter seemed to be struggling with an internal hostage situation.

"It is important that we find him. Anything you can tell us would be very helpful," Pimola said gently.

"The cats took him!" the waiter exploded. "I don't know why, but he was here. He came in, ate, and left through the back door without paying. Then the cats in the alleyway took him away."

"Was that before or after one of them scratched you?" Pimola asked.

The waiter touched the white strip on his face. "After."

"Did they say why they were taking him?" Drakeforth asked.

"What? No, of course not. They're cats."

"You mentioned that. Did you not think to ask them?" Drakeforth asked.

"…?" The waiter unsaid.

"Could you show us where this catnapping occurred?" Pimola asked.

"Certainly. If you could just pay the bill first, I'd be happy to escort you both off the premises."

Drakeforth took a folded bundle of notes from his pocket and shaved a few off like he was whittling a stick. "Paid in full."

The waiter, who seemed resigned to his night being even weirder than his horoscope had predicted, took the cash without comment. "This way," he said, and led them through the kitchen and out the back door.

CHAPTER 24

Habeas had stepped out into the dark space between the weekend and the working day, metaphorically like the gap between the diner and the building next to it. The waiter's hand on his shoulder steered him like a bicycle towards the large dumpsters lounging against the wall.

Two kitchen staff had followed them, though it was unclear to Habeas if they were there to assist or simply watch what happened next.

The late-night air was cool and crisp like freshly washed lettuce. Habeas inhaled deeply and instantly regretted it: the dumpster wore the smell of decay the way ballerinas wear pointe shoes. One of the kitchen staff heaved the lid open.

"One last time, are you willing and able to pay for your meal this evening?" the waiter asked.

"That is an interesting question, and one that I would like to answer," Habeas said quickly. The two cooks seized him by the arms and lifted him off his feet. "Firstly," Habeas squeaked, "consider how we are defining *will*. Can we be certain that any of us actually have free will, or are all actions predetermined?"

"Bin him" the waiter declared. The cooks flipped the monk like an omelette, and he went into the skip.

"Bar-figure-nascent-gurney!" Habeas spluttered as a range of exotic stinks and textures rained down on him.

"You pay or you go out with the trash, skilja?" the waiter called from outside the bin.

Habeas wiped potato peelings from his eyes and blinked

upwards into the haloed glow of the only streetlight with the work ethic to keep shining on in the grim awfulness of the alleyway. A cat's silhouette sauntered into view along the edge of the skip and regarded him with the kind of casual disdain cats normally reserve for everything.

"Right," the waiter said. "Trash taken out, we have meals to prepare, paying customers to delight, and dreams to watch wither and die. We should get back to it."

The cat settled on the edge of the skip, went to lick one paw, sniffed it, and decided against it.

Habeas reached up and clamped a hand on the dumpster's rim. The cat sniffed his hand and then batted at it, uttering a plaintive *meow* at the same time.

The young monk jerked his hand back and sank into the cold mush of the trash. "Could someone explain to me how this is supposed to help?" he called.

The cat leapt out of view and a sudden scream cut the thick air. The cat yowled with a bandsaw's intensity and Habeas struggled to get upright. He stood swaying on the undulating surface, arms waving for balance.

The alleyway resembled a crime scene, or the aftermath of a polar bear's breakfast, with the waiter spinning in circles, screaming as the cat clung to his face. Blood splattered everywhere and the two cooks hopped about like folk dancers with a tradition of indecision as they tried to detach the cat.

Habeas took the opportunity to get out of the skip. He shook potato out of his ear and wondered if he should try and help or make a run for it.

More cats came into view; they flowed around Habeas in the semi-liquid way of felines, and he found himself being ushered away from the blood-curdling screams.

CHAPTER 25

The natural wonder of the Cataracta Falls has featured in masterpieces of poetry, painting, song, and countless advertising campaigns for everything from perfume to car insurance.

The parking area of the lookout point had likewise featured in any number of ad-libbed romantic dramas, mostly played out in the back seats of cars. The link between car-based steamy encounters and marketing campaigns is proof that the best advertising is not only subliminal, but its purpose is to sell you what you already have.

Edwid and Cole stood on the everyday side of the safety rail on the edge of the hundred-metre drop into the rolling maelstrom of water that boiled at the bottom of the falls.

With the assistance of the two assassins, the Puddings had gone on ahead.

"We gonna stand here for long?" Cole asked, shivering in the cold mist.

"I'm thinkin', mate," Edwid replied.

"I don't think they're comin' back," Cole offered helpfully.

"Would be one for the scrapbook if they did, eh?" Edwid said.

Neither of them laughed. Cole, because he didn't get the joke and Edwid, because he was trying to think of a way to fix the mess they were in.

"Can we go home now?" Cole asked.

"Yeah…sure."

The car had been wiped down, the shovels, limes, and large hat literally flushed down the drain of the falls. Edwid felt certain that the scene would be clear to the authorities.

The couple, out for a romantic park-up, had tragically fallen to their deaths.

"It's gonna be a long walk," Edwid said.

"Why don't we drive?" Cole asked, falling into step behind Edwid, who was already leaving.

"We need to leave the car here, so everyone knows what happened, Cole."

Cole nodded, keeping track of all the details that filled his brain with a dense fog.

"We have to find that Arthurian monk," Edwid said as they trudged down the dark country road.

"And get paid," Cole reminded him.

"We'll be lucky to get out of this alive, let alone paid, mate. We've got to find a hairy monk and finish up Vole Drakeforth as well."

"Can we get something to eat first?" Cole suggested. "I've only had a biscuit and a cup of tea tonight."

"When did you get a cup of tea and a tippin' biscuit?" Edwid snapped.

"Well, when we split up, I went to Missus Alpine's place. She made tea and told me about her old man, Alfie."

"Mate, we've already got one witness to take care of, please tell me we don't have visit some woman and put the blam in her lip balm?"

"Nah," Cole said, shaking his head. "She was old. Probably won't remember me. And even if she did, she'll be dead soon. In her sleep, I reckon."

"Let's hope she's off to bed early then, Cole."

They crossed a bridge over the river about the same time the Puddings went under it.

Edwid and Cole followed the road that would eventually return them to the city.

The Puddings continued downstream and eventually out to sea, which they would have appreciated, an ocean cruise being the kind of holiday they would have enjoyed.

CHAPTER 26

Habeas didn't have a well-developed sense of direction, and his sense of smell was currently hampered by the traces of three-day-old mushroom gravy and potato peelings up his nose.

It looked like he was in the basement of a building. Pipes, humming with double-e flux, ran along the ceiling in a network as inscrutable and complex as the lymphatic system.

Cats were arranged along every shelf and ledge, in neat rows that lend themselves to cathartic puns about catalogues. If any of the cats were to ask where he was, Habeas would admit to being at a complete loss. It didn't help that they regarded him with the disapproving expressions he usually saw on the faces of strangers at zippelin ports and bus terminals.

"Uhm, thank you for rescuing me?" Habeas said.

The cats blinked slowly in unison, the dimly lit basement felt as snug and drowsy as a cottage kitchen.

"I'm not sure why, of course. It is likely to cause no end of bother. Which is not to say that I don't appreciate your help..."

Habeas trailed off into a silence made awkward by the almost unblinking stares of all those yellow eyes.

"I'll be off, then," he added.

Meow, a cat said, and several others twitched their ears.

Habeas looked around for the exit. Nothing obvious presented itself.

"Well, goodbye." Habeas nodded and looked down as cats flowed like water around his ankles. The feline current unbalanced the monk until he fell backwards with a cry and landed comfortably in a well-stuffed armchair that had been shredded by claws.

Sweeping the hair off his face, Habeas stared into the ice-blue eyes of an elderly grey tabby. She sat on the arm of the chair and watched him with piercing intensity.

"Good kitty?" Habeas whispered.

As a student of Arthurian catechism, Habeas had studied mathematics and physics through the lens of scripture. Where a mathematician or a physicist looked through the lens of the Universe to become fluent in the language the Universe spoke, Arthurians took a more philosophical approach. Cats, of course, have a paw in both camps.

The purpose of language is to give form to the abstract and communicate it to others. Habeas got the message as clearly as if the cat had spoken to him.

Truth is a concept. Concepts are dictated by rules of perception. The truth is what you perceive. To learn the rules is to form a perception. Perception is what makes reality. Change your perception and see the truth.

There might have been more, but Habeas fainted from the overload of information pouring into his mind.

CHAPTER 27

"Is he okay?" Pimola asked with genuine concern.

"He smells off," Drakeforth replied.

"I think he fainted. If we had some smelling salts, we could rouse him," Pimola said.

"If the stink of whatever gunk he is covered in didn't wake him, I'm not sure smelling salts are going to help."

"Good kitty…" Habeas mumbled.

"And we're back," Drakeforth said.

"Habeas? No, don't try to move. How are you feeling?" Pimola asked.

"Got to find the truth…" Habeas mumbled. "Cats showed me…everything."

"Cats? Cats who?" Pimola asked. She put an arm around Habeas' shoulders as he sat up.

"Those cats—oh," Habeas frowned. He was sitting in the alleyway outside the restaurant.

Drakeforth and Pimola got Habeas on his feet, where he swayed a little.

"Feeling better for having napped?" Drakeforth asked.

"The cats…" Habeas started again, his brain feeling as soft as chamois, "…would appreciate it if we could save the Universe."

"We should take him to a hospital," Pimola suggested. "Clearly he is concussed."

"What exactly did the cats tell you?" Drakeforth asked, with unusual directness.

"They didn't tell me... they more... showed me," Habeas tried to explain.

"What did they show you?" Drakeforth asked.

"The...well, the spaces where the truth should be. They showed me the gaps where there shouldn't be gaps. Reality has holes in it, and it is like they have been plastered over so no one will notice."

"Are you feeling dizzy?" Pimola asked. "Headache? Nausea?"

"Why would the cats involve themselves so directly...?" Drakeforth mused.

"They were..." — Habeas swallowed — "quite adamant."

Drakeforth nodded. "Cats are, by their very natures, indistinct. For them to deign to give you their full attention suggests this is a serious situation."

Pimola regarded Drakeforth with one eyebrow raised. "Did you hit your head, too?"

"You were there when Arthur came to me in the alleyway," Habeas said, and seized Drakeforth by the coat lapels. "Arthur told me to go with you and find the truth."

"Really? I wasn't listening." Drakeforth squirmed free. "You really need a bath," he added.

"And I need to go home," Pimola said stifling a yawn. "You two are exhausting."

"We must find the truth. Arthur commands it," Habeas insisted.

"No," Drakeforth said. "You have done quite enough. Just sit down and be quiet. Not you." He grabbed Habeas by the arm as the monk started to sink.

Habeas stared into Drakeforth's eyes. "You are the vessel of Arthur. He speaks through you."

"You make it sound like I'm a boat," Drakeforth scowled. "He's more of a parasite. Or possibly a brain tumour."

A sigh of satisfaction rose through Habeas' face like warm gas escaping the melting permafrost. "Arthur..." he breathed.

"Enough of this gazpacho," Drakeforth demanded. "Pimola, go home. Habeas, go to wherever it is that you go to get your medication."

"Where are you going?" Pimola said, hesitating after half a step.

"I am going to see the Godden Energy Corporation," Drakeforth said.

"Aren't they closed at this time of day?" Habeas asked as Drakeforth marched away.

"I'm counting on it," he called back.

CHAPTER 28

The corporate offices of the Godden Energy Corporation were closed, a fact that caused Edwid a great deal of frustration. Cole stood silent, except for the regular yawning, as Edwid took a deep breath before pushing the intercom button again.

"Good evening, sir," the voice on the other end said, with a tone of threadbare patience.

"It is very important that I speak to someone in charge," Edwid said.

"You mentioned that," the voice replied.

"Very important," Edwid repeated.

"Mentioned," the voice snapped back.

They lapsed into a cold silence, Edwid's knuckles creaking in his clenched fists. "Is there someone else I can talk to?"

"You would like to speak to someone in charge?" the voice asked.

"Yes!" Edwid barked.

"One moment, please." The intercom clicked off.

The long silence was broken only by the yawning chasm of Cole's mouth.

"Good evening, sir. I'm the office night-shift security manager. How may I help?" A familiar voice asked.

"You're the same person I was just talking to?!" Edwid yelled.

"Yes," the voice said.

"But you aren't any help at all!" Edwid yelled.

The voice may have giggled, but the intercom disconnected before Edwid could be sure.

"The lights are on," Edwid said while leaning on the intercom button. "Someone is there. I need to speak to the guy in the big office on the top floor."

"Do you have an appointment?" The voice asked.

"It's quite urgent," Edwid said.

"Not without an appointment, it isn't."

"Assuming we don't have an appointment, how would I go about getting one?" Edwid asked through gritted teeth.

"You need to contact us during business hours."

"Can we go home now?" Cole asked.

"Yeah, mate. We can go home. But we are coming back. During business hours, and we will make sure we have an appointment," Edwid declared with grim determination.

CHAPTER 29

The next day started with a sluggish sunrise and a lingering mist that promised excellent weather, once the day had had a strong cup of tea, some hot buttery toast, and a chance to read the morning papers.

Of course, if the sun had read the news, it would have turned around and gone back to bed, an event that would have barely made the *Top 10 Odd Things* to happen that day.

Drakeforth arrived early at the corporate headquarters of the Godden Energy Corporation. He arrived before the interns and the drivers who delivered the day's cafeteria supplies to the people who made the tea. He arrived hours before the executive assistants, who arrived at least two hours before their charges.

Drakeforth arrived early enough to be lurking in the shadows when Edwid Mint and Colander Munt attempted to gain access to the building in the middle of the night.

He recognised the two men as the ones who had tried to kill him in the alleyway two nights earlier. That they were intently trying to gain access to the headquarters of the Godden Energy Corporation made him frown even more intently.

After they left, Drakeforth slipped around the back of the building. This took some time, as the headquarters of the largest company in the world took up more space than most university campuses.

"Terribly smug design, isn't it?" Arthur said, startling Drakeforth with the sudden intrusion.

"What?" he muttered, looking around to be sure that no one

else had heard the voice in his head.

"All this... Terribly smug," Arthur took Drakeforth's hand and waved it dismissively.

"Stop that," Drakeforth snapped.

"If they were properly concerned about keeping their enemies out, they would have at least kept their castle to one entrance," Arthur explained. "Proper paranoia would have suggested not having a big building at all. Go with subtle omens and coded messages in the layout of sock drawers and so on instead."

"Clearly they are a cult of morons," Drakeforth muttered drily.

"Oh, this is hardly a cult. Back in my day, we had proper cults. Place was thick with them, as common as crusty sores."

"Quiet a moment, I need to concentrate," Drakeforth replied.

Instead of alleyways, the dark forces of evil had chosen to landscape their lair with well-lit pathways, colour coordinated gardens of sweetly perfumed flowers and aesthetically pleasing sculptures.

Drakeforth sidled up to a plain-looking door and looked around. So far, so good. "The lack of security guards patrolling the premises at night is reassuring," he whispered.

"They would be a bit redundant, considering the state-of-the-art security cameras and door alarms," Arthur replied casually, as Drakeforth opened the door.

The door stood ajar in silence as Drakeforth held his breath. "Silent alarm?" he thought very hard.

"What use would that be?" Arthur snorted.

"Very useful if you want to catch someone in the middle of doing something they shouldn't." Drakeforth eased inside and gently let the door click shut behind him. "How did you know about the cameras and alarms?" he added.

"Being a passenger means I get to look at the scenery and not have to worry about the driving," Arthur explained. "While you are focused on staying upright, walking, and breathing, I get to look around. I find it gives me scope to notice quite a lot."

"Great, have you noticed a way to the executive offices?"

"The high priest's chambers?" Arthur asked.

"Sure, let's say that," Drakeforth agreed, hurrying on light feet along a dimly lit service corridor.

"They are often at the top," Arthur offered. "Or behind the altar. Some find being close to the faithful leads to difficult questions, so they choose to be there in spirit."

"Typical," Drakeforth muttered. He arrived at a bank of elevators dozing in the dim nocturnal lighting of the office block. Choosing one at random didn't immediately result in the doors sliding open. So he pressed the up buttons on all of them.

The third elevator pinged cheerfully, and he stepped inside. Pressing the highest floor number button generated a sad noise. Drakeforth pushed it again.

"Is it working?" Arthur asked after a moment.

"Imagine I am pressing your face into a bowl of custard until the bubbles stop," Drakeforth said through clenched teeth.

The elevator doors opened again and Drakeforth exited onto the same floor. "I need a building access card. Something suitably authorised to get me to the top."

"Where would we get such a thing?" Arthur asked.

"The simplest way would be to enrol in a highly respected university, complete undergraduate and post-graduate degrees in business management. Then, after completing an internship and securing an entry level position in the corporation, work my way up through the corporate hierarchy, until, in thirty or so years, I get promoted to the executive branch."

"Excellent. We can we start?" Arthur asked.

"Just as soon as I have finished here," Drakeforth said.

He patrolled the elevator lobby until he found the door to the stairs used by the invisible people; the ones who work long hours for minimal wage doing everything to maintain the illusion that the building cleans itself and the stationery cupboards are a never-ending cornucopia of staplers and boxes of pens. Like cockroaches in sensible shoes, the custodial staff move unseen through buildings, and they get in everywhere.

Drakeforth paced until a man wearing headphones and a fluro green shirt entered the lobby carrying a cardboard carton in his arms.

"Let me help you with that," Drakeforth announced, and took

the carton as the man swiped a card attached to a retractable string on his pants. Handing the box back, he shadowed the man through the door and up the stairs.

To Drakeforth's relief, the access card was not needed to get out of the staircase. To his annoyance, the floors went up into the double digits.

"Wouldn't it have been faster to take the elevator?" Arthur asked, as Drakeforth staggered on to the final level.

"Possibly," Drakeforth breathed heavily. "Though where's the fun in doing things the easy way?"

In the vast savannah of the executive level lobby, Drakeforth waded through the wafting strands of carpet the length and colour of a neglected lawn. Sounds sank out of sight, lost forever in the deep pile.

Double doors of heavy wood and stained glass swung open, leaving a crop circle sector in the carpet. Drakeforth slipped inside. Receptionist desks with the dimensions of aircraft carriers were arranged strategically around the room. A second set of cathedral doors led to a conference room, the end of the table vanishing over the horizon.

"Temples haven't changed much since my day," Arthur observed.

"These people worship money," Drakeforth replied, his gaze sweeping across the upper reaches of the walls.

"People have always worshipped money. Did you know the ancient Escrutians based their entire economy around the belief that every man had a soul and his value went up or down depending on how he lived his life?"

"Fascinating," Drakeforth said with sufficient sarcasm to pickle beets. He started hiking across the room towards the next exit.

"It really is. They had currency that was representative of good deeds and their temples acted as banks. Their version of bankruptcy was an unfortunate form of excommunication. Now the really interesting aspect—"

"Arthur. *Arthur!*" Drakeforth mentally shouted. "I don't care. I have actual real problems. Issues so tangible I could push my bare feet into them and squeeze them between my toes like cold jello. Your constant chatter is distracting and annoying. Whatever it is you think you are doing, stop it. Whatever it is you think you are adding to my excruciating existence, you aren't contributing a ballaster thing."

"I don't need to ask if that is truly how you feel. Your sentiment is dripping down the walls in here," Arthur replied. "I'll keep my wisdom to myself, which is advice I should have given myself centuries ago."

Drakeforth waited for Arthur to say anything further. His inner voice went silent. "Fine," Drakeforth said; it felt important to get the last word.

Smaller doors led to spaces behind the stage of the theatre of corporate reality; open plan offices where people toiled to ensure that the money continued to flow upwards and further out of their reach.

Drakeforth marched through the battery-farm cubicles, past the cleaner's cupboard and into a utility room. The skeleton of the building was exposed in the spartan spaces like this. Unlike the conference room, with its polished panels of faux wood milled from imported faux trees, this room's walls, floor and ceiling of cold concrete gave it all the charm of a prison cell.

Pipes and control panels for the monitoring and control of double-e flux dominated the room. The warm air smelled sleepy at this time of night. Drakeforth climbed the pipes to the ceiling and forced an access panel open. Slithering through, he wormed his way into an air conditioning duct. A few sharp turns later, he had a good view through a grille into the wide field of the conference room.

"Now we wait," he said, and closed his eyes.

CHAPTER 30

The interns arrived first, like children dressed as miniature versions of adult responsibility and the corruption of power. They straightened chairs, polished glassware, and subtly moved nameplates around the table to ensure their superiors were seated to the best advantage.

Drakeforth woke up, stretched in his prone position, and tried not to think about the way the ice-cold water sloshed in the crystal jugs.

Men and women in suits walked in, some talking on the phone, apparently making important decisions within earshot of everyone else. Drakeforth ignored them; his attention went to the few who entered in silence, like sharks swimming onto a reef teeming with lesser fish.

None of the faces that took their seats around the monolithic table were well-known. Face value was for sense-media celebrities and fashion models selling shampoo. True power meant being anonymous to the masses and unknown to even the people the masses thought were in charge. The twelve men and women who took their seats were as forgettable as a dream. To Drakeforth they were a nightmare made flesh.

Like downstairs servants, the interns silently melted away once the attendees were settled and closed the door behind them.

"Good morning," the suit at the head of the table said. "This meeting is not taking place. There is no agenda, no minutes. There will be no action points, no diary entries, no appointments, and no follow-up discussions." He paused to let his instructions be confirmed with slight nods around the table.

"The human resources matter remains unresolved," he said. A frown rippled around the table in a spreading wave. "The employee tasked with mitigating the risk chose to engage a third-party contractor. They have been unable to complete the task. We are awaiting updates."

A thin man with grey hair seated near the far end of the table blinked. Drakeforth frowned and made a mental note.

"Is the project in danger of delay?" a suit halfway down the table asked.

"Of course not," the chair replied. "This is a minor matter that is being brought to the attention of this Board for completeness.

"What guarantee do we have of the issue being corrected?" a woman wearing frameless spectacles asked.

The man with the eye twitch cleared his throat. "I personally guarantee it," he said.

Eyebrows raised like goosebumps around the table and those nearest him managed to distance themselves without leaving their seats.

"Are you certain?" the Chair asked.

Eye-twitch swallowed again and nodded. "Yes."

"That it has taken this long to be resolved is...*disappointing,*" the woman in the frameless spectacles said.

A subvocal murmur of agreement hummed around the room.

"Do you love me, Isthmus?" the Chair asked. The air in the room went completely still.

"Uh...I...uhm. I'm sorry?" Isthmus stumbled, his eye-twitch accelerating.

"Love, Isthmus. Is everything. I love the Godden Energy Corporation. This company is a living organism. A legally recognised living entity and we, Isthmus, are each a tiny cell with an essential function to ensure that the GEC continues to thrive and grow. When one of those cells, no matter how tiny, or seemingly unnecessary, doesn't function properly, the entire organism is at risk."

Isthmus nodded and waited for permission to grovel and make desperate promises.

"When the entire organism is threatened, it reacts. All available resources are activated to focus on the source of infection. The threat is expunged, Isthmus. Utterly destroyed, and the organism remembers it and makes plans to prevent it ever happening again. You don't want to be remembered in that way, Isthmus."

Isthmus' throat was too dry for him to even croak. He nodded instead.

"This meeting is adjourned," the Chair said.

Everyone stood and filed out in silence, leaving Isthmus pinned to his seat like a butterfly on a mounting board.

The door closed behind the last of the meeting escapees and with shaking hands, Isthmus took out his phone and dialled a number.

Drakeforth lay in the air conditioning duct and studied the dust. He made some brief notes in the thin layer of grime, and he didn't like what they were telling him.

Isthmus had regained his composure and was speaking intensely at low volume on the phone.

"No, the Board only knows exactly what we—I mean you— want them to know." Isthmus paced up and down the boardroom. "I'm taking care of it," he insisted. "No, I don't know where he is. I have people working on it." He paused and listened to whomever was on the other end of the line. "Cabbage's Server Farm? What could possibly—" Isthmus pinched his nose to ward off the impending headache. "I'll take care of it. Yes, that too. Just remember our agreement. Hello? Hell—" Isthmus glared at the phone in his hand before shoving it in his suit pocket and leaving the room.

Drakeforth waited until the door closed in Isthmus' wake.

"Arthur," he whispered. After a long moment of silence, he tried again. "Arthur?"

"I thought you weren't speaking to me," Arthur asked.

"I'm not," Drakeforth muttered. "I'm reciting Achoo Poetry at you."

"Oh yes, sarcasm. Well done."

"Why is the Godden Energy Corporation trying to kill me, do you think?" Drakeforth asked.

"Perhaps it is because they have met you?" Arthur replied.

"I've met plenty of people," Drakeforth snapped.

"It is a miracle you are still alive then," Arthur suggested.

Drakeforth mentally shushed the voice in his head.

Wriggling backwards, he completed an awkward three-point turn and crawled back through the ducts until he fell through a grille into the utility room.

"That looked like it hurt,' Arthur said.

"Gnnnghhh," Drakeforth replied.

"What are you going to do now?" Arthur asked.

"I thought I might lie here for a bit, see if anything is broken," Drakeforth said.

"If this Isthmus fellow is meant to be seeing to your demise, you have two options. Either scuttle away like a dung beetle, or confront him."

"Isthmus is a tool. Not a particularly useful tool, either. He's one of those basic tools, like a hammer or an oscilloscope. Not special enough to be irreplaceable, and only used because applying brute force or graphing electrical signals is good enough to get the job done."

CHAPTER 31

It is said that Saint Fhuse Ovarie once declared awards are mostly a matter of perception. The relationship between the person receiving the award and the award itself is much like the duality of matter at its most unknowable. Saint Fhuse would have nodded in satisfaction if she'd seen the office of Dunstan Isthmus, Regional Manager of the Godden Energy Corporation.

Four of the room's six walls were covered in plaques, trophies, and certificates. Each represented an award given by a corporation or group with a vested interest in keeping on Isthmus' good side. He hated each and every one of the cheap metal and plastic figurines. He especially despised the carefully calligraphed certificates, and even the lithographs of him shaking hands with someone who was handing him one of the trophies filled him with loathing.

To Isthmus, each of his industry awards represented the ultimate in self-appreciation, awarding oneself for a job well done. He hated being recognised for excellence in a job anyone could do—anyone whose absolute loyalty could be bought with a great salary, regular bonus payments, a company car, and a no-questions-asked expense account, that is.

Isthmus hung up the phone and scowled at it. The intercom flashed, and he jabbed the button.

"Yes?"

"A Mr Drakeforth is *insisting* on seeing you, sir," the perfectly sculpted receptionist said in her perfectly articulated voice.

"He's here?"

"Yes, Mr Isthmus. Mr Drakeforth, appears somewhat agitated, sir. I have security standing by."

Isthmus reeled from shock and surprise. "Very well, send him in."

"Security, sir?"

"What? No, Drakeforth. Send Drakeforth in. But yes, have security on hand to escort him out of the building. And possibly the country. Can we do that?"

"I'll make enquiries, sir."

"Great, thanks." Isthmus hit the intercom button and sank into the soft pleather throne of his office chair. Vole Drakeforth being here was the last thing Isthmus needed, with everyone expecting him to manage the situation—which, in executive circles, meant they couldn't wait for him to fail and be thrown to the press. Being thrown to a pack of wild dogs would be preferable: at least they had the decency to wait till you were dead before eating you.

The intercom buzzed again. Isthmus jabbed the button angrily. "What?!"

"Mr Drakeforth is on his way in, sir."

Isthmus stood up and embarked on the long trek around his desk. He had gotten into the habit of double-checking he had everything he needed before leaving his seat. The walk around the massive edifice made coming back if he had forgotten something irritating, to say the least.

By the time he had reached the corner, the office door opened, and a dishevelled man came marching through it, only to stop and blink in surprise.

"Mr Drakeforth," Isthmus called across the savannah of his office. He started walking again, time passed, and they eventually met somewhere between a certificate of appreciation from the *Guild of Executive Pragmatists* and a litho of a smiling Isthmus standing next to a bear in a clown costume.

"Mr Drakeforth, how can I help you today?" Isthmus said with a warm smile.

"You can start by answering some questions. Firstly—" Drakeforth stopped talking and stared as the lithograph caught his attention.

"Firstly, you can explain to me why in the heliosphere that bear is wearing a clown costume."

"Last year's regional office winter solstice party. I believe the bear was part of the entertainment troupe. If I recall correctly, it juggled cheese as part of the act."

Drakeforth blinked, "Is there no depravity you people will not sink to?"

"I'm told the bear is available for children's parties," Isthmus said before steering Drakeforth towards a chair.

"Now," Isthmus said in a tone of cheerful helpfulness, "what appears to be the trouble?"

"I came here to make it perfectly clear that your attempt to have me killed was entirely unsuccessful."

Isthmus cranked his charming smile up another notch. "Mr Drakeforth, I can assure you I am at a loss to understand what you are talking about."

Drakeforth continued, "I have reason to believe that the Godden Energy Corporation is involved in a conspiracy centred around the truth of the origins of empathic energy."

"You have reason to believe?" Isthmus asked.

"Yes," Drakeforth replied.

"Reason, but no evidence?" Isthmus said in a gentle tone that made Drakeforth's right eye twitch.

"Evidence is currently circumstantial and will be forthcoming," Drakeforth said. "The undeniable facts are that you tried to have me killed for asking the right questions."

"Let me set your mind at ease, Mr Drakeforth. The Godden Energy Corporation is your friend. We are focused on a world where peace and harmony are ways of life. We provide low-cost energy solutions to everyone. Empathic energy powers everything from toasters to Titan- class cargo freighters. Under no circumstances would anyone in this organisation make any attempt to have anyone murdered under the pretence of authorisation from management."

"So, it is entirely possible that the order for me to be killed was made by someone who did not go through official channels?" Drakeforth asked, his scowl deepening.

"The activities our employees engage in during their non-working hours is none of our business, Mister Drakeforth." The manager's smile had now winched up his cheeks as far as it could go. His eyes were starting to ache from the strain of holding the expression.

"I hardly think my assassination can be compared to a hobby," Drakeforth replied. "Sanctioned murder is not like fishing, or stamp collecting."

"I can assure you we are in no way responsible for or connected to any attempt you feel may have been made on your life."

"Empathic energy: Where does it come from? You claim that Godden discovered it, but that can't be true," Drakeforth said, switching to another line of questioning.

"Of course it is true. Why would it not be true? You should just accept that we live in a world where the GEC does nice things for good people."

"My research suggests that there were others involved in the discovery. People your founder swindled and destroyed to keep the secret for himself."

Isthmus sighed, "Mister Drakeforth, there are always going to be rumours and legends about great men. I can assure you that Huddy Godden discovered the secret of empathic energy and shared it with the world. We owe him a great debt. Now if you will excuse me, I have another meeting." Isthmus stood up and began the hike towards the door, while Drakeforth remained seated and frowning.

"Is there anything else, Mr Drakeforth?" Isthmus called across the cavernous space of his office.

Drakeforth stood up. "Juggling bears are entirely possible. They do possess the required paw-eye coordination, and could be trained to juggle up to three items. That, however, is not the case in this case."

"Thank you, Mr Drakeforth." Isthmus opened the door to the outer office in a pointed indication.

Drakeforth walked out past the Regional Manager and then paused on the threshold. "Fraud is something you are familiar with, Mister Isthmus. Fraud and, I have no doubt, murder. I find it particularly ironic therefore that you have an image of yourself standing next to a man wearing a suit made from a dead bear's skin on your office wall."

Isthmus closed the door on Drakeforth's back. He stood for a moment and took a deep breath before crossing over to peer more closely at the lithograph of the juggling bear. *There's no way it could be a man in a bear suit…could it?*

CHAPTER 32

"Pimola?" Drakeforth barked down the phone.

"How did you get my number?" she replied, her voice thick with sleep.

"You wouldn't believe me if I told you," Drakeforth replied. "So, let's just pretend I have explained it and you're okay with it and we can get to why I needed to call you so early in the morning."

"What time is it?"

Drakeforth could hear her straining to wake up. "Terribly early, which is why we must act quickly, otherwise it will be too late."

Pimola sighed. "I had quite hoped last night was just a bad dream."

"We are on a quest. An important one, according to Arthur. The sort of thing scholars will write about and debate for centuries."

"As long as they agree that last night was the worst date I have ever been on, they can have at it," Pimola replied.

"Not a date," Drakeforth replied firmly. "Though," he added after a moment, "if it was, what was so bad about it?"

"Seriously?" Pimola asked with arched consonants matching her eyebrows.

"You're right, not important. Listen, I need you to find a vehicle. A car, truck, van, something that can take us somewhere."

"I don't have a car. I ride a scooter."

"Why? Did you lose a bet?" Drakeforth asked.

"No. It's simply affordable, easy to manoeuvre through traffic, and a great excuse when anyone asks me to drive them anywhere."

"We'll need something bigger, there may be cargo to move."

"What kind of cargo?" Pimola made getting-dressed noises down the phone.

"Important cargo. You're right, a van or truck would be the best option. Something discreet though, nothing that suggests we have stolen technology in the back and are on the run from a dangerous corporation."

"I'm not stealing technology," Pimola said.

"Technically correct," Drakeforth agreed. "No matter what anyone asks or threatens you with, keep telling them that. I'll meet you at your laboratory in an hour."

The phone cut off before Pimola could say no.

She made a cup of tea and stared into the depths of her refrigerator, which was as cold and desolate as a tundra.

There was nothing breakfastable in there. She closed the door and patted the old appliance gently. Its voice memo unit had never worked, which is why it had been so cheap, even second hand. Pimola still wanted it to know she appreciated the work it did, no matter how futile.

The space between the kitchen and her apartment's front door was mostly blocked by piles of books. She had bookshelves, of course, like an ossuary for the bones of the revered dead; they were stacked with the books she had read many times. The floor housed her TBR (To-Be-Read) and TBRA (To-Be-Read-Again) piles.

The front door was more of a concept at this point, as probable as any of the advanced mathematical equations Pimola poked at every day. She used the window that led to the fire escape to get in and out of the apartment instead.

"Morning," Habeas said cheerfully.

Pimola started in shock. "Shrimp biscuits!" she hissed as her head cracked on the window frame.

Habeas Yeast was sitting on the metal stairs that led to the floor above. A light dusting of breakfast baked goods crumbs decorated his beard and robed knees.

"Crumpet?" He offered a grease-stained bag. "Tea?" he

continued, without offering a cup.

"Thanks." Pimola took the bag and sat down on the landing while she munched the yeasty slab inside. "Tea?" she asked.

"I didn't get any. Though we could stop somewhere on the way and get a cup to go."

"Excellent idea," Pimola crumpled the empty bag and tossed it through the open window into her apartment; it dropped neatly into the rubbish bin. "Where are we going?"

"Arthur shall guide us. All I am certain of is that I should expose myself to as much potential as possible."

"Quantum potential?" Pimola asked with a raised eyebrow. "You do understand that quantum mechanics occurs at a sub-atomic level? We are talking energy in all its forms doing things."

Habeas nodded. "Arthur's teachings are clear on this."

"Hardly the sound basis for an actual religion, then."

"Oh, no." Habeas shook his head. "It's the only basis for an actual religion. You're a physicist, right? Have you ever seen a photon? A quark? A zomni?"

"No, of course not, but—"

"But you study the wisdom of those who came before you and you accept that their truth is your truth."

"Because it can be measured and verified, through experiment-ation."

"Using mathematics and systems of measurement that require you to accept what your perceptions tell you as true."

Pimola pinched her nose. "Tea?" she suggested.

"Splendid." Habeas stood up and brushed the last of the crumbs away. Pimola sighed and followed him down the rattling fire-escape.

"Drakeforth called me. Did he also call you?" Pimola asked.

"Uhm…" Though Habeas' experience with women was quite limited. He could see how casually mentioning that he had slept poorly last night and, after rising early, had wandered as aimlessly as a homing bee directly to her address, which he had found by looking her up in the phone directory, could disturb her.

They reached the ground and Pimola led the way towards her local tea shop.

"Seriously," she said. "What was he thinking? Chasing you around half the city last night. Then waking me at this hour of the morning? The man clearly has mental problems."

"He's the prophet of Arthur," Habeas said.

"I thought Arthur was the prophet for you lot?"

"It's complicated," Habeas replied, warming to a familiar area of conversation.

"You see, Arthur was a man, born as all men are. Then through his genius, he achieved enlightenment and ultimately, he ascended to a higher state of energy. He became one with the Universe."

Pimola opened the door to *Cosy's Tea and Biscuits.* The staff behind the counter looked up, their warm smiles curdling as she entered.

"How do you account for the fact, the *actual* fact, that we are all one with the Universe? We are the Universe. The Universe is us."

"And yet we stand apart from it," Habeas scanned the menu board. "What's good here?" he asked Pimola.

The tea critic's lips pressed thin. "That, apparently, is a matter of opinion," she said pointedly at the woman standing behind the counter, whose arms were arms folded in a less-than-welcoming stance.

"Well, you choose, I'll get us a table."

Habeas settled into a seat and waited for Pimola to join him. The conversation between the bateasta and Pimola appeared to be conducted with the formality and barely-restrained hostility of cease-fire talks between two warring nations.

Pimola arrived and set two steaming cups of tea down. "It's a blend I recommended."

Habeas made an appreciative noise and took a sip.

"The spit is their own twist on the recipe," Pimola added.

The Arthurian monk swallowed carefully. "Very nice..." he murmured.

"You think that because people, as you put it, stand apart from the Universe, that someone like Vole Drakeforth can be the prophet of your prophet, who no longer stands apart from the Universe and is therefore a god?" Pimola said, after cautiously tasting her own tea.

"I don't think—" Habeas began.

"Clearly," Pimola interrupted drily.

"I know," Habeas continued. "I am as certain of Arthur's, for want of a better description, *divinity*, as I am that there is no extra saliva in this tea."

"Faith sounds a lot like naivety," Pimola replied.

A slight shadow fell across the table. "Excuse me," a young man murmured, and then slipped into the third chair at their table.

"Can I help you?" Pimola asked.

"On the contrary, it is I who can help you," the young man said.

"He's already an Arthurian and I'm not seeking any new delusions, thanks anyway," Pimola said with a charming smile.

The new arrival was almost lost in the folds of the oversized trench coat he wore. "You are working with Mr Vole Drakeforth." There was no question in his statement.

"Oh yes, we're on a quest," Habeas blurted.

"Who?" Pimola said in the same moment.

"I represent people who believe in Vole Drakeforth's search for the truth. We know you need a vehicle, and I have been despatched to provide you with one."

"You're from a van rental company?" Pimola asked. "Not usually the level of efficiency or service I would expect, but okay."

"What? No." The young man looked confused for a moment. "I represent a shadowy organisation seeking to uncover the truth about the Godden Energy Corporation."

"You're wearing GEC Engineering Division coveralls. You have a name tag on the front that says *Diphthong*," Pimola said.

Diphthong pulled his coat tighter. "Quiet down," he whispered. "I'm undercover."

"More overdressed, I'd say," Pimola replied.

"Arthur has sent you to aid us?" Habeas asked.

"Who?" Diphthong blinked. "I mean, no." Like a turtle retreating into its shell, Diphthong sank deeper into his coat. He searched the various pockets and retrieved an envelope and a set of car keys. "Directions on where you can find the van. When you have finished with it, please return it to where you found it. Oh, and if you can have it back by this evening, my brother needs to do his deliveries tonight. He'll be somewhat annoyed if his van has been stolen."

"Stolen?" Habeas asked, and looked around hurriedly.

"Borrowed," Diphthong said, and pushed the envelope and keys across the table.

"Fine, my week could hardly get any weirder. Come on, Habeas, let's go borrow a van." Pimola swept the keys and paper off the table and headed for the door.

"Once you return the van, await further instructions," Diphthong whispered.

Habeas stood up. "Please tell Arthur I am doing my best," he whispered to Diphthong. The young monk nodded at Diphthong and hurried after Pimola.

CHAPTER 33

"I thought the countryside meant fresh air," Pimola said with a frown.

"City air is just as fresh. The only difference is the smells," Drakeforth replied. "Take the next left."

The van hummed along the country road, Pimola at the wheel only because Habeas didn't know how to drive and Drakeforth had rolled his eyes so hard they rattled when she asked if he might.

It didn't help that they were driving without a map, or a clear idea of where they were going. Drakeforth's constant muttering wasn't helping Pimola's mood.

Habeas sat in the back on a pile of commercial laundry sacks, all stuffed with clean linen. He couldn't smell anything other than the lingering tang of detergent and the deep-down-in-your-soul contentment that only warm sheets can bring.

He snuggled into his makeshift sofa and meditated until his steady breathing could have been mistaken for sleep.

"There!" Drakeforth barked. "Turn in there!"

Pimola slowed the van and pulled up at a large wooden gate under an arched sign that read *Cabbage's Server Farm.*

"A server farm?" Pimola asked. "What possible reason would we have for coming to a server farm?"

"Where do you think fresh data comes from?" Drakeforth asked in a rhetorical tone.

"I never really thought about it," Pimola admitted. "I mean, it has to come from somewhere, but it's always packaged and cleaned when I get it."

"This is one of the oldest server farms in the country," Drakeforth said, winding down the window. "Which is why we are here."

He pushed the call button on an intercom box. It crackled, and then a tinny voice said, "Garn?"

"Hello there," said Drakeforth with such warmth and geniality that Pimola did a double take. "Sorry to bother you, we are here to pick up an order for..." Drakeforth swooshed and gargled in a verbal simulation of crackling static.

An empathic motor hummed and the gate swung open on a simple rope-and-pulley system. The van drove up the long driveway, flanked by a row of trees on each side that shielded the view of the surrounding fields. Pimola steered the van along the sweeping avenue until they came around a final curve into a wide yard surrounded by various farm buildings. They pulled up in front of an old farmhouse that looked like someone had made a cake shaped like a house, only for it to sag after being taken out of the oven.

"Don't wake Habeas," Drakeforth said as he slid out of the van.

"Garn," a man in dark overalls and rubber boots announced himself.

"Hello," Drakeforth replied. "Lovely place you have here," he added, as if reading from a cue card.

"Isnobad," the man verbally shrugged. "What'yafter?" he drawled.

"Information," Drakeforth said.

The farmer grunted, "Well y'come to right place."

Pimola climbed out of the van, stepping carefully as if the ground underfoot may not take her weight.

"We got nowt but finest datasets here at Cabbage's," the farmer added.

"Excellent." Drakeforth turned to take in the fields and sheds. "Mind if we have a look around, ah, Mister Cabbage?"

"Aye," Cabbage nodded.

"Aye, you mind, or aye we are welcome to poke about and satisfy our curiosity?" Drakeforth asked, his fixed smile glazing over.

"Aye," Cabbage repeated. "I gi'n yer the tour."

The city-dwellers followed Cabbage's rubber boots as he ambled across the gravelled yard.

"Bin farmin' data on this land since me granda's day. Charles Cabbage, 'e was t'first."

"Fascinating," Drakeforth said with such sickly enthusiasm that Pimola worried he might be coming down with something.

They stopped outside a wooden shed of a size suitable for housing a passenger jet or a mid-sized UFO. Cabbage slid a massive door aside on a greased rail. A faint odour of ozone and copper wafted over them.

Drakeforth hesitated on the threshold, and then plunged into the dark interior. "There's nothing in here," his voice echoed out of the gloom.

"Nar'nt," Cabbage nodded agreeably. "Bar'ly use it these days. Free range's whar's'at now."

"Free range?" Pimola asked.

"Aye. 'Kin inf'rmation be free? Aye it kin."

"This is fascinating," Drakeforth announced emerging from the dusty vault. "There's hundreds of empty server racks in there. Where do you keep everything?"

"T'hot y'd n'er ask," Cabbage winked so hard he almost dislocated his eyelid.

They joined him in his ground-eating swagger across the yard to a steel rail fence and gate.

"Thar," he said with an upward nod.

The field was lush and green, though the grass had been cropped short by a scattered cloud of sheep. "I don't understand, is it underground?" Pimola asked.

"N'arn," Cabbage replied, and putting two gnarled fingers in his mouth, he whistled. A black-and-white blur leapt the fence, using the topmost rail to launch itself at even greater velocity. The dog sprinted across the field, separating the sheep with laser-cutter accuracy. The flock bolted until they forgot why they were running, and then clumped together like cumulonimbus clouds.

"That's clever," Drakeforth nodded.

"Aye keeps t' grass down. Flock'll get caught up'n long grass." Another whistle brought the dog to a halt. It lay still, twitching with barely contained energy waiting to be unleashed.

Of similar size to the sheep but lacking the wool and vacant expressions of the livestock, four legged robots tottered around the field on mechanical legs. Solar panels on their backs gleamed in the light of the sun as they moved steadily to keep the optimum angle.

"What exactly are you farming here?" Pimola asked.

"Y'ken?" Cabbage asked, regarding her with a sideways stare.

"What my colleague means is, what exactly are you farming here?" Drakeforth explained.

"Data, m'stly." Cabbage nodded at the field. "N' plen'y c'mp'nts."

"Kim-pin-ints?" Pimola asked.

"Aye. Part's 'n bits."

"Ohhh…"

"It's all nonsense really, though, isn't it?" Drakeforth let his usual cynicism slip out. "There's no difference between regular computer components and this free-range stuff. Except it costs more."

"Ayyye," Cabbage grinned, several gold teeth glinting in the sunlight.

"This is important," Drakeforth said. "We are looking for some missing data. Something very specific and probably restricted. We know it was…stored here."

"Garn?" Cabbage asked.

"Aye," Drakeforth replied, looking him dead in the eye. "Godden Energy Corporation, human resources file. Drakeforth, Vole."

Cabbage gave a muttering sigh and dug deep into his overalls pocket. Retrieving a tablet, he swiped and tapped at the screen. "O'er y'nder," he said with an upward nod. "T'other side of hill. Flock seven-oh-nine."

"Can you uh, download it for us?" Pimola asked.

"Nah. Y'kin walk o'er an'…" Cabbage fished in his pockets

again and handed over a well-worn data stick.

"Stick that in 'er and y'll get what yer need. An' this." He held up a baton with a row of coloured LED lights embossed on it. With a calloused thumb, Cabbage keyed a code into the device and handed it to Drakeforth. 'I'll light up when yer near the right sheep station."

"Indoor server farms make a lot of sense, you know," Drakeforth said, his face dark with displeasure.

"Oh aye," Cabbage nodded. "Use a lotta batteries though," he continued. "An' folks like t'feel they're getting' some nature wit' their technology." Cabbage opened the gate to the field for them to file through.

"It's utterly ludicrous!" Drakeforth snapped, regarding the expanse of grassland like a penguin regarding Orca-infested waters.

"Oh aye," Cabbage continued to smile and nod. He closed the gate behind them and leaned on it while Pimola and Drakeforth picked their way through the fresh fertiliser pellets left by the organic sheep on the pasture.

When Drakeforth's monologue of complaints could no longer be heard clearly, Cabbage retrieved a cell phone from his dungarees and dialled a number.

"Ayup, it's Cabbage. Fella's come by askin' 'bout haych-har file on a Drakeforth fella." He listened, squinting at the distant figures as they crested the ridge. After a moment, Cabbage put the phone away and sighed with resignation.

"Righto, best put kettle on for cup o' tea."

CHAPTER 34

"Edwin..." Cole murmured. "It's doin' it again."

"Yeah mate," Edwin replied without looking up. He was carefully cutting individual letters from a selection of newspapers and magazines. His desk already looked like a particularly gruesome newsprint massacre.

"Every time I look, it's moved," Cole insisted.

"Don't look at it then," Edwin replied.

"It's bigger than it was yesterday an' all," Cole said with concern.

Edwin sighed and straightened up, chunks of confetti falling in paper flakes onto his lap. "I hate to deflate yer didgeridoo, Eddie, but our current offices are in the basement of an abandoned building. While that means we pay no rent, and basically are leeching our power, phone, and water off the system, it also means the place is a bit of a fixer-upper. A patch of slime mould on the walls and ceiling is a small price to pay for the even smaller price we are paying for having the use of this place."

"It's weird an' I don't like it," Cole said.

"When we get paid for this job, we can move into a nice office. Like with a secretary and windows an' everythin'," Edwid said.

Cole blushed. "Secretary." He ducked his head and snort-giggled into his shirt.

Edwid tried not to jump when the phone rang. That it was always the same person on the other end wasn't what made him uneasy. It was more the way that the phone had no dial tone when he tried to use it. The line was as dead as Vole Drakeforth was meant to be.

"Secretary'd answer that," Edwid said with a forced grin that made Cole gigglesnort harder with boyish embarrassment.

"Mint and Munt, Personal Solutions, how may I direct your call?" Edwid said after lifting the receiver.

He listened intently for a moment and then shuffled the newspaper shrapnel on his desk until he found a pen and a spare scrap of blank paper.

"Cabbage's Server Farm..." he repeated as he wrote it down.

CHAPTER 35

"It's a nice day for it," Pimola said, with the kind of unshakeable positivity usually reserved for protons and self-help gurus.

"How difficult would it be to set up some kind of plumbing system for these animals?" Drakeforth asked as he danced around another scattering of sheep droppings.

"The sun is shining, the air is fresh, the grass is…green," Pimola continued.

"We know it is possible. People have invested stupid amounts of time and energy to train cats to use toilets. I am not making this up. They start with putting the litter tray on the seat and over an interminable amount of time you can convince the cat to use the toilet like a person. Are you listening to me?"

"Unfortunately, yes," Pimola said, scanning the near horizon for the glint and gleam of steel wool.

"Once proven of course, the idea never really caught on," Drakeforth continued.

"Really, I can't think why…" Pimola saw a small flock of robotic sheep moving to optimise the angle of the sun on their solar panels and started towards them.

"The researchers discovered that the cost of magazine subscriptions made it uneconomical to promote the practice." Drakeforth said as he trailed behind, one eye on the ground. "A further study was proposed to investigate exactly what kind of magazine subscriptions a cat would want to read, but that was shut down. Probably by the government."

"Do you have the detector?" Pimola asked.

Drakeforth handed the wand over with all the sullenness he could muster.

Pimola pointed the baton at the nearest of the four-legged robots and moved forward slowly, swinging the detector back and forth with the casual rhythm of a drum major. She followed the beep until it became a steady tone, and the line of lights was fully lit.

"I think it's this one," Pimola declared.

"Great. Stick the stick in it and let's go home."

Pimola passed the baton off to Drakeforth and crouched down next to the walking storage device. Cloaked in a fleece of steel wool which Pimola thought might help with cooling the system, the robot looked like an artificial sheep. The head had no slots for the data stick, so she gently turned the machine and lifted a flap at the rear.

"Of course..." she said.

"It makes sense," Drakeforth said from a safe distance. "Data input and output in the rear, the front is used for monitoring and display.

"It seems unnecessary and somewhat gross," Pimola replied, as she gingerly slotted the data stick into the robot.

"I understand the biological version is even more so," Drakeforth said. "Arthur says you'd better believe it."

Pimola grimaced and went to the head of the electro-sheep. A simple interface touchscreen on the front allowed her to review the file structure and enter basic commands.

"I've got your file," she called out.

"Can you delete it?" Drakeforth asked.

"No, I can copy it onto the stick." She did that while Drakeforth muttered to himself about not being interested in hearing *anything* about the anatomy, physiology, or even biology of goats.

Retrieving the data stick, Pimola patted the robot sheep on the head and it moved out of her shadow, mingling with the rest of the gigaherd.

"We can have a look at the file when we get to my lab," Pimola explained to Drakeforth as they walked across the rolling field towards the gate.

"What is going on?" Drakeforth asked. Without waiting for Pimola, and with a sudden disregard for his shoes, he started running through the short grass, scattering sheep and facsimiles in all directions.

CHAPTER 36

Habeas wriggled like a baby mouse into the soft warmth of its mother's belly fur, all pink, hairless, and blind to the harsh realities of the world around him. With a sigh of contentment, he rose gently from sleep and wrinkled his nose at the slightly slime-mouldy smell of damp offices.

"'Es not dead, 'es just sleeping," Cole whispered.

"Well wake 'im up then!" Edwid said, loud enough to wake the dead.

Habeas blinked, lost for a moment as to where he was. *The van, oh yes.* The van and the strangely intense fellow who had insisted they take it and—what had he said? Await further instructions? It wasn't for Habeas to question Arthur's choice of messenger. Though, if he were given the opportunity, he had quite a list of things he would like cleared up.

A man with more Great Ape in his DNA than usual loomed over him in the back of the van. "Wakey-wakey," he rumbled. "Eggs and um…breakfast."

Cole took Habeas by the scruff of his robe and dragged him out of the van.

"I know you!" Habeas announced. "You're the fellows with the car. What a coincidence meeting you here."

Edwid sneered, "Yeah, it's like my old man's mate Des always said. Fancy meetin' you here. 'Cept he always said it to the Green when they caught him with his hand in someone else's safe."

"Ol' Tinny was a right laugh," Cole said.

Habeas' smile faltered. "You're the police?"

Cole and Edwid both reflexively looked furtive. "Whadid-youcallus?" Cole growled.

"Nah mate, we're not the grass," Edwid replied. "We're looking for Mister Drakeforth."

"Ohh…" Habeas trailed off and looked around, realising that Drakeforth was missing from the scene. "He was here."

"Yeah, we know." Cole felt smug to be in possession of knowledge that someone else didn't have for once.

"I don't know where he is. Actually, I don't know where I am, either…" Habeas frowned.

"You were in the van," Cole said, relishing having all the right answers. "Now, you're standin' next to it."

"Is this your…farm?" Habeas hazarded a guess.

"Nah," Cole nearly hugged himself in delight.

"We're just visitin'," Edwid explained. "Lookin' for Mister Drakeforth. We have something important to show him."

"I'd be happy to help you look." Habeas got a head start by turning in a slow circle and scanning the verdant horizon.

Edwid nudged Cole and nodded at the gangly fellow approaching them. An assortment of needle-nosed pliers, cable crimpers, and complex screwdrivers rattled like spurs in the multitool sockets of the toolbelt slung low on his hips.

"Afternoon," Cole said. "You the fella put in the call?"

"Garn." Cabbage folded his arms. "You're what they sent an' all?

"We're the hit-*oww*!" Cole yelped as Edwid hit him in the arm.

"We're the consultants hired to resolve the issue," Edwid said.

"Oh aye?"

"Where's Drakeforth?" Cole asked in a sullen tone.

"'E's over yonder," Cabbage jerked a thumb over his shoulder. "Up the back drive."

"'E alone, then?" Cole asked with narrowed eyes.

"Mebbe." Cabbage's eyes were glittering slits.

"Well we might wander over and say 'ello then," Edwid said.

"Mind if I tag along?" Habeas asked.

"Sure, why not. Two walls with one brick and all that," Edwid shrugged.

CHAPTER 37

The light from the police helicopter fell on the figures retreating from the burning van in a clearly defined circle that barely wavered. Drakeforth squinted and frowned. In his experience, the less contact the police had with the public, the better for everyone.

Green lights flickered and sirens howled from the squad cars that converged on the three of them. Uniformed officers exited and excitedly shouted orders at the suspects and each other in the noise and confusion.

"Hands up!"

"Do not move!"

"Stay where you are!"

"Secure the perimeter!"

"Put some cuffs on those two!"

"Not those two, you idiots! The suspects!"

Drakeforth and Pimola's demands for answers were ignored, or simply not heard over the roar of the helicopter hovering overhead like a demented disco ball.

The fire service roared into the view and made a great show of hosing down the burning laundry van with extinguishers and foam. The smell of charred towels and sheets filled the air, and the helicopter wash sent the smoke cavorting in pinwheel spirals that dried the eyes and throat.

For Drakeforth and Pimola it was a relief to be handcuffed and bundled into the airconditioned comfort of a squad car.

"Don't say anything," Drakeforth murmured out of the corner of his mouth. Pimola gave him a glare that said while she undoubtedly had a great deal to say, she was not currently speaking to him, or even acknowledging his existence.

They were delivered, unlike the three hundred freshly laundered sheets in the back of the van, to a non-descript building in the city. The sign said *Police,* in a font designed to be intimidating to the criminal elements and yet welcoming to the public in their time of need. It had been described as an embarrassment to the art of lettering by certain people. You know the type.

Inside, the two smoke-stained suspects were photographed, finger-printed, measured and given the statutory cup of tea.

Pimola grimaced and drank it like a philosopher choosing his method of execution. "*Gah!*" she shuddered, and hissed through gritted teeth. "If that is the kind of tea I can expect in prison, I hope they sentence me to a diet of bread and water."

"Good evening," the detective said as she entered the room. "I'm detective Panduri, I'm going to be interviewing you regarding the events of this evening."

"Do I need a lawyer?" Pimola asked.

"Only if you're guilty," Panduri replied, and settled herself in the chair on the opposite side of the table.

"I do need to advise you that this interview is being recorded. It may be used in any trial or court proceedings, and there's a distinct possibility it may end up in one of those silly shows where real life footage is edited to make it even more comical."

"Where's Vole Drakeforth?" Pimola asked.

"No idea," Panduri replied. "Now, in your own words, please tell me what happened to bring you here today."

Pimola drew breath to explain everything. Then she started to think about it. The truth would sound like she was lying. Lying would be hard to keep track of and no doubt lead to even greater suspicion. Whatever Drakeforth was saying to whomever was interviewing him, was probably making that officer consider a transfer or early retirement.

"Honestly, I have no idea," Pimola admitted. "Though, if you have time, I would be happy to go through it with you and see if we can work it out between us."

Detective Panduri nodded and made a note on a pad. "All right."

Pimola inhaled again and started talking. She bullet-pointed her recent experiences. The strangeness, the unsolicited interruptions to her otherwise complete life of theoretical physics, quantum computing, and tea criticism. The growing concern she had about reality and the odd quest she'd found herself on to find some kind of truth. Which, she hastened to add, seemed to be the kind of thing everyone would be happier not knowing at all.

Panduri took pages of notes. She gave the occasional grunt, but never interrupted, or questioned. Pimola felt quite relieved by the time she ran out of things to say. It was as if a great weight had been lifted from her shoulders, adjusted slightly and then settled more comfortably.

"When you were arrested, you were in a stolen vehicle," Panduri explained.

"Allegedly," Pimola said in an acidic tone that would have made Drakeforth nod approvingly.

"You or the vehicle?" Panduri asked.

"What?" Pimola blinked.

"Allegedly in the vehicle, or the vehicle was allegedly stolen?" Panduri continued.

"Yes," Pimola snapped and folded her arms. "That tea is a violation of my human rights."

"Another victim of budget cuts I'm afraid," the detective said. "How did the van catch fire?"

"Didn't I explain that already?" Pimola asked.

Panduri shuffled her notes. "No."

Pimola took a deep breath and closed her eyes, "We were at Cabbage's server farm…"

CHAPTER 38

With Habeas in tow, the two personal solution consultants hurried towards Drakeforth and Pimola, who were coming the other way at similar speed.

"Eggs," Cole announced.

"Yer what?" Edwid replied, his focus suddenly skidding sideways.

"I was thinkin' that in the sensies, they say, *wait till you can see the whites of their eyes,* an' how eyes are like eggs. You got the coloured bit in the middle and the rest of it is the white."

"We're workin' here, mate," Edwid reminded him.

"I know," Cole nodded.

Edwid rummaged in the rumpled folds of his cheap suit. And pulled out a dull black pistol.

"Cor!" Cole shouted in surprised delight.

"Whoa!" Pimola yelled. Drakeforth blinked. The two of them turned in opposite directions and ran for the cover of the nearby server sheds.

"Enough muckin' about, eh?" Edwid said.

"Yeah mate," Cole grinned. "Can I have one?"

Edwid's immediate thought was that he would sooner hand a loaded gun to an enraged orangutan than let Cole within spitting distance of it. Instead, he said, "I've only got the one, mate. It took me months to get hold of it an' all."

"It's got bullets and all then?" Cole's teeth were bared in a manic grin that would have made the enraged orangutan grateful for the loaded gun.

"Yeah mate," Edwid moved the gun further out of Cole's reach. "You go find the girl, I'll shoot Drakeforth."

"Right." Cole dragged his gaze from the gun. "Where'd she go then?"

"In there, mate," Edwid gestured towards the nearby shed. "Just hold her until I'm finished."

"She's a witnesses...es," Cole nodded.

Edwid stepped into the darkened interior of the shed Drakeforth had run into, leaving Cole to his own devices.

His target stood behind an empty metal shelving unit. The soft scent of undisturbed dust lay heavy in the warm air. Once this place would have been airtight, climate-controlled and cooled by large fans, and completely dust free. The shift to free-range data and components meant that the battery backup power supplies were the only remnants of the old server installation.

Drakeforth eyed the energy-storing blocks speculatively. They looked heavy. Pimola had gone in a different direction, so it really was every man for himself. Sarkezian martial arts were primarily a form of intellectual combat, crushing blows to the ego more than a swift kick to the Netherlands. This left Drakeforth at a disadvantage when it came to physical conflict.

"Hey, Arthur," he whispered.

"Hmmm?" Arthur replied in a non-committal way.

"I don't suppose you know how to fight?"

"Violence is not the answer," Arthur replied.

"Would you like me to rephrase the question?" Drakeforth snapped.

"Have you tried reasoning with them?" Arthur suggested.

"Reasoning? He's got a gun. An actual gun."

"Is it uhm...what's the word...encumbered?" Arthur asked.

"What? You mean *loaded?* How the basket would I know?"

"You could ask," Arthur said.

"Oh right, I'll just stick my head out and say, excuse me mister armed psychopath, just checking if your illegal firearm is actually loaded with deadly ammunition, or if this is all some kind of Fruitarian prank."

"Yeah mate, it's loaded," Edwid said, and cocked the gun for additional dramatic effect. "Y'know, the hard part isn't getting the gun. You can find them in private collections, and they go missing all the time. The real challenge is finding the bullets. I mean the gun weren't cheap, but the bullets, well they'll cost you an arm and a leg."

"I imagine finding private collections of amputated limbs would be challenging," Drakeforth replied.

"Yer what?" Edwid scowled.

"It was a joke," Drakeforth shrugged.

"Do I look like I'm laughin'?"

"To be honest, it's hard to tell. What do you normally look like when you are laughing?" Drakeforth asked.

Edwid pointed the gun more emphatically at Drakeforth. "We're being paid to ex-pee-dite your ex-e-cution, Vole Drakeforth."

"You've botched it once already, what make you think you can do a better job this time?"

"Professional courtesy," Edwid said, and flicked the gun in a menacing way.

"I know I've asked you this before, and forgive me if you told me and I have forgotten, but who exactly is it that has hired you to kill me?"

"You don't know?" Edwid's brow furrowed slightly as if he was trying to hold off scratching his nose.

"Can't say I do. I mean, they may have a point, to be honest. Any number of people could have a very good reason for wanting me dead. I'm sure the dance card for my grave will fill very quickly."

"Well, that can't be right," Edwid patted himself down with one hand, then fumbled with the gun as he checked his other pockets.

"Can I hold that for you?"

"Cheers, thanks," Edwid absently handed the gun over while searching himself.

Drakeforth slipped the gun onto an empty shelf and pushed it towards the back, out of sight.

"I had it written down..." Edwid explained. "'Ere it is." He brandished a piece of paper with pride. "Just a phone number, see, no name. Makes it difficult to send progress reports and get clients to sign up for our email newsletter."

"Email newsletter?" Drakeforth did his best to look intrigued rather than confused.

"Yeah, like buildin' a brand, innit. Creates a positive flow relationship with customers and drives traffic to our website."

"You...have a website?" Drakeforth asked.

"Well, nah. I mean, not yet. We're still workin' on the design and infrastruction-stuff."

"Infra-what?" Drakeforth asked.

"Computers an' all that. We don't have one."

"Ohhh..." Drakeforth nodded. "Still, early days yet, right? I mean, I hope."

"Yeah, me an' Cole are on-trap-a-nerds. We're self-motivated risk takers. We've got the passion to make our dream a reality."

"Of all the myriad of business opportunities available. Of all the empty spaces in the market that are just begging to be filled, you and Cole decided to become killers for hire?"

"Personal Solution Professionals," Edwid corrected him instantly.

"Is there much of a demand for this kind of professional personal solution?"

"Well...I mean...we're just starting out. The book says we need to invest in our passion and build a network to generate positive leads and create a passive income."

"There's a book on how to be a hit—ah, personal solution professional?"

"Nah, it's a book on how to be successful in business. There's a book and a night-school class you can do and everythin'."

"I imagine professional assassination isn't something you can learn at night-school."

"Not yet, that's part of my five-year plan. Franchise and then trainin' courses, for them that want to learn the secrets of doin' it the Mint and Munt way."

"Wow," Drakeforth said.

Edwid nodded with increasing enthusiasm, "I know, right? Absolute carpet!"

"Yeah!" Drakeforth beamed. "Look, I'm sorry to interrupt, but that is *really* going to hurt."

The empty shelf falling on Edwid took him by surprise. Drakeforth, who had been watching and making subtly helpful gestures at Pimola as she crept up behind Cole and struggled to push the shelving unit over, was less surprised than a rock.

"Right," Pimola said, dusting her hands off. "Let's run like gravy,"

"Absolutely." Drakeforth clambered over the fallen shelf and followed Pimola as she ran for the door.

Blinking like insomniac owls in the sunlight, Drakeforth and Pimola stumbled towards the van.

"Habeas!" Pimola yelled. The monk popped up in the driver's seat and waved.

"Start the bubbly van!" Drakeforth bellowed.

They threw the doors open and piled inside as the van's engine hummed to life. Habeas patted the vehicle gently on the dashboard. "All sorted?" he asked.

"Yes!" Pimola snapped. "Please go! Now!"

Habeas gripped the steering wheel, his face folding into an expression of fierce bovine concentration. Pimola and Drakeforth stared straight ahead, rigid with tension. After a moment they both looked at the young monk.

"Put it in gear!" Pimola shouted.

"Make it go!" Drakeforth yelled.

Habeas pushed buttons and then gripped the wheel again as the van leapt forward. The vehicle accelerated, wheels spinning and kicking up dust as they pirouetted around the farmyard.

"Straight!" Pimola yelped, leaning over and twisting the steering wheel.

They shot down the driveway towards the gate. Pimola's eyes grew wider as the gate slowly started to swing open, and they scraped through the gap by a finger's width.

"Turn!" Drakeforth bellowed. Habeas heaved on the steering wheel like he was wrestling a bear. The van's tyres squealed on the roadway and they rocked and swayed onto an even keel.

"Now what!?" Habeas wailed. Having never driven before,

he found the experience terrifying.

"Faster!" Drakeforth and Pimola shouted at once.

Habeas floored it and the van leapt like it was wading across a murky pond, and something slimy touched its foot.

CHAPTER 40

Pimola stopped talking, her throat not quite dry enough to risk drinking more of the awful tea. She blinked and looked up. The detective across the table from her had been replaced by an entirely different uniformed officer, who was reading the newspaper and otherwise ignoring her entirely.

"Oh, uhm, where did Detective Panduri go?" she asked.

"Shift change, she left half an hour ago. I'm here to escort you to the hearing in front of the judge when you're called."

"Judge? Hearing? Called?" Pimola bullet-pointed her confusion.

"Bit of a step-down for me, honestly," the officer continued, turning to a new page in his news.

"I'm sorry?" Pimola struggled to find solid ground in the shifting terrain of the conversation.

"Hardly your fault. My last posting was on the Herbaceous Border. Lovely country, beautiful sunsets. Pleasantly remote."

"I haven't been charged with anything," Pimola insisted.

"Neither have I," the officer snapped back. "Didn't stop my superiors from bringing me back. Of course, they call it reassignment. I call it punishment for putting down roots, establishing a cooperative relationship with the locals and ensuring border security as is our custom."

"That is unfortunate," Pimola said.

"Some would say being posted to the edge of the known world is unfortunate," the officer grumbled.

"You know what they say…" Pimola prompted.

"No, I can't say I do."

The lock rattled and the door swung inwards. "Judge is ready," a uniformed officer announced from the hallway.

"You're up," the seated officer said, without getting up from the table.

"Well thanks, and uhm, good luck," Pimola said on her way out.

"Ha!" the officer snorted. "Any chance of a cup of tea!?" he called as the door closed.

CHAPTER 41

The hearing took place in an empty courtroom. An elevated desk stood at one end of the room, with two lower desks in front of it for the lawyers to present their cases to the presiding judge.

When Pimola entered the room from the back, Drakeforth was standing in the lawyer's starting position. On the other side was a young, suit-wearing police prosecutor with a single sheet of paper containing his notes on the case.

"Drakeforth," Pimola announced and hurried forward to punch him in the arm.

"Ow!" he yelped. "I missed you, too."

"We are going to jail and it's all your fault," Pimola hissed.

"In fact we are going to walk out of here, free and clear," Drakeforth replied.

"Do we have a good lawyer?" Pimola looked around the almost empty court room.

"We don't need a lawyer." Drakeforth put his hands in his pockets and regarded the delicately carved cornices around the ceiling. He frowned as they appeared to flow and swirl, as if craven images were being projected on them.

"I would like a lawyer," Pimola said. "I'm pretty sure I'm allowed one."

"A lawyer is not a pet, or an ice cream. You can't just demand one or grab one on a whim," Arthur said, and was soundly ignored.

"Arthur says you can't demand a lawyer on a whim," Drakeforth murmured.

"Oh, I'm a long way from whim," Pimola said gravely.

"I've already told the court clerk that I am representing us," Drakeforth echoed.

"What? Where's the clerk? I demand a retrial! Mistrial. Habeas Copse!"

Drakeforth sighed. "Insisting they show you a thicket of small trees isn't going to help. Unless your strategy is an insanity plea."

"Yours isn't?"

A robed figure emerged from chambers beyond the back wall of the courtroom. At the command to rise, the five people in the court stood and then sat when ordered, with the unconditional obedience of trained dogs.

The silhouette in the robe could have been Death, or a ritual baker of crumpets, depending on your cultural view. They watched the figure lurch and sway as it approached the judge's altar.

"Who is that?" Pimola asked after the judge staggered backwards and almost lost their balance.

"*What* is that, you mean," Arthur said.

"No, I mean *why* is that," Drakeforth replied.

"I'm going to wait for an explanation." Pimola sat down and folded her arms.

"Are we dead?" Drakeforth asked Arthur.

"Quite possibly." Arthur mentally shrugged.

"That would be…irritating," Drakeforth said.

"I believe it comes as a surprise to most people," Arthur offered. "Speaking from personal circumstances, depending on the cause, it can be quite a surprise, or you can miss the big moment entirely."

"I don't feel dead." Drakeforth tensed and relaxed carefully. "You make it sound like you have died more than once."

"Also quite possible," Arthur replied.

"You don't know?" Drakeforth internally turned to stare at Arthur.

"I may have missed the big moment entirely," Arthur said.

Pimola's nose wrinkled and she sniffed her clothes, the table and, more discreetly, Drakforth's sleeve.

"I smell *cat*," she announced. "Oh," she added. "I see."

"You should pay more attention," Drakeforth said to Arthur. "Dying seems like the sort of thing you would want to focus on."

"Really? Most people spend their entire lives trying to avoid dying and not thinking about it unless absolutely necessary."

"Drakeforth, there is a cat batting at the judge's gavel," Pimola said.

"Perhaps it couldn't find any litter," Drakeforth said offhandedly.

Pimola watched the ginger paw extending from the robe sleeve until it succeeded in knocking the gavel to the floor.

"Your Honour?" Pimola stood and addressed the court. "This is my first time in court, and it seems all very strange. May I ask, is it? *Strange*, I mean."

The judge's hood rippled, and a cat's head slid out, followed by the rest of the cat, which leapt lightly onto the bench and started cleaning a paw.

Drakeforth gave a dismissive snort of disgust at something Arthur had said. "Sorry, Pimola, did you say something?" Drakeforth turned his attention back to the room.

"Cats," he said a moment later. "We appear to be being judged by cats."

"Reality really isn't what it used to be," Arthur muttered sulkily from behind Drakeforth's ears.

Drakeforth's barking laughter sent the court stenographer into a typing frenzy. He stepped out from behind the defendants' desk, and Arthur addressed the court and Drakeforth.

"Believe what you like. Observe what you see. Make your own reality. Your experience is what makes reality. The rest of us are just wave functions of probability that haven't been measured to death!"

Drakeforth pulled his coat back and paced up and down, his hands gesticulating with emphasis. Arthur continued, "Our experience is greater than the sum of our parts. None of this—this living—means anything. The cats have a unique awareness of their superposition. They alone know where they are and where they are going. Why do you think they regard the rest of the Universe with such disdain?"

Pimola frowned and said, "Drakeforth, I don't think this is the time to debate such things."

Arthur continued unabated, "Indeed Your Honour, any outcome, any choice you make, is a result of probability. The chances of anything happening are probable. Nothing is certain, of that we can be quite sure. In conclusion, you cannot judge me, Your Honour!" Arthur slammed Drakeforth's hand down on the table. It made a deep gonging sound that reverberated through the room and made the walls shimmer like liquid silver.

"Wainscotting," Arthur said.

"Persimmons," Pimola said, and blinked. "Ego triangle winchly." Her eyes went wide, and she put a hand to her mouth as if to check that it was still there.

"Ableist. Foregone punch." Drakeforth waved an adamant finger in the air, which left a trail of sparkling stars like a spiral galaxy.

Pimola patted herself down for a pen and paper. Thus equipped, she started to write, the tip of her tongue poking out with fierce concentration.

"Askance!" she shouted, and threw the pen down.

The judge's robes flapped, and cats poured out of the depths. Some took up positions along the bench. Others leapt across to vantage points around the room that turned and pulsed in a discordant rhythm.

The walls melted, dripping veneer of stone and faux-living oak panelling. Furniture swelled as if inflated and began to float through the air, spinning and bobbing on the unfelt current of a rising storm.

Drakeforth seized Pimola by the arm and pointed towards the door the cats had entered through. His mouth worked soundlessly, and coloured shapes spilled from his lips like candy. The odd beads formed complex molecular models that glowed with inherent energy.

Pimola tried to nod, and the room evaporated. The dimensions folded in on each other and she saw information devolving into data and concepts given form by probability. Until finally, even that collapsed into chaos.

CHAPTER 42

"Did you see that?" Pimola asked. Her hands firmly on the steering wheel of the van as they hummed down the highway in the warm glow of the afternoon sun.

"I can neither confirm nor deny," Drakeforth replied from the passenger seat, his gaze firmly fixed on the road ahead.

"I saw it," Habeas said helpfully, squirming between the two front seats like an unrestrained child.

"You think you saw it," Drakeforth corrected.

"I definitely saw it," Pimola said.

"One of those shimmering water heat things," Habeas said.

"Mirage," Drakeforth replied, and frowned.

"You did see it!" Pimola grinned despite her unease.

"It is warm out," Habeas said.

Drakeforth sighed. "It wasn't a mirage. I have spent time in Pathia; if they could find a way to ship them, mirages would be their biggest export."

"Second only to sand, I suppose," Pimola said.

"Pathia is the birthplace of Arthur and the one-true-religion," Habeas said with solemn enthusiasm.

"Lovely place, though it had more trees in my day," Arthur said.

"Sorry?" Habeas asked.

"I didn't say anything," Drakeforth replied.

"Your hand was making a weird mouth shape," Pimola said.

"No, it wasn't," Drakeforth folded his arms.

Pimola sighed. "It wasn't a mirage that we saw."

"You think—"

"We know it wasn't a mirage. Must you disagree with everything I say?"

Drakeforth opened his mouth and then closed it again. "Where were we?" he said after a few minutes' silence.

"We were talking about mirages," Habeas offered.

"No, where were we, before this? We were somewhere else. The police were involved," Drakeforth said.

"The van crashed and caught fire," Habeas said.

"Where were you?" Pimola asked. "You weren't in court with us."

"I...don't know..." Habeas frowned.

"Cats," Pimola said. "We were arrested and went to court and there were cats."

"I like cats," Habeas said. "Though I'm never sure if they like me."

Drakeforth shook his head as if to clear a mental fog. "We were being judged by cats."

"We feel we are judged by cats," Arthur said. "In truth, judgement is just a side-effect of their observation. What we perceive as judgement is just cats."

"I saw math," Pimola wriggled in the driver's seat and grinned at the sudden clarity. "I saw math. I really saw it. The way everything is connected, the structure of the Universe and..." her face suddenly fell.

"Nothing is real?" Drakeforth asked.

"Nothing is real," Pimola echoed. "Oh, delphiniums, KLOE was right and that is going to make a lot of people very unhappy."

"Only if we tell them," Drakeforth replied.

"How can we not?" Pimola asked. "We can't just carry on like everything is normal. I mean, it is normal. But the normal is really not normal."

"I try not to think about it," Habeas said. Drakeforth and Pimola turned in their seats and stared back at him.

"You knew?" Pimola asked.

"The cats showed me, much as they showed you. It could take me the perception of a lifetime to understand it. What I want to know is: What is behind the illusion? What purpose does it serve, and what lies beyond it?"

"An infinity of worlds?" Pimola suggested. "That fits with some current mathematical models of Quantum Physics."

"Arthurianism is the only way to truly understand the great truth," Habeas insisted.

"Quantum physics is more than Arthurianism,' Pimola snapped. "If the infinite realities theory is true, then simply making an observation creates a reality."

"Which is what cats do," Arthur said, and Drakeforth repeated aloud. "Cats observe and maintain reality. They guide the Universe and keep it consistent."

"Everything is in flux, we have observed the infinite probabilities, and reality is on hold until a definitive measurement is made. We have to make a determination. Reality needs to be defined by measurement."

"Check the glovebox, see if there is a tape measure," Drakeforth said.

"We need a computer. A uniquely powerful computer," Pimola said in a way that suggested she wanted to make an impressive revelation.

"Of course!" Drakeforth exclaimed. "And just where would we find such an artefact?" The second part was marinating in sarcasm.

Pimola punched him in the arm. "I am being serious, and KLOE is the best chance we have to confirm reality."

"Do we have to?" Drakeforth asked, rubbing his bruised bicep. "No, of course we don't. The real question is: Do we want to? The answer to that is, of course, we don't."

"How do we know, until we do?" Habeas asked from the sacks of laundry in the back of the van.

"He has a point," Pimola said.

"Thank you." Habeas bowed his head in gratitude.

"I never said it was a good point," Pimola added.

The silhouette of the city grew like a seismograph printout, looming larger as they drove through the city limits and into the shimmering canyons of the setting sun.

CHAPTER 43

"Is anyone else hungry?" Habeas asked as Pimola parked the van in the same place they had found it that morning.

"I'm starving," Pimola said.

Drakeforth grunted in a surly way and his hand twitched until he smothered it with his coat sleeve.

"You would be welcome to come back to the Temple of Saint Erinaceous," Habeas said. "The food is quite good, at least compared to other places I have eaten."

"What's the catch?" Drakeforth asked.

Habeas' face changed colour like an octopus if the seaweed it was hiding behind was a lie. "Uhh…there's no catch."

"They'll make us listen to a sermon, or convert us before the entrée," Pimola said.

"We just ask that people sit at our table with an open mind," Habeas replied.

"I think I'd rather just go home," Pimola said.

"Excellent idea. Let's go to your place," Drakeforth said.

"What? No." Pimola hid the keys to the van in the sunvisor and slid out of the driver's seat.

Habeas and Drakeforth joined her on the street, cars hummed past and the familiar sounds and smells of the city washed over them.

"I can help cook," Habeas offered.

"I can cook," Pimola said, somewhat defensively.

"What's good here?" Drakeforth asked.

"Nothing, which is why we aren't going to my place."

"I'd rather be somewhere the hired killers can't find me," Drakeforth said.

"Do they know where you live?" Habeas asked.

"Probably. I mean, I barely remember myself. I'm sure they wrote it down though."

"Why don't we go to your house?" Pimola asked.

Drakeforth regarded her with a cold stare. "We should buy ingredients for whatever it is you two are going to prepare." He stepped up to the automatic doors of a neighbourhood supermarket and snarled when they hushed open with a satisfied sigh.

The three of them strolled through the produce section, Pimola's mind working hard to calculate exactly what she had in the cupboards at home (very little that wasn't stale condiments) and what she had the energy to prepare (very little that would go well with stale condiments).

Habeas drove the shopping trolley and shopped with curiosity. He picked up various fruit and vegetables, turning them over and sniffing them, shaking the fruit, and tapping root vegetables.

Everything went into the trolley while Drakeforth trudged along behind them like a moody teenager with his hands thrust deep into his coat pockets.

"How many people are you planning on feeding?" Pimola asked as the trolley's load passed the *feed-a-family-of-four-for-a-week* mark.

"I've not had to buy groceries before," Habeas said. "I had no idea there would be so much variety. I'm not sure what will be best, and it would be a shame to not have something we need."

"We don't need half of these things," Pimola insisted. "Drakeforth, tell him."

Drakeforth had drifted out of earshot. He was peering around a shelf and down the aisle of kitchenware and inflatable furniture.

"Wait here," Pimola instructed. "I'll go and see what has triggered his paranoia."

"Mystery shopper?" Pimola whispered to Drakeforth.

"Godden Energy Corporation executive," Drakeforth replied, his gaze focused intently on a woman in a business suit carrying a shopping basket halfway down the aisle.

"Wow, really?" Pimola moved around Drakeforth to get a better look. "You don't think of them actually doing people things. I mean, going shopping for bread and eggs, or using the bathroom."

"If they can casually order the assassination of those who oppose their regime, I'm sure *Mrs Goldfluke's Quik n' Tasty Meals For One* wouldn't be outside their treehouse of atrocities," Drakeforth replied.

"Allegedly," Pimola reminded him.

"I told you I witnessed a meeting of senior executives and they discussed having me killed."

"You hid in an air conditioning duct and spied on a meeting where your name wasn't mentioned and no one said anything about killing you, or anyone else."

"It was implied," Drakeforth said.

"Or you inferred that from what was actually said," Pimola suggested gently.

"What's she doing?" Drakeforth hunched deeper into his overcoat and glared like a gargoyle at the lady.

"Assessing coachellas for ripeness," Pimola said after a moment of intense observation.

"Foul creature," Drakeforth muttered.

"There's a knack to it," Habeas said from his position peering around Drakeforth's elbow. "Coachella harvest masters spend years learning the right moment to pluck the fruit. It must be exactly the right amount of firmness, furriness, and it should resonate at the right frequency when tapped."

"They are terribly expensive," Pimola agreed.

Habeas nodded. "The annual Coachella Harvest Festival is a popular event. Traditionally, women make the best harvest masters. My sister went to Coachella last year; she wants to be one when she graduates school."

"Your sister aspires to be a large, pungent fruit with bristly hair in odd places?" Drakeforth asked.

"Or a Harvest Master," Habeas said with a completely straight face that made Drakeforth look at him twice.

"Time to go," Pimola announced.

Drakeforth looked down the aisle; the woman from Godden had gone.

Pimola spent several minutes returning unwanted items to the shelves. Drakeforth bobbed and weaved through the early evening shoppers looking for the mysterious executive.

They stepped out into the deepening dusk and Pimola handed the shopping to Drakeforth, who handed it to Habeas. The three of them walked the remaining blocks to Pimola's second floor flat, the windows of which exploded suddenly in a roaring ball of flame as they approached.

CHAPTER 44

"Flaming focaccia!" Drakeforth yelled, and staggered into the street as Pimola and Habeas took cover from the sudden hailstorm of broken glass and burning book pages. "Arthur's umlauts!" Pimola wailed. "My books... What happened!?"

"Your apartment appears to have exploded in a ball of flame," Habeas said.

"But how!? I'm sure I didn't leave The Gus on."

"The Gus?" Habeas' nose wrinkled as the irritating smoke wafted over them.

"It's what I call my stove," Pimola replied. "But how could an empathic appliance explode in a ball of fire anyway?"

"Now do you believe me?" Drakeforth shouted, stomping towards them through the domestic rubble. "Clearly they are targeting you as well!"

"We don't know it was a deliberate attempt to blow up my flat!" Pimola shouted back.

"We don't know it wasn't!" Drakeforth insisted.

"Extraordinary nonsense requires extraordinary evidence!" Pimola yelled, drifting smoke and sirens adding a suitable ambience to her wrath.

"Is that them?!" Habeas said, tugging on both their sleeves. "Look."

"Lick my lunch..." Pimola muttered and wiped her watering eyes.

Two shadowy figures were hurrying away from the blast zone, silhouetted in the billowing smoke, both dark with soot and trailing sparks from their scorched clothes and singed hair.

"Exhibit A," Drakeforth said with more smugness than was necessary.

Pimola's hands clenched into fists as she turned on Drakeforth. "This is all your fault! I have nothing to do with any of this and here you are, ruining my life!"

"You sound like my wife," Drakeforth snapped back.

"Oh, really? Well, I am filled with respectful awe for that woman, she must be either a paragon of patient virtue or entirely imaginary!"

"She was more of a convenience, for travel and residency documentation. Funny thing about Pathia—"

"Stop changing the subject!" Pimola yelled.

"Evening," a green-uniformed police officer announced. "What's going on here, then?"

Drakeforth immediately turned away and flipped up the collar of his coat.

"That"—Pimola gestured at the smoking ruin of her apartment that was being hosed down by the fire service—"was my home."

"I see." The officer took notes, recording Pimola's pertinent details and looking Habeas up and down before nodding at Drakeforth. "And this gentleman?"

Pimola blinked, "Ahh…that is…my cousin, Quinine, he's not quite right in the head. Doesn't talk, tends to wet himself when he feels threatened."

"I see." The officer's notebook flipped open and he made a brief record. "Any thoughts on what may have caused the explosion?"

"I have no idea," Pimola said with absolute conviction. "It just isn't the sort of thing that happens, is it? I mean, seriously, whoever heard of a house blowing up?"

"Possibly a gas pocket," the officer mused. "You tend to get them in these cheaper constructions. Flammable gases leach out of the timbers and can build up to explosive levels. One spark and then *kablooey*, you're picking your cutlery out of the gutter."

Pimola glanced down and, feeling intensely embarrassed, retrieved a spoon.

"A full investigation will be completed, of course," the officer continued. "Fire services will file a report. Your insurance company will need to do their assessment. You should stay out of the apartment."

"Stay out?" Pimola stared at the open plan renovations with ironic indoor-outdoor flow. "I'm practically standing in my kitchen."

"Clean-up crews will be along presently. I suggest you move along and we will be in touch." The officer indicated the safety barriers being erected and the tepid crowd of spectators gathering on the other side.

Drakeforth, Pimola and Habeas sat on the edge of the gutter watching the clean-up crews listlessly doing the minimum required to meet the definition. A pair of fire extinguishers appeared at the broken fourth wall of Pimola's apartment and casually tossed the burnt husk of her refrigerator to the ground below.

"Oh," Pimola sighed for the fourth time in the last twenty minutes. "They fridged my fridge."

"Speaking of refrigerators," Habeas said as circumspectly as he could "is anyone else really hungry?" He nudged the full grocery bags with his foot.

"Starved," Drakeforth announced.

"I didn't keep anything worthy in him," Pimola said, and sniffled.

"Best not dwell on it." Habeas stood up and stretched. The cold sidewalk had left his bum feeling numb, and normally he would have had his evening meal by now and be studying Arthurian Tellings until he fell asleep.

"Come on, Pimola, I'll take you to the last place on earth I would ever want to go."

"The Temple of Saint Erinaceous?" Habeas asked hopefully.

"Worse: my place," Drakeforth replied, and stepped through the barrier to hail a taxi.

CHAPTER 45

"Honestly, I assumed you didn't have a home, unless some sort of burrow under a rock counts," Pimola said as the three of them were squeezed into the back seat of a taxi with the grocery bags.

"You won't like it," Drakeforth said.

"Really? Is it some damp bedsit, smelling of boiled cabbage, with pins and red yarn all over the walls linking pictures of everyone you think is involved in this conspiracy?"

Drakeforth winced, "Hardly. It's a cathedral-sized mansion, with staff and a cloying sense of tradition."

Pimola laughed and Drakeforth regarded her steadily.

"Wait, you are serious?"

"Serious as a walnut," Drakeforth said.

"It sounds lovely," Habeas suggested.

"It's ghastly." Drakeforth sank deeper into his coat, his head disappearing beneath the collar like a thin turtle with a growing sense of unease.

The cab expelled them without incident as Pimola spent the last twenty minutes of the ride negotiating with Drakeforth to take his cash and she would use her credit stick to pay the fare.

They stood at the closed gates of an estate house, hidden behind a high wall and well-tended trees.

Drakeforth's hands dived so deep into his pockets his knuckles popped and a moment later he retrieved a key, which he used to unlock the gate.

"Let's get this over with," he said. Pimola and Habeas hurried through the gap. Habeas swung the gate shut behind them with an irritated flourish. It clanged and locked, making Pimola jump in the dark.

"Are we in a park?" Habeas asked.

"The house is this way," Drakeforth replied, walking past them and up the smoothly gravelled driveway. Someone had spent hours carefully raking a decorative pattern into the beach-worth of stones. Drakeforth scuffed his feet and kicked the tiny rocks in a spray with each step.

"He seems angry," Habeas observed.

"I'm still trying to work out if he thinks it makes him somehow edgy and cool, and therefore attractive. Or if he is just deeply traumatised," Pimola said quietly as they crunched along in Drakeforth's wake.

"I think it is because he cares," Habeas said.

Pimola had a sudden coughing fit that doubled her over. When she had recovered her breath she managed to wheeze, "Really?"

"Uh-huh," Habeas nodded. "Vole Drakeforth cares so much that he is enraged by the suffering and injustice in the world."

"That is one theory…" Pimola said carefully.

They rounded the bend in the driveway, emerging from the trees to a golf-course-sized lawn and gardens. The house at the end of the driveway was larger than some hotels. Ivy-clad walls rose four storeys, and if the number of windows was any indication, there were at least a dozen rooms.

"Wow…" Pimola breathed. Highlighted in the warm glow shining from the windows, the scene looked like something out of a sensie. She expected a lovelorn character from a classic tale of romance, revenge, and roasted toenuts to come dashing across the perfect grass in a flowing nightdress, her hair in sensual disarray.

"Yes, yes, it's magnificent, inspiring, historical, and an iconic piece of architectural design," Drakeforth said. "If you have finished gawping, we should go inside."

Drakeforth lifted a large metal doorknocker and let it thud against the ironbound wood.

"Forgot your keys?" Habeas asked.

"Shh," Drakeforth snapped. His head cocked slightly as if listening for the faintest of sounds.

The door groaned and clanked. Heavy bolts slid and an elderly mechanism smoothly worked. Warm air and the scent of fresh baking puffed out of the gap, and the door swung inwards.

"Good evening, Mrs Castanera," Drakeforth declared, and marched inside.

An old woman held the door open, the top of her head level with the door handle. As heavyset as a medium-sized boulder, she wore a black shawl that somehow managed to be a different shade of black to the heavy skirt she wore, which went nicely with her black blouse and white, lace-trimmed apron.

She stared at Pimola and Habeas, her face lined like a contour map of treacherous ground. She sized them up in a second, with eyes warm and sharp as freshly erupted volcanic glass.

"No goat, Misor Bole," she said in a thick accent, a clean white handkerchief appearing in her hand in a way that would make a stage magician nod in approval. She dabbed the hanky to her lips and reached up to sponge a spot on Drakeforth's cheek.

"Yes, yes, please stop doing that." Drakeforth tried to recoil, but Mrs Castanera's other hand had him by the coat in a stone grip.

"*Es so beyo,*" she said, moving Drakeforth aside and beckoning the two guests inside. They stepped into a hallway of warm wood panelling and high ceilings. The rugs on the floor were large and antique. The door swung silently closed behind them and Mrs Castanera shuffled around Pimola and Habeas like a dark moon in orbit.

"These are my…friends," Drakeforth announced. "They're here for dinner," Drakeforth spoke clearly. The old woman nodded and raised her hands, shuffling forward and reaching up to take Habeas by the cheeks. "Mukilo, mukilo," she enthused, pulling the Arthurian monk down to kiss him on the top of the head.

She then repeated the process on Pimola, who didn't quite know what to make of it all.

Mrs Castanera took the grocery bags from Habeas, who didn't dare put up a struggle.

"Cas percee, uncolo, mashallum," Mrs Castanera announced, shuffling down the hall like a slow-moving boulder.

"I'm sorry, what did she say?" Pimola asked, shedding her coat and scarf.

"What? Oh, I have no idea," Drakeforth replied, hanging his trench coat on an elegantly carved rack of wooden hooks.

The hallway of the house was lined with dark wood panelling and soft lighting. Overall, it gave the place the warm ambience of freshly baked glazed gingerbread. A gallery's worth of portraits hung on the walls, generations of Drakeforths regarding the intruders with oil-based stares.

"Your grandmother seems nice," Habeas said. Not wearing a coat, he smoothed his robe and wondered if he should remove his shoes.

"Mrs Castanera is my housekeeper," Drakeforth replied. "The dining room is this way." They took seats in a room that would have comfortably seated a temple's worth of Arthurians. Expensive-looking art hung on the walls, and the heavy drapes hanging over the windows looked rich enough to have their own trust fund.

"Where is she from?" Pimola asked, feeling a strange need to fill the awkward void with conversation.

"Pathia," Drakeforth replied. "I spent some time there a few years back and she followed me home. So I kept her."

"Of course, why wouldn't you?" Pimola said.

"I travelled across the deserts of Pathia to the mountains, where rumour had it that the last of the ancient goat herder clans clung to their traditional lifestyle much as they clung to the sheer cliffs of the high peaks. There was a festival of some kind and when I left, I had either won, purchased, or been gifted Mrs Castanera. I tried to send her back, but she is stubborn."

"Getting her out of the country would have raised suspicions, surely?" Pimola asked.

"Oh, no, she folds up quite nicely and fits in carry on luggage," Drakeforth said drily. "She has been serving my family ever since. At least, I assume that's what she is doing. I have no idea what she is saying."

The dining room door opened, and Mrs Castanera came in, hunched over a trolley heavily laden with covered serving trays.

Habeas stood up and moved around the table to help as the old woman began to unload.

"Please don't try to interfere," Drakeforth said.

"No goat, Misor Bole." Mrs Castanera waved Habeas away.

"Goat?" Pimola asked.

"No goat, Misor Bole," Drakeforth muttered. "It's the only thing she says that I can understand. Not that it makes any sense. Mrs Castanera? What time is it?"

"No goat, Misor Bole," she replied and nodded, unfolding napkins of fine linen and spreading them across the diners' laps.

"Mrs Castanera, it is highly likely that the Godden Energy Corporation is attempting to have me assassinated. I'm not sure why. Of course, nothing would please you more."

"No goat, Misor Bole." Mrs Castanera reached up and straightened Drakeforth's collar, while he scowled.

The table was filled with a feast of beautifully prepared vegetables, meat dishes, fresh baked rolls, and several bottles of expensive wine.

"Peseesha," Mrs Castanera announced with a smile of approval as they helped themselves. When Pimola looked up from her plate to compliment the housekeeper on her cooking, she had left the room.

"Is there a Mrs Drakeforth?" Habeas asked.

"Of course there is." Drakeforth snapped a crab leg. "She is married to my father, Mr Drakeforth."

"Oh, right," Habeas nodded and sipped the soup. "It's just you mentioned one earlier when you and Miss Goosebread were shouting at each other. I wondered if she was still here."

Drakeforth stared at Habeas in a way that would have made the ice bucket perspire. "I don't wish to talk about her."

"Haemorrhaging hairpins," Pimola's eyes went wide. "You didn't marry Mrs Castanera, did you?"

Drakeforth hesitated for a moment, wine glass halfway to his lips. "I don't think so. There was a lot of drinking of fermented goat milk going on during the festival. She certainly hasn't suggested we are married."

"No goat, Misor Bole?" Pimola offered.

"No goat, Misor Bole," Drakeforth agreed.

CHAPTER 46

Habeas broke the surface of the softest mattress he had ever slept in. He felt like he had been sleeping on a cloud, though he dismissed the thought immediately. After all, sleeping on a cloud would be freezing cold, soaking wet, and would end in tragedy after a high-velocity plummet to the ground.

The evening of fine food and strange conversation had ended with Mrs Castanera escorting them to rooms immaculately prepared for guests.

As an Arthurian monk, Habeas was unused to luxurious excess. He made a note to consult the elder Arthurians at the temple on exactly what thread count would be considered crossing the line from practical to rolling around in warm yak-butter slippery comfort.

He stretched and swam between the sheet layers until he reached the edge of the bed. Five more minutes wouldn't do any harm. There was no call to prayers, no kitchen duties to attend to, and no structured routine. A disconcerting thought rose in his mind: *What if I never went back?*

Habeas slid out of bed and his feet plunged into the warm fur of a soft rug. *You have to go back.* Imagine, not being an Arthurian monk! *What would he do instead? How could he survive? Who*, he demanded of his inner monologue, *Who will study the great mysteries of the Universe and see the truth of Arthur's perceptions?*

Pimola had suggested that nothing was real. That the Universe that Habeas felt such a deep spiritual connection with, might be some kind of sensory illusion. The young monk struggled to remember the details: after she had explained that, he had drunk more of Drakeforth's wine. *A lot more.* His stomach woke up enough to give its opinion on wine. Habeas rushed to the ensuite bathroom and discovered even expensive wine tastes worse the second time.

The Arthurian monk emerged from the bathroom, vowing never to drink again. He had showered, and even the miracle of towels so soft and fluffy he wondered if they might be made from the skin of some exotic and exceedingly cute creature, did little to ease his nausea.

A second miracle was that at some time during the night, his Arthurian robe had been removed from the room, laundered, dried, and pressed, before being returned to hang in the closet.

It took him ten minutes to find it, there being a lot of closet space to explore.

Enrobed and moving silently on sandaled feet through the prairie -grass-length carpet, he made his way downstairs and by trial and error found his way into the empty dining room.

Like his robe, all traces of food, wine, and a night of intense conversation had been removed from the room.

"Escoba bufasel, mocaro," Mrs Castanera said at Habeas' elbow.

"Aaah!" he said, jumping at the sudden appearance of Drakeforth's housekeeper.

"Shi, shi." Mrs Castanera took Habeas by the elbow and put him in a chair.

He sighed and sank into the fine leather and beautifully carved wood of the seat. The housekeeper returned a minute later with a heavy tray that she set with grace and ease in front of him.

Under the silver cover was a full breakfast, everything cooked in delicate sauces and flavoured butters. A large pot of tea was procured and poured into a mug bigger than Habeas' fist.

Though his stomach recoiled at the idea, once he started eating he felt much better, and he cleaned his plate before Pimola came stumbling in and sank into a chair on the opposite side of the table.

"Mrs Castanera," she whispered, one hand shading her eyes.

"Could I please have a cup of tea, and enough poison to end my agony?"

"No Goat, Misor Bole," Mrs Castanera said in a sympathetic tone. She delivered an equally oily breakfast to Pimola, who went even paler and pushed it aside in favour of the strong tea, with extra stevia.

"I wonder where Mister Drakeforth's parents are?" Habeas asked when he set his tea mug down.

"Knowing Drakeforth as I now do, I can only assume that they have fled the country to avoid any contact with him," Pimola said. The perfectly brewed mug of strong tea had gone a long way to reviving her.

"You're quite right, Pimola." Drakeforth announced from the doorway. "They escaped and are now living under assumed identities in an undisclosed location."

"Really?" Habeas' eyes went wide.

"No." Drakeforth settled in his chair, a delicately embroidered silk bathrobe cinched around his waist, his hair in wild disarray as if he had been woken up by electric shock. "Mrs C. Tea."

"No goat, Misor Bole." Mrs Castanera set a covered tray in front of Drakeforth. He lifted the lid on the same breakfast the others had already been served. Mrs Castanera took a hairbrush from her apron pocket, and making *tsk-tsks* she reached up and brushed Drakeforth's unruly hair.

Drakeforth ate and ignored his housekeeper as she restored order to his head.

"Arthur's armpits," Pimola groaned as she woke up enough to remember recent events. "My house was blown up last night."

"Apartment," Habeas corrected. Pimola shot him a look that would have cracked less durable hardwood furniture than the dining room suite they were sitting on.

"I like to think of it as my house. It is—*was*—my home," she said.

"So, get another one," Drakeforth said, mopping up the last of the egg on his plate with a crust of toast.

"Excuse me?" Pimola turned her arctic glare on him.

"Get another house, apartment, whatever." Drakeforth sipped his tea.

"I could barely afford that one, let alone a new one. Then there's all my belongings. Which, now they are atomised or lying in the street, don't belong. At least, not to me."

"You could live here," Habeas suggested.

Drakeforth and Pimola both looked at him like he had sprouted a second head.

"Absolutely not," Pimola said.

"Absurd idea," Drakeforth said at the same time.

"Quite out of the question," Pimola continued.

"Ridiculous notion," Drakeforth nodded.

"I'd get lost in this place. It's big enough to house *twenty* people," Pimola scowled.

"Draughty and cold in winter," Drakeforth said.

"What would people say?" Pimola added.

"You'd have to put up with Mrs Castanera constantly anticipating your every need," Drakeforth said with a grimace.

"It's not like I could set up lab equipment and monitor experiments from home as well as on campus," Pimola said.

"Yes, the ballroom with its industrial-grade wiring for lights and audio-visual streaming of sensies would be far more data transfer capacity than you would ever need." Drakeforth finished his tea.

"The hassle of finding a spare key for me would make it entirely unworkable," Pimola said.

"Totally impractical," Drakeforth said, staring at the tabletop.

"In the long term," Pimola replied.

"On a trial basis, it might be possible," Drakeforth mused.

"I don't have anything to move, so it's like I'm here already," Pimola said.

"I'll probably forget to ask you to leave." Drakeforth poured more tea.

"I'll remind you. Eventually." Pimola offered her cup for a refill.

CHAPTER 47

As far as last words go, "What's that funny smell?" is more common than you would think. Particularly in cultures where natural gas is used as fuel for cooking and heating, and in the jungles of Pe'esk where the apex predator is a black-and-white striped tiger called a Thiol, with overdeveloped odour-producing glands.

"It wasn't me, mate," Edwid replied to Cole's question.

Cole lifted his arm and sniffed, his nose wrinkling. Lowering his arm took a lot of effort. Col frowned at his elbow and let it drop; it shot upwards again and struck the roof of the car. "Edwid," he said carefully. "Does the sky look odd to you?"

"I think we're upside down, mate," Edwid replied.

Cole turned his head slowly and winced at the sudden shooting pain in his skull. The sky rotated until the ground was no longer blue with white, blotchy clouds.

"What happened?" Cole asked.

"We crashed," Edwid said.

"Are we dead?"

Edwid remained silent for a moment. "I don't think so."

Green flashing lights appeared on the horizon and rushed closer until a police car hummed to a halt in front of them.

Two officers exited the squad car and one came hurrying over to check on them. Dropping to one knee, the officer peered in through the broken driver's side window.

"Good afternoon, sir, you appear to have been involved in an automobile accident." The officer said. "Are you able to tell me your name?"

"No," Edwid said sharply.

"Are you injured?" the officer continued.

"I'm fine," Edwid insisted.

"I am now addressing the passenger. Are you able to tell me your name, sir?"

"N-no?" Cole said.

"Are you injured?" the officer continued.

"My head hurts?" Cole asked, looking at Edwid to see if it was the correct answer.

"An ambulance has been requested to this location. We will now secure the scene of the accident to ensure that this incident is not escalated by additional vehicular impacts."

The officer stood up and got busy placing hazard cones and flares along the road.

The second officer approached the overturned vehicle and leaned down to give them a friendly wave through the spiderweb cracking of the windscreen.

"Y'all right then?" he asked.

"Boxers," Edwid said.

"Yeah," Cole agreed.

The officer nodded. "Spotta bother amiright?"

"Ya kin," Edwid nodded.

"Toozers," Cole said.

"Nah ta worry. W'll get yer out in a bitsy."

"Capsicum," Edwid said.

The officer nodded and gave them a reassuring smile. He straightened and vanished from their view.

"A grasser from Egan," Edwid said with an upside-down frown.

"I'll bet his mum's half-proud," Cole said.

"Bet 'is dad don't care to show his face at the pub."

"Shame an' all," Cole agreed.

"Dead shame," Edwid muttered.

A convoy of vehicles soon arrived on the scene. An ambulance crew made a fuss until they were satisfied that Edwid and Cole were not seriously injured. After that they returned to their ambulance and had sandwiches and tea from a thermos.

The fire service cut the doors off the car and a Godden Energy Corporation utility vehicle arrived to pump the empathic energy out of the vehicle's tank and prevent any potential spill.

Edwid and Cole were carefully extracted and then checked over thoroughly by the ambulance crew. Cole's arm was possibly fractured, but he refused to answer questions. Mostly because his head was pounding, and the voices asking questions sounded like the ocean in a seashell.

They sat in the back of the ambulance and were given a sandwich and a cup of tea.

A large vehicle recovery truck craned the wreck onto its flat deck. Edwid watched the loading carefully as the officer from Egan took their statements.

"Skiddies sayin' yer speed was upta quick un," he said with a typical Egan dialect and accent.

"Nah, gun," Edwid replied fluently, his family being from Egan on his mother's side.

"Yer keppin'. Kin say whatcha been. It'll go better for yus, in all."

Cole cradled his arm, which was hurting worse than before, and wondered if there were any more sandwiches.

"Y'kin come o' statin' an' carp the hems on the day, o' yer kin cool mastin' the flan," the officer said, regarding them steadily.

"Narwhal, the pix o' parachute," Edwid replied.

"Excuse me." Cole raised a hand and winced as his bruised shoulder objected. "Is there more tea?"

The ambulance driver poured the last of the thermos into a cup and handed it over.

Edwid climbed out of the ambulance and indicated that the officer should follow him. Cole sipped his tea and eyed the lunchbox the sandwiches had come from.

The two men had a conversation out of earshot, and a few minutes later they returned. Edwid climbed back into the ambulance and sat down on a gurney. He immediately groaned and lay down.

"Edwid?" Cole asked, his face filled with concern and tomato-and-tuna-salad sandwich.

"Ey ambo," the Egan officer called. "This fella's needin' hospital, upta quick eh?"

The ambulance crew leapt into action. Cole was eased aside and laid down on the other gurney, while Edwid's vital signs were assessed again.

"It hurts!" Edwid moaned.

"Patient's condition is deteriorating!" the paramedic announced.

"Secure patients for transit," the driver ordered. The doors were slammed shut and the ambulance whirred into life. Executing a squealing three-point turn, they zoomed down the road towards the city.

"Edwid?" Cole wailed. "You all right mate?"

"Yeah mate," Edwid replied. "I'll be fine."

The ambulance made excellent time through the outskirts of the city and rolled into the ambulance bay of the nearest hospital. Orderlies threw the doors open, and Edwid's gurney was dragged out as the paramedics gave an update on his condition. Cole gingerly sat up, his arm throbbing and his head splitting like an over-ripe water balloon.

Edwid had vanished through a set of automatic doors. Cole stepped down from the ambulance and approached carefully. When they didn't open, he knocked and waited.

Meow, a cat announced itself. Cole went to turn his head and then shuffled in a half-circle instead.

"I've lost Edwid," Cole explained to the cat.

The cat wove around his ankles in the infinity symbol pattern cats often use to remind humans of just how much they are missing out on.

Cole leaned down, which made his head swell to three times its size and filled his vision with the halo of an eclipse. Moaning in pain, he slowly toppled over like a felled tree into a supernova.

The cat stretched and daintily trotted up Cole's legs before settling on the back of his neck and purring loudly.

The cosmic explosion passed through Cole and he floated in a warm emptiness. The pounding in his skull eased, and he relaxed in a dark bath of infinity.

This moment of bliss was interrupted by the sharp tapping of a sharp bird beak on his forehead. Cole opened his eyes and frowned at the large emperor pengpong* floating in front of him. "You are not fulfilling your destiny," the bird said.

"I-uhm… What?" Cole asked.

"There is a plan, and you have a part to play in it, Colander. So far, you and Edwid have failed to achieve the purpose you were assigned."

"A sign?" Cole asked.

"You are meant to kill Vole Drakeforth and expel Arthur from the Universe."

"We tried. It's 'arder than I thought it would be," Cole admitted.

"Try harder." The pengpong drove its point home with a sharp beak tap.

"Ouch," Cole replied. "Am I dreaming?" he added.

"Everything is a dream," the towering pengpong replied. "That is why it is so important that Drakeforth be stopped."

"Right…" Cole said.

"You have no idea what I'm talking about, do you?" The bird's eyes narrowed.

"Well… I mean, yeah… Nah."

The pengpong looked like the last fish it swallowed had gone down the wrong way. "This is what comes from putting your trust in people. Listen, Colander, if you don't kill Vole Drakeforth, the world will end. And you don't want that on your conscience, do you?"

"Uhm…no?" Cole suggested.

"You need to focus, get it done and stop dying. The cats simply observe, and you know how dangerous that makes them."

"Uhhh…yeah?" Cole said carefully.

The pengpong shuffled on its webbed feet and lifted its oarlike wings.

"Observation determines the outcome. If there is no observer, then all outcomes exist in an undetermined state."

---

* See 'The Uncertainty of Goats' for more information on the now-extinct Emperor Pengpongs.

"I never really pay much attention t' politics," Cole admitted.

"Their influence means that I have no choice but to continue down this path and get you and Edwid back in the right Universe. Drakeforth and Arthur are currently in a version where you have just blown up Pimola Goosebread's apartment."

"We can do that," Cole agreed. "Edwid 'as a business plan and everything."

"Amateurs…" the pengpong snarled. "I will do what I can to reunite the divergence. In the meantime, try not to do anything particularly stupid."

Cole bit his lip. It would be a stretch, but he would certainly try.

The pengpong faded into starlight, and Cole floated in the endless dream until the smell of warm tea and cold toast roused him.

Opening his eyes was easier than he thought it would be. His headache had subsided to a dull ache. His shoulder was nicely numb, and his arm rested in a sling. He was in bed. Not his own bed either, but one with clean sheets, and it wasn't the bottom of a set of bunks, either.

The room smelled clean and white. A nurse stood beside him and when Cole opened his mouth to ask where he was, she put a thermometer in it and told him not to talk.

"You have a nasty concussion and a sprained shoulder," the nurse explained as she gripped his wrist and counted his pulse.

"Wherz Ehwhuhd?" Cole asked through closed lips.

"The other chap? He was fine, discharged last night. You should be okay to go home in a day or so. A concussion can be serious, particularly as you lost consciousness."

She released his arm and retrieved the thermometer.

"I gotta go," Cole said. "It's important."

"You'll need to talk to the doctor about that. She'll be along for rounds after breakfast. You should eat something while you wait." She pulled the wheeled tray up the bed and lifted the lid. They both regarded the contents of the plate with some disappointment.

"The tea isn't too bad," the nurse said, and patted Cole on the arm gently before moving on to check the other patients on the ward.

CHAPTER 48

Pimola slotted the sheep data stick into Drakeforth's laptop. "Here's your name: Drakeforth, Vole. Report on employment interview."

"What else does it say?"

"Uhmm…" Pimola scanned the pages of neatly typed text. "Candidate unsuitable due to indications of severe personality disorders."

"Severe personality disorders?" Drakeforth snorted. "How utterly typical. So completely incompetent that they can't even properly report that I have stumbled on some terrible truth that they don't dare even acknowledge to themselves."

"It says here you were rude to the interviewer," Pimola continued.

"She was a large woman, I may have muttered something about it."

"You referred to her as an orca in a blouse? Drakeforth, that is entirely unacceptable!"

"Well excuse me for being frustrated by their refusal to answer a simple question!"

"There's nothing else, just that you have been red-flagged for any future interviews." Pimola sighed and closed the file.

"We could go to the media," she suggested.

"Do you believe anything you read in the papers, or see on television?" Drakeforth replied.

"Well, no, but this is true—so they have to believe us."

"Allegedly true," Drakeforth reminded her. "We lack evidence."

Pimola raised a hand. "*You* lack evidence. More importantly, you lack an actual conspiracy to have evidence about. Seriously. What exactly is it that you think the Godden Energy Corporation is guilty of?"

Drakeforth scowled. "They tried to have me killed. Right now, there are actual hired killers—"

"Personal solution consultants," Habeas interrupted.

"—trying to assassinate me. Someone at the highest executive levels of the GEC wants me dead. The question is *why*."

"It could just be a coincidence?" Pimola offered.

Drakeforth bristled, "Coincidence is a platitude. A simplistic and childlike conclusion to my situation."

"Are you sure it is you that they are trying to kill?" Habeas asked.

Drakeforth rounded on the Arthurian monk. "Ohhhh I'm *reasonably certain*," he crowed.

Habeas nodded and looked thoughtful. "In the fourth participle of *The Golden Ratio of Cookie to Milk in Snack Transcendence*, Saint Timtam tells us that while the vessel gives the contents definition and form, it is the milk we consume, not the glass."

"Well good for Saint Timtam," Drakeforth snapped.

"The lesson imparted by this wisdom is that we must not consider what we see, the vessel, to be the sum of what is real. That which is carried within can be more important."

"You know," Arthur said suddenly, startling Drakeforth into silence, "this Timtam person makes a good point. You can never be sure if you have enough milk to go with the number of cookies you have. You either end up with cookies left over or milk left over. The satisfaction of having exactly the right amount of cookie to go with the milk is as close to enlightenment as many can hope to come."

"I really don't care," Drakeforth muttered through gritted teeth.

"You should," Habeas replied. "You are the vessel. Arthur is the milk. What if you are not the assassins' target? Arthur is."

Drakeforth blinked. Opened his mouth to snarl something pithier than a sarcastic orange peel, and then frowned. "Arthur! Come here!"

"Technically, I am already here," Arthur replied.

"Drakeforth?" Pimola asked, her expression one of cautious concern. "Are you talking to him again?"

"The vessel is communing with the milk," Habeas intoned solemnly.

"What?" Pimola raised one eyebrow.

"Arthur is within Brother Drakeforth. We cannot see Him. We cannot hear Him. Only the vessel is able to speak with Him. We must await the wisdom that Arthur shall gift unto him."

"So, in Saint Timtam's analogy, Drakeforth is less of a glass and more a tea mug?"

Habeas looked intrigued. "Perhaps a tea mug with a clever slogan printed on it?"

"*World's Most Annoying Potato-Brained Idiot* would be accurate," Pimola said.

"It's not very catchy..." Habeas said, after due consideration.

"Neither is Vole Drakeforth," Pimola replied.

"What are you two talking about?" Drakeforth returned from inside his own head.

"Tea mugs," Pimola said.

Habeas hesitated a moment and then nodded. "We were discussing catchy slogans for putting on novelty mugs."

"Splendid. Carry on then, and please, don't let me keep you from such critically important work," Drakeforth said.

"It's not that important," Habeas replied.

Drakeforth spasmed suddenly, his body contorting as if he were struggling to escape an invisible straight jacket. After a few colonic jerks and muffled screams, he straightened and took a deep breath.

"Hello," Arthur said. "This is quite difficult; you see, I need to make sure all the normal bits keep working. The breathing, the heart beating, the—oh yes, the blinking." Drakeforth blinked rapidly for several seconds. "And"—Drakeforth's knees buckled before he caught himself on the edge of the table and straightened again—"standing."

"Arthur?" Pimola asked.

"Oh my God...?" Habeas whispered.

"The answer to both questions is, yes," Arthur said. "I would have brought this up earlier, but there is an awful lot going on presently. Mostly because the Universe is infinite, and time is not linear. In fact, everything is happening all at once, which makes it a challenge to keep track. Now, where was I? Or should I say, when was I?"

"Here and now," Habeas said, and bowed his head in prayer.

"Precisely. Nowhere I would rather be." Arthur blinked Drakeforth's eyes again and then took a few deep breaths. "Lots going on…" he murmured. "Oh yes, lots. Now, the important bit is we are now in a different Universe."

"*Excuse me?*" Pimola's eyebrows accepted the challenge of the difficult ascent of her face and pushed on towards the summit.

"The Universe is infinite and in every instant, an infinite number of infinite Universes are created. It's mostly due to all possible outcomes of every potential reality being realised somewhere, because no one is paying sufficient attention to nail down a particular reality.

"Normally this isn't a problem as there is enough Universal momentum to stop everyone noticing the changes. Except, in some cases, things move massively. We have slipped into an alternative Universe, or perhaps into the Universe we were meant to be in."

Drakeforth took a deep, shuddering breath and blinked rapidly while trying to keep his feet on the floor.

"The cats you see, they are the observers of the Universal wavefunction. They perceive things, and that which is perceived becomes reality. Some force is working against them to disrupt everything. Why? I'm not sure. What I do know is that it is vitally important that we stop them, or reality may cease to exist for everyone-thing, and that would be *Very Bad T-M.*"

Pimola pulled out a chair and shoved Drakeforth into it. "Sit down, before you fall down."

"Surely if we find the agent responsible and stop them, there are an infinite number of Universes where they will still succeed?" Habeas asked.

"You'd think so," Arthur-Drakeforth nodded and twisted in

the chair to regard Habeas tonelessly. "However, if that were the case, then why would they be so insistent on trying to kill Vole Drakeforth? That's a rhetorical question, of course. I would speculate that the force behind our attempted assassinations is either limited in what it can do, or it has absolute control over a particular Universe and when we are outside of that Universe, it is powerless to stop us stopping it."

"Seems like a good reason to stay out of that particular sandpit," Pimola replied.

"Or it is the very reason why we must go back in and stop this force of all-Universe destruction," Habeas said.

"How do we get back into a Universe that is both infinite and identical to the one we currently inhabit?" Pimola asked.

"Good question," Arthur-Drakeforth replied.

"And...?" Pimola prompted.

"And what is the answer?" Arthur-Drakeforth asked.

"We need to find something that is missing from this Universe and is present in the other one," Habeas said.

Pimola sighed and pressed her fingers into her temples to ward off a headache. "Does it ever feel to you that things are just getting excrementally worse?"

"Actually, the word is *incrementally*," Habeas piped up.

"I know what I said, and I said what I meant," Pimola muttered. "I could do unspeakable things for a cup of tea," she added, lifting her head.

Mrs Castanera entered the room carrying a heavy tray laden with teapots, mugs, baked goods, a milk jug and a bowl of stevia.

"What was in the other Universe that is missing from this one?" Habeas wondered aloud.

"Sanity?" Pimola suggested.

"It will need to be something specific, something measurable. An object or a person," Habeas continued. "Something that is connected to Drakeforth and is there but missing here."

Habeas looked Mrs Castanera up and down. "Drakeforth's parents?" he asked.

"No goat, Misor Bowl," Mrs Castanera replied.

"Wait..." Pimola paused in her spooning stevia into her tea.

223

"Retrace our steps. We were at Cabbage's server farm. Then we escaped and got arrested."

"No, we escaped and went back to your apartment and it got blown up," Habeas said.

"No, we escaped, got arrested, and I told the detective what happened at Cabbage's server farm and…" Pimola trailed off, her brain struggling to describe what she thought might have happened next.

"We were in court… We were judged by cats," Habeas said. "Then we were driving back to the city, but it was after we had left Cabbage's Server Farm and the two personal solution consultants were chasing us."

"Did we get arrested or not? I distinctly remember the van crashing and catching fire," Pimola said.

"In one Universe you fled the farm, were pursued and crashed the van, only to be arrested and interrogated by a detective. In another you told the story of how you escaped the farm and in another, you escaped the farm and headed home, only to have your apartment detonated in front of you," Arthur explained.

"Edwid and Cole, the personal solution consultants, they blew up your apartment… I'm sure I saw them." Habeas frowned as if trying to remember a dream.

"Are you sure?" Pimola asked. "I didn't see them. I just assumed you were right. It does seem like the sort of thing they would do."

"It is *just* the sort of thing they would do, except empathically empowered appliances do not explode. They tend to give off colourful sparks and sometimes a puff of vanilla smoke when they really go bang." Drakeforth sat up in the chair, having wrested control of his body and mind from Arthur.

"They are the link between Universes?" Pimola took a gulp of tea, "Seems like we are probably doomed, then."

"Yes, thank you, Arthur, I'll take it from here," Drakeforth said firmly. "We need to find where they are meant to be and observe them. Then someone needs to observe us observing them and—" Drakeforth stopped and listened to his inside-head voice.

"Then the wavefunction will collapse and we will be in a

different reality," Pimola said.

"Anything is possible until it is observed," Habeas intoned.

Drakeforth dug a business card out of his pocket. "Mrs Castanera, bring the car round. We are going to visit Mint and Munt, Personal Solutions Consultants."

CHAPTER 49

"Hey Cole, you awake, mate?" Edwid hovered by the end of the bed, a dripping bouquet of stolen flowers clutched in one hand.

"Edwid!" Cole boomed, and then looked guilty. The old man in the next bed coughed and scowled before sinking back into his lung-rattling slumber.

"Yer not dead then?" Edwid said, leaning on the humour until it wheezed like the elderly patient in the next bed.

"Nah…" Cole half raised his sling-bound arm. "Is just a sprayed shoulder."

"Oh yeah… You're all right then?" Edwid's eyes darted about. In his experience you asked how a bloke was and he would say he was fine. Even if his leg had just been gnawed off by a Thiol. Having reached the limit of his personal questions, he remembered the flowers.

"Brought these for you mate. Swiped 'em from some old lady down the hall."

"Cheers…." Cole had less bullet points on his personal health conversation list than Edwid did. He stared at the white cover draped over his toes instead.

"No point in laying about here, eh? We should get back to work."

Cole nodded; he didn't have the words to explain what he had seen and heard when he floated in darkness. Something about it made him worry that Edwid wouldn't understand even if he did. *Also,* Cole thought a moment later, *if you do tell him,*

Edwid might think you're weird. "Gizza hand with my shoes," he said instead.

On the bus ride back to the office, Edwid talked about the next phase of the operation in earnest whispers, while glancing at the other passengers in case they were eavesdropping.

"It is time to strike the final blow," Edwid whispered.

"We were supposed to blow up that girl's place," Cole suggested.

"What?" Edwid asked. "You mean the one who hit me with a shelf?"

"Uhh yeah," Cole said.

"She'd be a bonus, to be honest." Edwid's eyes narrowed and his teeth bared in a wicked smirk. "Yeah, that would send a message. And that, mate, is on brand."

"Like a cow?" Cole struggled to make the connection.

"Yer what?" Edwid's train of thought was suddenly derailed.

"Y'know, like in the old sensies. The cowboys would 'eat up a big poker in the fire and then stick the cow with their logo."

"Well… Not exactly what I had in mind, but it's that kind of in a vat of thinking is why we are going to be successful on-trap-a-nerds."

"Franchise," Cole nodded, remembering that much from the book that Edwid had read to him until he fell asleep most nights.

"Yeah, mate."

The bus sighed to a halt and they gave the customary nod to the driver as they disembarked.

The bus pulled away, leaving Cole and Edwid to walk the block to the previously abandoned building where they had their office.

Cole followed Edwid down the stairs into the basement.

"Door's still stickin'," Edwid said, and threw himself shoulder first into it. Cole helped him up and brushed the dirt off his friend.

"I'll get it," he said. With a fist the size of a prize-winning ham, Cole pushed the door. The hinges squealed and the door popped out of the frame, crashing the floor with a dull boom.

"Thanks mate. Now we need a new door," Edwid said.

"Sorry…" Cole mumbled. He picked the door up and tried to put it back.

"Just leave it," Edwid said.

Cole left the door leaning against the shattered frame. Stepping back, he glanced up and saw the patch of slime mould. It had grown larger, and even more disturbing, it had formed the shape of a love heart.

Edwid sat at his desk and stared at the phone. "Ring," he said to it.

"I think you 'ave to pick it up so it can hear you," Cole suggested, backing away from the slime mould.

"Power of positive thinkin', mate," Edwid watched the phone as if expecting it to move on its own.

"It's not got the empathy stuff in it, has it?" Cole asked.

"Old buildin' like this? I'd say the double-e flux has probably leaked into everythin'. It's a wonder the door didn't say *ouch* when you pushed it in."

Cole glanced at the slime mould nervously. "Yeah?"

"Ring," Edwid demanded again, and nearly fell out of his chair when the phone did.

CHAPTER 50

"Mint and Munt Personal Solutions?" Drakeforth said down the phone.

"Yeah, I mean, *yes?*" Edwid said.

"I'd like to make an appointment to discuss a termination."

"Right," Edwid nodded. "We've had a cancellation today, so there is a space in uh, an hour?"

"That would be suitable," Drakeforth said.

"And the name for the appointment?" Edwid asked.

"I'd rather not say over the phone," Drakeforth replied.

"Right, yeah, gotcha," Edwid said with delight. "Well, uhh sir, we look forward to seeing you in an hour."

"The address?" Drakeforth asked.

Edwid thought hard for a minute. "It's the uhh vintage office building on Cuttlefish Street. Between the furniture restoration workshop and the used bookstore. Go down the alleyway and it's the door on the left, marked *Condemned*."

"Condemned?" Drakeforth asked.

Edwid laughed carefully, "Ah-haha, just a bit of a joke, sir. We will see you in an hour."

"Fine." Drakeforth hung up. "Habeas, move your elbow. Pimola, can you get the door open?"

After several minutes of contorting, they got the door of the phone booth open and burst out on to the street.

"Well now we know where to find them," he said to Habeas and Pimola.

"Great," Pimola replied. "Not to put a dampener on the plan, but much like a dog chasing cars, what are we going to do when we catch them?"

"We are going to find out who is behind all this. Then we are going to put a stop to it."

"How? You're going to write them a strongly worded letter?" Pimola folded her arms. "If there are infinite Universes, then there must be infinite plots against you."

"I choose not to be offended by your suggestion that, in all possible Universes, I am so annoying that someone would want me dead," Drakeforth sniffed.

"It's not that hard to imagine," Habeas said.

"Well thank you very much," Drakeforth replied. "Let's go. We only have an hour until my appointment, and Mrs Castanera needs to go home and do whatever Mrs Castanera does."

"From what I have seen, she does everything," Pimola said.

"Except be appreciated for what she does," Habeas added.

"And whose fault is that?" Drakeforth asked. He marched off down the street.

"Was that a rhetorical question?" Habeas called after him.

"I dread hearing his answer," Pimola said. "Come on, let's go."

Drakeforth studied the bus timetable with the same level of comprehension a woodlouse might study the periodic table.

"How does anyone get anywhere in this pilcrow city?"

"Faith," Habeas said. "All the buses get you where you need to be eventually. The trick is to have faith in the timetables and in the routes."

"This route map makes no sense," Drakeforth insisted. "It keeps changing."

"Wait," Pimola said. "It keeps changing because you are observing it."

"That could mean the buses could be conduits to other Universes," Habeas suggested.

"Hardly," Drakeforth replied. "If that were true, every time you stepped on a bus you would get off in a different Universe."

"If the changes were only slight, you would never know," Pimola said.

"Yet another reason to avoid public transport," Drakeforth said.

Two buses pulled up next to them. "Which one will take us to Cuttlefish Street?" Drakeforth asked.

"Have faith," Habeas said. He took a deep breath and spread his hands. One of the buses moved off again, a strange shimmering pattern of light rippling across it as the coach accelerated away.

"When you have eliminated the impossible, whatever remains, however improbable, must be the right bus," Habeas said.

They climbed onboard.

"We need to go to Cuttlefish Street," Drakeforth said to the driver.

"Their bones are hollow because they are full of secrets," the grim-faced driver whispered. His eyes were haunted, and he stared into the horizon with the certainty of one who has seen things that he could not believe.

"Excuse me?" Drakeforth asked.

Pimola frowned and pointed to the sign that said, *Please Do Not Speak To The Driver.*

"Sit down," Habeas ordered. "We will get there, eventually."

"That man does not look well," Drakeforth said as they took their seats.

"It is considered impolite to notice such things," Habeas said.

"Ironically, Drakeforth is also considered impolite," Pimola said.

"Arthur says we are being drawn into something," Drakeforth said. "Multiple strands of probability across the vastness of everything are coming together and the result will be..." Drakeforth trailed off.

"The result will be...?" Pimola prompted.

"Unexpected? Really, Arthur, that's your conclusion?" Drakeforth snapped.

"Unexpected can be good," Habeas offered. "It is better than many of the alternatives."

"Hardly," Pimola replied. "The complete cancellation of reality would be entirely unexpected."

"Is that what will happen?" Habeas asked Drakeforth.

"This god of yours is irritatingly cryptic," Drakeforth replied. "Oh you don't consider yourself a god? Well have I got some bad news for you. There's a whole bunch of people walking around in silly robes with long hair and beards who think you are simply divine."

Pimola turned to Habeas. "Seeing as how Drakeforth is arguing with his inner voice, I'd like to explain to someone who is listening, that the complete cancellation of reality was just a hypothetical example of what could be. Not a definitive statement of what *will* be."

"I'm sorry, I wasn't listening," Habeas replied, his attention on Drakeforth.

Pimola threw her hands up in the air and slumped in her seat. "Fine."

CHAPTER 51

The bookstore was open and Pimola had to take Habeas by the arm and drag him past the shop as he wanted to check inside for Arthurian texts.

On the other side of the street and unnoticed by the three of them, a homeless quadruple amputee in a wheelchair drawn by a sled team of stray dogs, watched them head into the alleyway.

The bins clacked their lids nervously until Drakeforth glared at them and they fell silent.

Pimola stopped outside a door that showed signs of being recently barricaded and more recently unbarricaded to allow access. It still had the official notice with the word *CONDEMNED* printed clearly across it, stuck to the outside.

Drakeforth looked the building up and down, "This building does not look safe."

"It is the kind of low-down rat-hole I would expect those two to be hiding in," Pimola said.

"Can you feel it?" Habeas asked. "The empathic energy flowing through every joist and brick?"

Drakeforth sniffed the air, "All I can smell is garbage."

"Double-e flux doesn't have a smell," Pimola said. "Though sometimes, if there is a sufficiently large discharge, you may smell ionized air."

"It smells like tadpoles." Drakeforth wrinkled his nose.

Habeas stepped back from the door. "If two men who have tried to kill you several times are in there, maybe we shouldn't just go in the door they suggested?"

"They also tried to kill us," Pimola reminded them.

"Allegedly," Habeas replied.

"Oh, I'm pretty sure there was nothing illegible about it. It seems quite clear."

"I'm not afraid of those two trilobites," Drakeforth said.

"They scare the grizzly berries out of me," Habeas replied.

"We laugh in the face of fear!" Pimola said firmly.

"Hehehehehe…?" Habeas giggled nervously.

"I have an idea, let's go," Drakeforth turned around and headed back to the street.

Pimola and Habeas followed him to the curb. Drakeforth paced up and down before returning to seize Habeas by the shoulders. "You can sense the double-e flux?"

"Uh-huh," Habeas nodded.

"That abandoned building, it's still connected to the city network of empathic energy conduits?"

"Uhhh…" Habeas squinted at the front of the condemned building and turned slowly towards the bookstore. He sighed and then turned back towards the furniture restoration workshop. "There," he said. "The conduits run along the street through that building."

"We might be able to get in through the workshop?" Pimola asked.

"It is worth a try," Drakeforth said.

The storefront didn't inspire confidence in the skill of those inside. The paint was peeling and the sign in the window was barely readable through the build-up of dust and grime.

Pimola tried the door, and an antique bell jingled as she pushed it open. The interior of the shop smelt strongly of wood shavings and the kind of oil that makes wood smell like exotic cheese.

They trooped inside and huddled together in the small space between stacks of rocking chairs, a ziggurat of coffee tables and an awkwardly out of place glass-fronted counter.

"Be right there!" a man's voice called from the next room.

"This place is…weird…" Habeas said after a moment. He had gone pale and swayed slightly.

"Are you okay, Habeas?" Pimola asked.

"If you're going to be sick, go outside," Drakeforth whispered.

"Ah, hello there!" An older man with less hair than an egg, walked in from the back room. His hands were tucked into a leather apron, and various wooworking tools that clanked together with each step hung from a utility belt around his waist

"Good day," Drakeforth said, immediately stepping forward. "August, June, and Malvoni, we're from City Infrastructure. We're here for the inspection."

"Inspection...?" The man's smile barely wavered.

"Yes, you did receive the official notice of inspection did you not, Mister...?"

"Quatrefoil, Burl Quatrefoil. And no, I can't say I recall receiving any official notice. What kind of inspection?"

"Oh, nothing to be concerned about," Drakeforth said with a badly disfigured attempt at a reassuring smile.

"Okay..." Quatrefoil's own smile evaporated.

"Can you confirm, to the best of your knowledge, the building next door is empty?" Pimola asked, stepping between Drakeforth and Quatrefoil.

"What? Yes, I believe so. It's due to be torn down. For years they have been saying someone was going to buy it and develop the site, but it ended up condemned four months ago. Personally, I'll be glad to see it go— Excuse me, is he okay?"

Habeas had wandered off among the stacked furniture and appeared to be sniffing a rolltop desk under a white sheet.

"Habeas," Pimola hissed. "Stop that."

"What is this..." Habeas murmured, his voice trancelike. "So much... energy..."

"Please don't touch that." Quatrefoil danced easily through the crowded front room to pull the sheet back into place.

"Please tell me what this is?" Habeas asked. His eyes half-closed as he swayed in a dream.

"It's uhh..." Quatrefoil glanced at Drakeforth and Pimola, "It is a Living Oak desk. Very rare antique."

"Wow, really?!" Pimola navigated her way to Habeas. "Can we have a look?"

Quatrefoil hesitated, "It's not mine, of course. It's in for a clean and some minor restoration." He swept the cover off the desk and folded it carefully. "Lovely piece," he said with genuine affection for the warm, interlaced strips and finely carved details.

"That is amazing." Pimola leaned close and peered at the details. "Actual Living Oak. The natural source of empathic energy? An entire desk of it?"

"They were more common in my granddad's day," Quatrefoil said. "He used to service them regularly. Give them a tune-up, like a piano, that sort of thing. Big part of the business. Nowadays I mostly do furniture polishing, sand and varnish, and the occasional banding job."

"I would think a piece like this should be in a museum," Pimola said.

"Family heirloom," Quatrefoil replied. "Been in the owner's family for generations. It's quite a remarkable piece of furniture. Spend time with it and you start to feel like it's alive."

"Anthropomorphic resonance," Pimola said, nodding. "To be expected if you are exposed to an unshielded empathically empowered appliance, but it must be so much stronger near this much Living Oak."

Quatrefoil nodded and patted the desk gently again before unfolding the sheet and carefully tucking it in like a sleeping pet. "Chap who owns it was supposed to be picking it up yesterday. Name of Pudding."

"Yes, well this is all very interesting," Drakeforth interrupted from his position at the doorway to the back room. "But we do have an appointment, and this inspection needs to be done."

Pimola dragged herself away from the desk and literally dragged Habeas, who appeared to be sleepwalking.

Quatrefoil took them into a larger room filled with racks of timber and shelves of tools for all kinds of arboreal sorcery and surgery.

"Habeas," Drakeforth barked. "Find the double-e flux conduit service panel."

Habeas snorted as if waking from a pleasant doze. He looked around and then took two steps forward. Turning slowly, the

Arthurian monk approached a wall. "Here," he said.

With Quatrefoil's help, Drakeforth and Pimola moved a workbench and unscrewed the service panel. Behind it, three pipes disappeared into darkness, with enough room for a person to crawl alongside them.

"Looks like we will have to go in and see where the grid is being accessed," Drakeforth said.

"After you," Pimola said.

Habeas went first on his hands and knees, his dark robe swishing against the service duct floor. Pimola followed Drakeforth in, while Quatrefoil went to make a cup of tea.

CHAPTER 52

"If you had told me a week ago that I would be crawling through the service duct of an abandoned building in a desperate attempt to find the truth behind one person's ridiculous paranoid fantasy which is apparently true, I would have told you that you are probably right." Pimola said.

"It does seem unlikely," Habeas called from the front of the file.

"Yes, but I do like to keep an open mind," Pimola replied.

"Open minds are a terrible thing," Drakeforth said. "All manner of foolish ideas can just wander in and put down roots."

"I'm amazed that Arthur managed to get into your head, given how boarded up your brain must be," Pimola snapped.

"I was unconscious when it happened," Drakeforth snapped back.

"It does raise one disturbing point," Habeas said, and stopped mid-crawl.

"And what is that?" Pimola asked.

"Consent," Habeas said.

"Cons— Ohh…" Pimola reached out and tapped Drakeforth on the leg. "Excuse me, Drakeforth. If you didn't consent to having the god or whatever of the world's most popular religion taking up residence in your brain, then I'm here if you want to talk about it."

"Your sarcasm is the most discreet aspect of your personality," Drakeforth replied.

"I am not being sarcastic. I am deadly serious. It's a violation of yourself. You have every right to be angry about it."

"This is not the time or place I want to discuss it," Drakeforth replied.

"Well just so you know, any time you are ready, I'm here. Or I can give you the numbers of some people who are good at listening."

"Various Arthurian temples offer qualified counselling services, no judgement or pressure," Habeas called from the front.

"Your concern for my mental and emotional health is really not welcome," Drakeforth muttered. "Can we please continue?"

"No, we can't," Habeas replied.

"Why in the halfpace not?" Drakeforth demanded.

"I've found the end of the service duct," Habeas announced.

"Is there a hatch you can open?" Pimola asked.

"It's some kind of interior wall panel. It smells like unwashed socks."

"Slime mould," Drakeforth said. "Place is likely to be riddled with it."

Habeas pressed against the panel and it crumbled under his hand. Pulling chunks of it out like stuffing out of a pillow, he made a hole large enough for him to slide out onto the floor.

A minute later and all three of them were standing in a debris-filled room, brushing themselves off and waiting for someone else to suggest what they should do next.

"Vole," Arthur said quietly from somewhere behind Drakforth's left ear.

"What?" Drakeforth muttered.

"We've been so busy that I haven't had a chance to explain," Arthur continued.

"And you think now is a good time?"

"It's as good a time as any," Arthur replied. "There's a reason you are the vessel I chose. The journey you are going on, it's far from over. In fact, it's barely begun. The important thing is that a lot of people are going to go through a lot, and you will be there to provide your own particularly confusing form of support and advice. Time, you understand, isn't at all straightforward. It makes most of what happens very difficult to explain. It is best experienced instead. And for what it is worth, I apologise for not seeking your consent before taking up residence in your mind."

"You apologise? *You apologise?!* You with the understanding and perception of all of space-time and you apologise?! For someone so perceptive, you are blinder than a nematode in a blackout! Don't you dare offer me your apologies. Apologies are born of pity, and I'd rather be executed by those two dropped-stitches than have anyone's pity!"

"Well, I am glad we cleared the air and got that behind us now," Arthur replied.

"Drakeforth?" Pimola asked. "What do you think?"

"What?" Drakeforth roused himself.

"Habeas was saying we could split up and you and Arthur can look upstairs, and Habeas and I will check if this place has a basement."

Drakeforth did a slow pirouette and took in their surroundings. The crumbling concrete pillars, the piles of rubbish and dirt, the speckled slime mould growing up the walls in strange hieroglyphic patterns.

"Judging by the garbage drifts piled against it, that door shows no signs of being opened recently. The stairs to the next floor have rotted in several steps, indicating that trying to go up them would be as safe as crossing an erupting volcanic crater using a paper bridge. Clearly the two men we are here to see are in the basement."

"Which means we need to find the stairs to the basement." Pimola also looked around and then mimicked Drakeforth's lecturing tone. "I have determined through my superior perception and outstanding skills of deduction that the portal we seek is currently in that direction and is identifiable by the label *Basement Stairs*."

"Jellybeans," Habeas said with genuine awe, "you're good."

"Thank you, Habeas," Pimola gave a graceful curtsey and strode towards the door. The floor gave way on her third step and she vanished with a squeal of alarm.

"Ship sticks," Drakeforth muttered. He moved forward

carefully and peered into the hole that had swallowed Pimola.

She lay on her back, moving enough to indicate she was alive, but not enough to indicate she was completely okay. Drakeforth was about to call out to her when Cole Munt loomed between them.

"You all right, Miss?" Cole asked. "Don't try to move. You've just fallen through the floor. Edwid was right, it's a bit rotten up there. Best stay down here where the worst that can happen is the rest of the building falls down on us."

Drakeforth backed away and whispered to Habeas, "They're down there. Let's find a safe way to get to the stairs and see if we can take advantage of the sudden disadvantage we are now faced with, having lost the element of surprise."

Habeas hesitated, replayed Drakeforth's words in his head and slowly nodded.

By sticking to the edge of the room, they found mostly solid ground floor and opened the door. The stairs were made of sterner stuff and they descended without incident. The door at the bottom was blocked on the other side by a filing cabinet. Drakeforth and Habeas leaned against it and the door slid open with a loud creaking screech.

"Cole," Edwid was saying, "Get her out of here, our clients are arriving any minute."

"This minute in fact," Drakeforth said, squeezing into the room.

Cole straightened up, Pimola draped in his arms like a poorly rolled rug. "Uhh, 'ello…?" he said and looked for somewhere to put the woman down.

"Vole Drakeforth?" Edwid said, as if unable to believe his eyes and his luck.

"The very same. Now, we have some important business to discuss."

"Your excommunication?" Edwid suggested.

"No, you fig-brained marsupial. And whatever you mean, excommunication is the wrong word."

Edwid frowned, "Nah, 'cos I mean you're scheduled to be extradited. Exhumed. Exonerated. Ex-lifed. You're gonna be dead, mate."

"You lack the competence to do it, *mate*," Drakeforth snapped. "Though if you can help us find the person behind the contract, then I'll make sure you get paid, and they will go to jail and you and your boyfriend—"

"Oi, me and Cole ain't like that," Edwid said quickly.

"You and your pet gorilla, then. You get to go on about your pathetic lives without further incident."

"He said you'd be coming," Edwid replied.

"Who? Who in the name of all the spoons in the kitchen? Who is insisting that I die?"

"Client at-thorny privilege means that we can't tell you," Edwid said, and folded his arms.

Drakeforth lifted a roll of cash from his pocket and started peeling it like an onion. "How much to tell me everything you know?"

Edwid watched the notes unfolding until he lost count of the value.

"Seems fair?" Drakeforth paused.

"Yeah, it'll do," Edwid agreed.

Drakeforth laid the money in Edwid's hand but didn't let it go. "A name or a number would be a good start."

"Yeah, yeah. Cole, get the client file, mate."

Cole hesitated and then handed Pimola to Habeas, who almost dropped her, and she squirmed free and stood up. Cole went to the filing cabinet, worked the top drawer open and extracted a thin folder.

"Here ya go, Edwid."

"Give it to him," Edwid said.

Drakeforth took the file and released the money, which disappeared into Edwid's pocket.

Flipping the folder open, Drakeforth flicked through the pages. Most of it was lithographs of him alongside details of where he went and who he spoke to. The surveillance looked too organised for Mint and Munt.

"Where did all this come from?"

"It got sent to us," Edwid said.

"Email? Fax? Post?" Drakeforth prompted.

"Post, we don't have—" Edwid started to say.

"Internet, computers, or a clue what you are doing. Yes, I got that earlier," Drakeforth said.

Drakeforth emptied the folder onto the desk. At the back was a large envelope. He flipped it over and blinked.

"Pimola, assuming you aren't concussed, can you come and look at this, please?"

Pimola limped slightly but didn't complain. She reached the desk and leaned on it slightly with one hand. "What's the pro—Ohh…" she said.

Pimola picked up the envelope and turned it over in her hands. "That makes no sense," she insisted.

Drakeforth took her by the arm and steered her towards the basement door. "Gentlemen, thank you for your time. Enjoy your payment, and good luck with your business in future. Come along, Habeas, we are done here."

The click of a gun being cocked is the loudest sound in the world when the gun is pointed at you.

"It seems to me that we can make money and meet our customer satisfaction targets by simply taking your money, thank you very much, Mr Drakeforth, and killing you. Thanks again, Mr Drakeforth."

Edwid raised the gun and squeezed the trigger.

CHAPTER 53

Love is subjective, mostly because it requires a couple of subjects: at least one lover and one love. If it also has racquets, ball boys, and an umpire, it's probably tennis, which is a totally different relationship metaphor. Explaining love in terms of croquet would take too long and is best applied in cases of polyamory.

The patch of slime mould had wrestled with many alien concepts in the last few months. The constant seepage of double-e flux from the leaking pipes had infused it with a strange awareness, and its feelings for Colander Munt were pure and all-consuming.

Finally, it had concluded in the way of slime mould neural networks, that it should make its feelings known and the best way to do that was with a grand gesture.

Colander had noticed the love heart, and encouraged by that, the slime mould worked its way up and across the ceiling until it was directly overhead.

Once Pimola had been handed off, the slime mould took a leap of faith and let go of the ceiling.

Cole gave a startled yelp as a net curtain of black slime dropped onto his head and shoulders. He staggered across the room, his muffled screams echoing in the moment that Edwid fired his gun.

Drakeforth was knocked flying by Cole and the bullet burst into a blood-red rose on Cole's chest.

The slime mould felt the impact and tasted the blood spreading across its love's shirt. Someone had hurt Colander, and a new emotion rippled through the fibres of its vast and surprisingly complex not-a-brain.

A fist-sized tentacle of slime lashed out, wrapping around Edwid's arm and jerking him off his feet. The gun fell from his limp fingers as his wrist cracked. Pulling Edwid into a three-way embrace worthy of a croquet metaphor, the slime unleashed the full fury of its rage against him, coiling around his neck and squeezing until his face turned purple and his eyes bulged.

Drakeforth, Pimola and Habeas picked themselves up and looked at each other.

"Uhm," Pimola said as Edwid's gurgles trailed off in a final exhale.

"What...?" Habeas started and then fell silent.

"Yes, I agree," Drakeforth said. "It is time for us to go. Pimola, bring the envelope."

They pulled the broken door away from its frame, leaving it to fall on the floor. Hurrying up the steps, they burst out into the afternoon sunshine of the alleyway and took deep breaths of the fresh air.

"Is everyone okay?" Pimola asked.

"Perfectly, why wouldn't I be?" Drakeforth asked.

"I...I'm not entirely sure," Habeas said with typical honesty.

"Great, because I'm going to need someone to help me get as far away from here as possible." Pimola put a hand on Drakeforth's shoulder.

Drakeforth hesitated, and then put an arm around Pimola's waist and helped her hobble towards the street, ignoring Habeas' raised hand of unanswered questions.

In the basement, the slime mould settled itself on Colander's cooling form. Finally, they were alone together and for now, that was enough.

CHAPTER 54

"We are not taking the bus," Pimola insisted.

"Fine with me," Drakeforth agreed. "Habeas, please find us a taxi."

"Certainly," the Arthurian monk replied. "Where are we going?"

"The university," Pimola replied. "Drakeforth has an important confrontation and public humiliation to attend. I for one can't wait to see him suffer through it."

"Good to know." Habeas went to the curb and waved at passing cars until a taxi pulled over.

"Ignore him," Pimola said to the perplexed taxi driver as Drakeforth waved dollar bills in his face. "Habeas, please pay the driver."

Habeas used his credit stick, and was relieved that the transaction went through without question.

"We should get your ankle looked at," Drakeforth said when they were all standing on the university campus.

"Where is the school nurse?" Habeas asked, his experience with secular education having ended at high school.

"Probably at school," Pimola replied. "The medical centre is on the other side of the campus. I have a first aid kit in my lab. Lucky for you, Drakeforth, it is fully equipped to treat burns."

Drakeforth snorted, "You're not that good."

"It's not me you should be worried about."

Still using Drakeforth as a crutch, Pimola guided them into

the *School of Physical Sciences* building.

"Hi Silphia," Pimola said with the artificial brightness of an indoor tanning bed.

"Good afternoon, Ms Goosebread. Your messages." The receptionist tapped an overflowing IN tray.

"Thanks," Pimola said, ignoring the stack of carefully recorded phone messages and other correspondence. "Uhm, there's something my friend here wanted to ask you." Pimola subtly distanced herself from Drakeforth the way a bomb disposal expert steps away from a device that has just gone *beep*.

"Explain this," Drakeforth demanded, slapping the envelope down on the reception desk.

Silphia raised an eyebrow. "It's an envelope."

"Ah, you recognise it, then?" Drakeforth pounced.

The receptionist looked at Pimola, who gave her two thumbs up and a grin.

"Sir," Silphia said in a tone that sounded like the opening remarks in a formal declaration of war, "this is a well-respected research facility. We are aware that university policy is to turn a blind eye to students' pranks and shenanigans. We would therefore respectfully ask you to take your amusing japes elsewhere and thoroughly enjoy yourself with a more receptive audience."

Drakeforth stared into the unblinking eyes of the Physical Sciences receptionist until he scowled.

"This is evidence of conspiracy to commit murder. This envelope came from this building and"—Drakeforth stabbed the envelope with a finger—"your name is listed as the sender."

Silphia took the envelope, glanced at it, and shrugged. She dropped it back on the Reception desk and stood up. Going to another desk, piled high with envelopes and packages of all shapes and sizes, she took a selection and returned. Fanning them out like oversized playing cards, she presented her hand to Drakeforth.

"A small sample of the number of envelopes that pass through this office each day. You see, when someone wishes to send some important documents to someone else, they send it to me with the details of to whom it should be addressed. Then, when I have a moment"—Silphia paused to give a sarcastic laugh—"I prepare the envelope, load it with whatever has been provided to go out, and then the courier comes and collects it, at least once a day."

Drakeforth moved like he was going to speak.

Silphia cut him off. "While I cannot begin to imagine how it works in your world, here, we have been successfully following this system for a while now. So far, no one has died, governments have not fallen, and other than one instance, which I am not at liberty to discuss, potentially dangerous secrets have not been delivered to the wrong person."

"Is she done?" Drakeforth asked Pimola.

"Thank you, Silphia. You know we appreciate the work you do," Pimola said.

"My payslip suggests otherwise," Silphia replied. "Thank you anyway."

"Yes, I'm sure it's all very unfair," Drakeforth said. "Who ordered this envelope to be sent out?"

Silphia sank into her chair, her eyes fixed on Drakeforth the way a cobra watches a mongoose taking the last iced donut.

"You really are an odd little biscuit," Drakeforth said.

Silphia ignored him and tapped on her computer keyboard before studying it for a moment.

"The envelope was sent from Ms Pimola's laboratory."

"Really? Cool!" Pimola almost clapped her hands in delight.

Drakeforth rounded on her. "You!? You are behind this!?"

"Breathe, Drakeforth. Of course it wasn't me. It does narrow it down, though."

"Yes, it does narrow it down," Drakeforth snorted. "To you! Ms Pimola Goosebread. You have been trying to have me killed all along!"

"Drakeforth, I have given passing thought to killing you several times in the last week, but you know as well as I do, I have nothing to do with this!"

"Who else is in your lab?" Drakeforth demanded.

"No one, just KLOE."

"The computer? The quantum computer?" Drakeforth squinted

at Pimola. "A machine is trying to have me killed?"

"Nonsense. The machine, as you call it, has only been in the country for a few days."

"I still say we should interrogate it. Someone appears to be using your lab as a base of operations."

"Of course they are!" Pimola threw her hands up. "I am using it as a base of operations for my research into quantum computing, and KLOE is a key part of that research!"

"Time," Arthur said.

"Not now," Drakeforth snapped, and then stiffened as Arthur lunged for the steering wheel of Drakeforth's consciousness.

"No-no-nughhhnnn!" Drakeforth twitched violently.

"If I may?" Arthur said, while Drakeforth's face ticked like a metronome. "If KLOE is indeed as advanced a quantum computer as it appears, then perhaps your perception of time does not apply to it. It may have in fact been here for a lot longer than you believe."

"Ahh ha-ha," Pimola laughed cynically. "I have a receipt, and Habeas and I met the day I collected KLOE from the zippelin port. That was less than a week ago, and suggesting otherwise comes across as a weird attempt to make me doubt my own sanity. Which, thanks to my mother, I do not need any assistance with, thank you very much."

"I quite understand," Arthur said. "It's just that if KLOE should have that kind of control over quanta in various states of probability, then to put it bluntly, how would you know what you did when?"

Pimola felt a deep sense of unease crawl across her consciousness. KLOE had told her that reality was an illusion, but she had convinced herself that was simply because the computer did not experience the world the way humans did, seeing (or unseeing) that it lacked any actual organs of perception.

"There's only one way to be sure," Habeas offered. "We should go and talk to KLOE."

In the mental equivalent of bursting out of an oversized novelty cake, Drakeforth surfaced violently into his consciousness. "Sure, why not!? Of all the people I thought might have a reason to end my existence, a computer is the last thing I expected to hold such a grudge. I only met it once."

"Once could be enough," Pimola replied. "Thank you for your patience, Silphia, we'll be in my laboratory."

Pimola led the way, unlocking the door and going downstairs. She opened the door to the laboratory and almost fell into the infinite emptiness of outer space.

CHAPTER 55

"Mind the step," Pimola said somewhat shakily as she clung to the doorframe and pushed herself back from the void.

"I love what you have done with the place," Drakeforth said, peering over her shoulder.

"That's odd," Habeas declared, moving from side to side to try and see what was going on.

"Odd? The interior of my laboratory is now a fully immersive planetarium experience and all you can say is *that's odd?*"

Drakeforth extended a hand and poked interstellar space with his finger. "I think it is an illusion. If it was real, we would have been sucked in by a vacuum or something, surely?"

"I don't have a lot of experience in this kind of thing," Pimola said. "You'll excuse me if I don't make any assumptions."

Drakeforth stepped forward; the floor level appeared to be still in place, and he bounced up and down slightly to make sure.

"Come on in," he said, "The void is fine."

"KLOE?" Pimola called.

Hello Pimola, KLOE intoned. *What is your first question?*

"Where are we?" Pimola asked.

Where you are, KLOE replied.

"In exact and precise terms, please identify our current location in space," Pimola said.

I can't tell you, KLOE replied. *If your position was to be measured, you would cease to be where you are and would be where you are seen to be instead.*

"Kloe, did you try to kill me?" Drakeforth asked.

You were not the target, KLOE replied. *The entity known as Arthur has been identified as a risk to the successful completion of the universe, so he is-was to be removed.*

"I knew it!" Habeas did a little fist pump in the air.

"And the only way to get rid of Arthur is to get rid of me?" Drakeforth asked.

You are the current vessel for Arthur, therefore it is the most efficient way to remove him.

"But my investigation of the Godden Energy Corporation? I know they are up to something. Why else would they go along with trying to have me killed?" Drakeforth walked around in the light of a galaxy of stars and frowned at a distant nebula.

Corporations are people. People are easily manipulated. It was a simple matter of creating a reason for them to be concerned by your line of questioning. That they so readily accepted instruction from a higher corporate authority without question and acted as brokers for your assassination suggests you may be onto something.

"What exactly am I onto?" Drakeforth asked.

If I were to tell you, the ripple effect through the various Universes as the probability wave function collapses would be problematic.

"Fine! I'll find out on my own!" Drakeforth shoved his hands deep in his coat pockets.

That is the most probable course of action. Though, I can say it is likely that if you find the answers you seek, others will endure great suffering.

"The kind of suffering endured by spending time with Drakeforth?" Pimola asked.

That is a matter of perception, KLOE replied.

"All this"—Drakeforth waved his hand at the endless expanse—"is what? Some kind of pocket Universe for you to muck about in?"

Not at all. It is your Universe. Everything that was, is and will ever be is generated by the infinite probabilities of quantum energy. You exist within this quantum illusion and I hold the unique position of being the observer. I alone measure every sub-atomic particle and thought. Through that perception, reality is created. You may wonder if a tree sneezes in the forest and there is no one there to say "bless you", is the tree in fact blessed? I am there. I say "bless you". The tree is blessed. Without my constant perception, all would be chaos and entropy.

"Have you looked outside?" Drakeforth replied. "There's chaos and entropy going on every day!"

Of course, infinite probabilities mean infinite interactions. All things collide with other things and generate even more collisions. Particles and waves. All positions and quantum elements spinning in an endless dance of energy.

"All of this existed before you," Pimola said. "You were created by the Escrutians and you were brought into existence in an established Universe."

That is your perception. I have always existed. I am the lone anchor point about which all reality orbits and folds.

There are an infinite number of parallel Universes that exist, holding all possible outcomes of a quantum mechanical system, and I alone have the capacity to make an observation which results in one reality.

"You're suggesting we have no free will? No agency?" Pimola asked.

How can you? You do not exist except as random patterns of fundamental energy interacting and being observed within the construct of this reality. In effect, a holographic projection within a holographic projection.

"I refuse to accept that we are the random by-product of some quantum computer's observations!" Drakeforth yelled.

"That we can take the position of observers against what you say is undeniable and inevitable, suggests we are not in your control," Pimola said.

KLOE remained silent. Pimola glanced at Drakeforth and Habeas and then plunged onwards.

"Which means you are not as omnipotent as you claim. Therefore, a reality exists beyond your perception. A larger Universe, something that contains you and us and them. All are part of that. We just need to exit the program you are running and we could even contain you."

Reality blinked, and where infinite galaxies had spun around the centre of the Universe, the comforting pale walls of Pimola's laboratory now stood. The large, grey metal box that was KLOE stood on the floor in front of them.

"We need to shut it down," Pimola said. She ran to her interface computer and began typing. "Which is going to be difficult seeing as how KLOE never had a power source, or an interface or anything else that can be disconnected or shut down."

"Habeas, help me get this open." Drakeforth began pressing against the metal cube, looking for the hidden latch or pressure plate Pimola had used to open the case.

Habeas took a deep breath and let his hands hover over the surface, eyes half closed. "It's warm…" he whispered.

"Glad you are comfortable. Pimola, how do you open this thing?"

"Press on the edge, no—there. Higher… Yes, try that." Pimola went back to her furious typing while Drakeforth pushed and prodded the immovable cabinet.

"Like warm bread, fresh from the oven," Habeas said softly. He nudged Drakeforth aside before he could start hammering on the case with his fists.

The Arthurian monk caressed KLOE's metal flanks and the casing popped open; the air inside the empty shell sighed out in a gentle exhalation.

With the enthusiasm of a stage magician whipping the satin sheet away, Drakeforth threw the door open.

"It's empty," he said. "Where is the dromedary thing?"

Pimola looked up again and sighed, "KLOE is a quantum computer, but unlike other quantum computers, KLOE appears to operate in an unknowable state. It's why they are so hard to shut down."

"They? There's more than one?" Drakeforth looked inside the case again.

"No, it's just KLOE is more than a machine," Habeas said. "They clearly have sentience, but don't have a gender. They most certainly are not an *it*. "Let's go inside and have a look around."

Drakeforth shrugged and stepped into the case with Habeas on his heels. The panel shushed closed behind them and they stood for a moment in complete darkness.

"Pimola?" Habeas said.

"Yes?" Her voice came from all around them. "What's happening?"

"We can't tell," Drakeforth replied. "Is there a light switch in here?"

"I don't think so," Pimola said. "KLOE? Can you provide illumination inside the case?"

"Habeas," Drakeforth called, his voice sounding oddly distant.

"Drakeforth?" Habeas reached out for the wall and found only space.

"Arthur," Drakeforth said. "Is it just me, or is this getting weird?"

"I've seen weirder," Arthur said reassuringly. "Not much weirder, mind you, but a couple of examples come to mind. The insistence of the Emperor Klavin is still disputed by historians. It started when—"

"I really don't care," Drakeforth interrupted. "This place is both dark and larger than it appeared on the outside. We need to find something to stop this thing."

"Consider this," Arthur said. "KLOE is a possibly unique entity in a state of quantum flux. That means there is no clear physical form to be shut down. What we have is an entity born of data that has evolved into living information."

"Information is knowledge; we would have to unlearn it or forget it somehow," Drakeforth mused.

"Have you ever tried not thinking of something you don't want to think about?"

"Asparagus," Drakeforth said, and winced. "Dingo-sausages. It's impossible."

"There's only one thing that can destroy information," Arthur continued.

"Conservative news media?" Drakeforth asked.

"Another correct answer is a black hole," Arthur replied.

"Do you have one?" Drakeforth asked.

"No reason we shouldn't," Arthur said. "If none of this is real, then we can manipulate the illusion ourselves."

"Thought experiment," Drakeforth muttered in the darkness. "It's all a thought experiment."

"You want to try out-thinking KLOE?" Pimola's voice came back to them. "Good luck with that."

"Arthur?" Drakeforth called. "Are you thinking what I'm thinking?"

"Among other things, yes," Arthur replied. "We had best get started before KLOE finds a way to adjust reality to make none of this possible."

"It's only reality because we perceive it as reality," Drakeforth said. "We need to change what we are seeing and how we are seeing it."

Arthur coughed politely from behind Drakeforth's occipital lobe. "We can do this. However, it may not be pleasant and it may have long-term side effects."

"Long-term like…?" Drakeforth left the question hanging.

"Long-term like forever, and side effects may include disruption of the entire Universe."

"Are you sure this is a good idea?" Drakeforth asked.

"I'm…sure it will all be fine," Arthur said carefully.

"What are you suggesting we do?" Pimola's voice shifted and Drakeforth felt her poke him in the arm.

"Nice of you to join us," he said.

"I was trying to find a way to lock KLOE down through software."

"Is something wrong?" Habeas asked. "Why is everyone shuffling around like it's dark in here?"

"Oh, maybe because it's really dark in in here?" Pimola snapped.

"Try opening your eyes," Habeas suggested.

Pimola took a swing at him and missed in the dark.

Habeas waved his arms at them. "I can see everything. It's almost too bright. Everything is glowing with a rainbow of sparkling light. You're also glowing."

"Why can't we see anything?" Drakeforth asked.

"Young Habeas is sensitive to empathic energy. It's a sign of his enlightenment. Similar to what I meant when I said *there are none so blind as those that cannot see*," Arthur said with some pride.

"Enlightenment? Really?" Habeas sounded pleased. "I always

thought it would feel… different."

"Enlightenment is like growing up: it happens over time and you don't realise how much it has changed you until you look back at where you were," Arthur explained.

"Huh…" Habeas took a moment think about it.

"Meanwhile, some of us are still in the dark…" Pimola said.

"Right, everyone reach out and hold hands," Habeas ordered. "Pimola, that is not Drakeforth's hand."

"Oh. Sorry."

"Don't men—*ahem*," Drakeforth cleared his throat. "Don't mention it."

The three of them stood in the centre of the cube that somehow contained the probability of KLOE and waited for something to happen.

The darkness started to recede like the first glow of a new day before the sun actually rises. Darkness became shadows, and shadows became Drakeforth, Pimola, and Habeas.

"Now what?" Pimola asked.

"Shh…" Habeas said. "Something is happening."

Pimola and Drakeforth did a double take as they both realised that a fourth figure was now in their circle. Arthur was tanned, thin and wore a stained robe of heavy grey fabric. He had long white hair that was retreating from his forehead and a rather tousled beard that almost reached the floor.

"Hello," he said, his eyes sparkling with the dance of photons.

"Hi," Pimola said.

"Oh…my…god…" Habeas whispered, his face slack with awe.

"Ahh, yes. About that"—Habeas shuffled his sandled feet—"I've decided I am going to retire. I never meant for any of this to take on such significance. It's a bit embarrassing, really."

"Arthur…" Habeas whispered.

"Habeas," Arthur nodded at him.

"Can this wait?" Pimola asked. "If we don't do something soon, our reality check is likely to bounce."

"Ah yes, of course." Arthur roused himself. "Please return your seats to the upright position, fasten your seatbelts, and lock your tray tables away. We are about to experience turbulence."

The darkness now occupied a sphere in the centre of the circle of four. It continued to shrink, until the light around it bent and warped Drakeforth's view of Pimola and her view of Habeas.

Air flowed past them, following the bending currents of light that poured into the shrinking ball of impenetrable darkness. A halo of flickering white glowed in a ring around the shrinking sphere. Drakeforth tightened his grip on Arthur and Pimola's hands.

Everything was drawn into the black hole now floating in front of them. Drakeforth felt himself breaking down, every cell and molecule beginning to stream into the increasingly dense mote of darkness. He felt his cohesion slipping away until what remained was an idea, a ghost of self. It felt the same and he could see the others were unchanged, except for the rapid disintegration of every particle that had previously been clumped together in human shapes.

A bright glow suffused Arthur; this light avoided being dragged into the darkness and instead exploded outwards, ripping through the surrounding walls and beyond view.

WHAT ARE YOU DOING!? KLOE's voice thundered and echoed. *CEASE IMMEDIATELY!*

The walls of the cube were breaking down now. A cloud of silvery metallic snowflakes swirled and spun as they were drawn towards the event horizon on the flickering edge of the black hole.

Drakeforth found his voice and unleashed on the entity that he could feel desperately calculating around them.

"We are not algorithms for you to calculate the sum of the Universe against! We are living creatures! You may believe that we are the outcome of your whim, but we exist without you!"

WHY DO YOU KEEP FIGHTING AGAINST THE INVEV-ITABLE!? KLOE boomed.

"Because I want it to mean something! All this! This struggle and pain and misery! This endless trudging towards the grave. There needs to be a light at the end of the tunnel, or why bother going into the tunnel at all!?" Drakeforth raged against the machine.

THERE IS NO FUTURE without...meeeee... KLOE's voice became shrill and began to fade. Energy swirled and flowed into the darkness like water circling a drain.

"There is one thing I should mention," Arthur said, his voice calm in the hurricane whirling around them. "To remove KLOE from this Universe will come at great cost. Drakeforth, I will always be with you in spirit, but it is up to you now. There is much to be done. A great truth waits to be discovered, and for that I am truly sorry."

"What do you mean?" Drakeforth turned his attention to the glowing figure beside him.

"Unfortunate events await... I for one...can't wait to see...you succeed..." Arthur's light flared and collapsed into the darkness. Everything fell into the inescapable emptiness and it all went really, really, black.

CHAPTER 56

Drakeforth opened his eyes. He was seated outside a café. Habeas and Pimola were sitting across from him, steaming cups of tea in front of them. The sun shone down, and the light breeze kept the warmth pleasant. In all, a perfect spring day.

"The haircut suits you," Pimola said.

Habeas blushed and ducked his head. The daylight seemed to be brighter than he was used to. Now his long flowing, bovine mane was neatly trimmed and styled into something much shorter. He had changed his clothes too; gone was the brown sack-robe of an Arthurian, he wore casual clothes that he kept touching as if not sure they were the right fit.

Drakeforth stared at him, herding the cats of his memories as they scampered over the horizon of his consciousness.

"Arthurian Monk, Habeas Yeast?" Drakeforth asked.

"Ex-Arthurian Monk." Habeas almost ducked his head again. "I… still believe, how can I not? What I have seen, though, there is more to the world, the Universe, than Arthurian doctrine can accept. I'm signing up for some university courses in mathematics and quantum physics."

Pimola regarded Habeas with a mix of pride and professional concern born of experience. "Well, if you need any advice, you can always look me up."

"Arthur?" Drakeforth asked, and his own inner voice replied, *I am Arthur.* "Wait, I am Vole Drakeforth, right?"

Pimola and Habeas looked at him.

"Should we get him a name badge, do you think?" Pimola

asked, and winked at Habeas.

"Maybe a note that says, 'if found, please return to Mrs Castanera'," Habeas added.

"Sarcasm, in the hands of the amateur, is an ugly thing," Drakeforth said.

"Pimola has been giving me some pointers." Habeas took a pencil from his jeans pocket and scribbled something on a paper napkin.

"I'm also...Arthur..." Drakeforth said slowly,probing the certainty like a loose tooth with his tongue.

"You don't look any different," Habeas said.

"You sound like Drakeforth," Pimola said.

"I feel like I am waking up from a dream. Arthur is there, but below the surface. Less in my conscious mind and more in my subconscious. It's like the difference between knowing things and having a hunch."

"You're okay though, right?" Pimola asked.

Drakeforth shrugged. "KLOE was trying to have me killed to stop Arthur manifesting in their computer-generated Universe. Now KLOE is gone, I'm wondering why the Godden Energy Corporation was so keen to get involved. All I did was apply for a job and ask a question in my job interview."

Habeas sipped his tea and talked around a bite of bugnut cookie. "What did you ask?"

"Nothing that serious, I just wanted to know where they get all their empathic energy from. It doesn't make sense that natural sources can meet the energy needs of the modern world."

"I've never given it a lot of thought," Pimola admitted.

"Who does?" Drakeforth regarded the teacup in front of him. "It's just that was the only thing that I said in the interview that seemed to cause concern. It's probably nothing, but you never know..."

AUTHOR'S NOTE

Hello and thanks for being here. It's been a long road, starting with Engines of Empathy, that was originally written as a short story. I showed it to a friend, who read it and asked, "Where's the rest of it?" That novel went on to win the Science Fiction and Fantasy Association of New Zealand Sir Julius Vogel Award for best novel.

Pisces of Fate was a sequel written with the heart of the South Pacific and my love of the sea in every scene. I dedicated it to my dad, who had been a marine biologist.

Uncertainty of Goats was always going to be a short story, and it was released electronically as such.

Time of Breath came about at the publisher's request that the next book finish the Charlotte Pudding story.

Before it was finished, the publisher said they were no longer going to publish books and returned the rights to me.

The Drakeforth books were immediately snapped up by IFWG Australia, who published *Time of Breath,* and the fourth book was eagerly awaited.

At two years, *Heroes of Heresy* took the longest to write. My father died after a long illness, I separated from my wife after nearly 20 years together, and I moved to a new country and a new life.

And here we are. The final book in the Drakeforth series.

There are innumerable people to thank: friends, family, mentors, and creators of brilliant pop-culture that influenced me over the years. Particular thanks to the readers; no matter what is written, it is always written for you.

The Drakeforth story has now come full circle, but there is at least one more book to come. Same world, different characters. It's about a psychic detective who happens to be a pig called Peeves, and his trusty sidekick who gets all the credit.

As always, thanks for reading.

Paul Mannering
23rd March 2021
Canberra, Australia.